A WORLD ON THE ISLAND'S EDGE

A WORLD ON THE ISLAND'S EDGE

Book I of the Golden Dolphin

MATTHEW RUDD REYNOLDS

Interior Illustrations by Talia Threadgill

Contents

for my wife Shannon and mother Sharon

The Island of Grey Cove

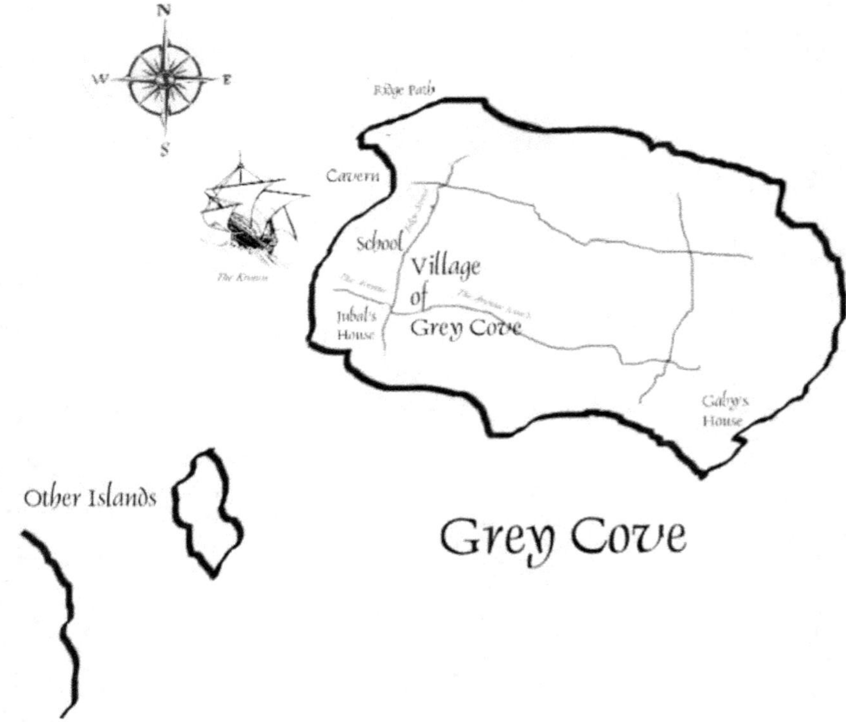

One

Song in Sunset

"I'm sorry, Andi," her teacher said.

No, you're not sorry, Andi thought. *Not at all.*

Trying not to lose her temper, Andi began again. "Miss Dugger, I don't think you saw what you think you did the other night."

"Oh no," Miss Dugger replied. "I saw what I saw." She turned to Andi with a plastered smile on her face. "It'll be okay, Andi. Everything will work out in the end. Your needs will be met; your brother's needs will be met. Even your grandmother's." She seemed oddly insincere, but Andi could not tell why.

Andi then did something daring. She met her teacher's eyes, letting all the anger she felt in that moment flow into them. Her teacher recoiled slightly before a shadow of anger appeared on her face. Andi turned her back on her teacher and slammed the classroom door hard behind her. She smiled, thinking of Miss Dugger jumping at her desk.

Leaning against the wall out in the hall, Andi gathered her breath in. This could not be happening. It just *couldn't.* Adjusting the strap of her overalls, Andi pulled her backpack up onto her shoulder. A tear dropped down her cheek. Andi wiped it off angrily, knowing that she couldn't walk out onto the playground crying. All she had to do was walk through the playground to the gate, and she would be free of all of this. *For now, anyway,* she admitted begrudgingly.

As her feet hit the concrete asphalt of the playground, she heard Gaby yell her name. Andi kept walking, hoping that the girls would think the wind from the sea had drowned their voices out. She did not want to talk to anyone right now, least of all Gaby. But Gaby kept calling after her until Andi stopped.

"What?" She finally replied.

Gaby jumped down from the jungle gym, her entourage gathering around her as she walked right up to Andi. "What'd Dugger want with you?" There was a note of jealousy in Gaby's voice. Andi almost laughed. Gaby didn't have to be jealous of anything. It was true that Ms. Dugger seemed to pay more attention to Andi than the other students, but now Andi knew why.

"I got the top grade on the English composition paper," she answered. It *was* true. Ms. Dugger had used this as an opening, before getting to what she really wanted to say to Andi.

Gaby's faced flashed with jealousy. Then she retorted, "Bet she wanted to talk to you about your *retard* brother." She tapped her feet on the playground. "Right?"

Andi slammed her backpack into Gaby's face with full force. Gaby flew backward onto the asphalt playground, her nose bleeding. Gaby began to cry, clutching her arm.

Andi's heart was stone cold. She stood over Gaby, saying nothing. The playground was quiet. The girls from behind were staring at them. Andi spoke to Gaby through clenched teeth.

"You can say whatever you want about me. But not about my family."

Gaby screamed, "You think you're better than everyone else. Don't you?"

Andi gritted her teeth as she picked up her backpack. She walked to the school gate. Finally, she turned back to where Gaby still lay.

"I don't think I'm better than anyone ... except for you." The rage welled up in her again. She swung her backpack in an arc again as a threat.

"Don't *ever* say anything like that again. *Not ever!*" Andi screamed. She ran off toward Edge Street, sobbing. She could hear the other twelve-year-old girls crowding around Gaby. She brushed her chestnut hair back behind her, as if she were brushing all of them away. It wasn't enough.

Andi cried as she walked up the little road. Few cars came this far up the island of Grey Cove. Most stayed below in the village, near the shops where the ferry was. She wasn't worried about anyone seeing her. Thank God it was Friday. She didn't have to worry about facing Gaby or any of those girls until Monday. Or Ms. Dugger, for that matter. The meeting with her teacher sat like a stone in Andi's stomach. She drew her breath in shakily. Her feet found themselves on a dirt path climbing up toward where her home was.

Home. The path rose sharply as it diverted west from Edge Street, making it quite a climb. The rise flattened out to a jutting crag of rock. The rock was known to the island residents as the cliff, offering any who came this way amazing views. *But never like today.*

She rarely came home this late, and the sun was already dying in the distance. Andi stood there for a moment, transfixed by the golden sheen the sun gave off. Its light bounced off the waves. She shook her head in wonder. It was always cloudy, obstructing the views of the other islands. Not today. Their outlines were quite clear, stretched against the sun on the sea.

She felt the ground move beneath her feet. Stunned, Andi stumbled to her knees before catching herself. An earthquake? Here? Andi was alone. Nervously, she drew in her breath.

Out of nowhere, she heard singing. It didn't sound like anything she'd heard before. Andi strained to hear more. A definite sound of many voices joining like a chorus. Joyful noises forming themselves into words of a language she did not understand. Andi turned around. There was no one behind her. She turned back. The sound was coming from the ocean. Thousands of whales, dolphins, sea lions, seals, and even more were gathering in the bay below her cliffside home. She could only see the bay from where she stood — any closer, and her view would disappear entirely.

Even a huge gathering of bald eagles flew over the small indentation of sea that was almost private to Andi's home alone. Heads of the watery creatures rose above the water. Their voices rolled over Andi like a towering wave of sound. The wings of the eagles and other birds seemed to beat in accordance with the many cadences of song coming from the water. She sat down in awe. The vision soothed Andi's lingering anger from the playground incident. The worries she was carrying about the meeting with Ms. Dugger began to fade.

There were so many different species! The song hit notes Andi had never known existed. Her heart began to thud inside her. Surely the earth itself was shaking with the music. Or was she imagining this? How was it possible—both the gathering of the animals and the unearthly song?

Her eyes darted toward the village of Grey Cove below. She figured that everyone would be on the beach listening. But there was no one. No cars moved on the few roads she could see from her vantage point on the cliff. Nobody was taking pictures. Very few could see the bay from below, but there should have been at least a few people who heard the song. The few stars of early evening twinkled, almost in accordance with it. The waves crashing against the cliff echoed the intonations coming from the water.

Two figures shot out of the water. Andi blinked. It was not a trick of the light. The creatures danced in the air. They encircled one another in a gyrating movement. Their dance matched the harmony of the song she was hearing. Andi gasped. The creatures were *dolphins. Golden* dolphins. They shone with a golden sheen, lit as if from beneath by orange and yellow fire. Their skins shimmered with varying hues of flame.

Andi leaned forward on her knees, trying to see them. One was larger and older—the other was younger. Andi understood. This young, golden creature had just been born. She was sure of it. It was so tiny compared to its mother, less than a third of its size. Its mother was about eight feet long, but Andi could not be sure. It followed its mother's movements with a childish enthusiasm. The mother's movements were more graceful and restrained.

The dance of mother and child ended with the setting of the sun. The many singing creatures disappeared below the sea, suddenly isolating the girl. Andi found herself lost in loneliness. How could she ever explain this to anyone? Who would believe her?

Andi did not know how long she'd sat there looking out to the sea. Darkness had fallen. She knew Grandma Bea would worry, so she began walking toward her home. The stars were high in the sky as she approached the large stone cottage. Gray rock inset, the house rose out of the cliff as if shaped out of it. The fact that her house was older than time relaxed her. It meant that it would keep standing. Its timelessness stood out against everything else that was changing.

The house stood on the cliff facing out toward the sea. The exterior walls of the house were of rectangular stone, its colors alternating between gray, chalk white, tan, and dark brown. Grandma Bea had explained that the cottage was from an older time. Like those of the Welsh, English, and Scottish. It loomed up before her in the dying light.

The door opened before Andi's hands reached the old brass doorknob. Her grandmother Bea stood framed by the doorway. She watched Andi, her lined face asking for an explanation.

"You're late." The voice was sure and clear, which helped unclench Andi's insides. She gave her grandmother a weak smile as she entered. A fire roared in the fireplace. It covered more than half the wall of their living room. Andi looked at the fire and then back at her grandmother speculatively. *So far so good.* Even better than Andi had hoped for.

The interior of the house was cast in a dark wood, save for the stone fireplace. The often-cloudy days on the island did not bring a lot of light inside. Still, all Andi cared about was that it was *home*.

Andi fell back onto the worn but comfortable old couch opposite the fireplace. Her grandmother sat next to her. Grandma Bea's hair was a dirty, stringy gray. On her good days, it was clean and silver, but today she looked a mess. *Still,* Andi reasoned, *it could mean she's been out of it all day and now it's one of her good times.*

"Why so late, Andi?" The reflection of the fire on her grandmother's cheekbones reminded her of the dolphins—the swirling, fiery, golden colors of the two dolphins she'd seen earlier.

Andi traced her fingers on the brown coffee table in front of them. She finally asked, "Did you hear the singing outside? You know, did you ... see anything out there?"

"Singing? Well, no. Not all the way out here," her grandmother answered, perplexed.

Andi changed the subject. "How's Artie?"

"He's been anxious." Her grandmother regarded Andi curiously. Andi knew she wasn't in trouble for being late. She wasn't going to be grounded or anything like that. Her grandmother just needed an explanation.

"Grandma...you remember when you went to the store the other night?" Her grandmother nodded. "Ms. Dugger, my teacher, was there. At the store." Andi looked at her grandmother for confirmation that she understood. She got none except for a slight frown. "She said you didn't recognize her, that you were lost. She made me stay after school today. She wanted to know if you were all right."

"And what did you tell her?" Grandma Bea asked, her eyes sharp.

"I told her that—I told her that you'd been taking a new medication. That you were just getting used to it. But she wasn't satisfied with that answer. Grandma, she said she drove you home in her car from the store. Ms. Dugger said you were mumbling strange words the whole drive back."

"Was I?"

"That's what she said. Grandma, I think she called a social worker. From Social Services. They may be sending someone over, you know, to check us out." Andi ended with a slight plea in her voice, looking at her grandmother's face. Had she understood? Andi chose not to mention the fight with Gaby.

Her grandmother stared into the fire. There was no answer.

Andi began tentatively. "Grandma, they'll take us away. They will. And none of us will be together. I'd have a different set of foster parents than Artie. What would become of you? We need to figure this out. We need to figure out a way to stay together. We can't let Ms. Dugger win."

Andi nudged her. "Grandma?"

Her grandmother looked up vacantly. She scanned the living room. Maybe she was looking for something. Andi nudged Grandma Bea again, hoping to keep her from disappearing. Her grandmother turned to her, frowning. "Dugger?" she said.

"My sixth-grade teacher," Andi answered, her heart sinking.

"Dugger?" The light had gone out of Grandma Bea's eyes.

Andi rose and went to a bay window that overlooked the sea. Andi could see the waves beyond the cliff. The moon shone on the water. Tapping her fingers against the glass window, she left fingerprints on the pane. The fingerprints faded from the glass, only their outlines remaining visible.

Grandma Bea was a shell of who she used to be. Her awareness, her memories had disappeared. The outline of her was like the fingerprints still on the pane. An edge, a shape. Andi could not see the woman her grandmother once was. Her grandmother was a smudge of her former self. Wasn't life supposed to be more than that?

Andi pursed her lips together. She wasn't giving up. She couldn't. Detectives and policemen dusted for prints, finding them when no one else could. Andi planned to dig down into her grandmother's memories. From that, she would find a way to save herself and them, to keep them together. She wouldn't lose Artie, nor would they lose their grandmother. They would find a way to beat the odds one way or another. They *would*.

As if on cue, she heard her brother's slow footsteps thud on the stairs above. He was looking for her. She turned around. Grandma Bea had fallen asleep in front of the fire. Putting a blanket on her grandmother, Andi turned to Artie.

"Hi," Andi said, smiling at her twin, who'd entered the room. She looked at his wild blond hair, so different from her own. Who would guess that they were twins? They had the same clear-as-glass green eyes, but that was it. He was blond and fair while she was brunette and darker. Andi put her hands on Artie's arm. He didn't always like touching, but this time he didn't object.

Artie held his favorite toy in his left hand, a silver slinky. She could hear its rings coiling backward and forward. The slinky possessed

a springing rhythm. A rhythm to a music that existed only in Artie's own mind. He wrapped his arms around her, still holding the slinky in his left hand. She found both the hug and sound of the slinky soothing.

Andi released him from her arms, holding him at a distance. He said one word. "Late?" It was a question without reproach, something Andi was thankful for. He just wanted to know why. And why wouldn't he? He was all alone most of the day, especially now with Grandma the way she was.

The official story was that Grandma Bea homeschooled him. Andi knew better. Artie homeschooled himself. He'd gone on to higher math, leaving her forever behind. Every time he tried to show Andi his advanced formulas, she shrugged her shoulders. She did not understand them. The only thing she could do was tell him how proud she was of him, which made him beam. Andi's pride was real. She knew his formulas were correct.

Pulling herself away from Artie, she asked, "Did you see—" She paused. "Did you see or hear anything from outside?"

Artie looked at her oddly. "Heard *something*. What?" he said, his eyes luminous with curiosity.

Feeling overwhelmed, Andi decided to drop the subject. She smiled, sticking her tongue out at him before saying, "Baby brother," trying to tickle him. He frowned, not liking the reminder that Andi was two minutes older than he was. She tickled him on the stomach. He broke out into a wide smile.

"Some things happened at school," Andi continued. That much was true. "So tell me about you. Hungry? Should I make crackers and cheese?" He nodded.

Andi walked quickly into the kitchen. Artie put his hand on her shoulder as she began to get crackers and cheese. This was enough to bring tears to her eyes. Artie always knew when something was wrong. Andi couldn't fool him. Without him saying anything, she turned and collapsed on his shoulder. "Oh, Artie," she said, crying. "I'm so afraid. I'm so afraid."

Her twin held her in his arms, the slinky still dangling in his hand.

For a moment, she and Artie were the two golden dolphins dancing together in the sea.

Two

A Door Into an Unknown Room

That night, Andi found herself jerked awake from her sleep by a voice whispering, "*Help me ...*"

Andi sat up in her bed, confused. She checked her clock. It was after midnight. She waited to see if she heard anything more. For a moment, there was nothing. Then the voice came again. "*Help me.*"

Andi slowly slid out of bed and wrapped herself in a robe. She checked Artie's room. Her twin was fast asleep. Creeping down the stairs, she turned on the hall light to see if Grandma Bea was awake in the adjacent bedroom. But Grandma Bea's head lay on her pillow; she was fast asleep.

Again, the voice came. "*Help me.*"

Andi's nerves were now on edge. She moved into the living room, peering through the back window to the ocean beyond. The moon hung over water so still it looked like glass.

The voice came again, this time more insistent. "Help me."

Scared as she was, a wild, irrational hope popped into Andi's head. "Mother?" She hesitated. Again she spoke. "Mom? Is that you?"

The voice came again, this time no longer a whisper but clear and distinct. And now the malevolence behind the voice as it repeated the words was unmistakable: "I'm trapped. Help me." The voice sounded like rock scraping on rock. Nothing like her mother's, Andi realized.

"Who are you?" Andi shouted into the darkness. "What do you want?"

Andi heard footsteps upstairs. *Great.* She'd woken up Artie. She heard him coming, his slippers padding on the stairs. He entered the room, his bleary-eyed face half in darkness. Artie stared at her quizzically.

"Do you hear it?" she asked him. She motioned in the air, trying to pinpoint the source of the noise.

The evil voice erupted into a wail. "Help me!" the voice screamed, its tone angry, demanding. Andi felt chilled, as if the voice were screaming out for blood.

Like a siren, it reverberated throughout the room. Andi screamed, falling to her knees as she covered her ears with her hands. Artie approached her, examining her with a puzzled look.

"You can't hear it?" Andi asked, dumbfounded.

Her twin shook his head no.

As she removed her hands from her ears, Andi listened. There was nothing. She rose to her feet. Smiling reassuringly at Artie, she walked around the house, looking. Finally, she looked outside the window.

"Don't," Artie said, his expression agitated and grieved. She understood why.

"That's not what I was doing," Andi explained. "I wasn't—I wasn't looking for where Mom—" She stopped.

"Not there," Artie said to her firmly.

Not there, Andi repeated to herself bitterly as she led her twin upstairs to their bedrooms. *Not anywhere.* As she lay in her bed wide awake, Andi listened for the voice but heard nothing. Was she going crazy? Like Grandma Bea? Maybe everything was becoming too much for her. She finally drifted back into an uneasy sleep.

***

The next morning dawned bright and cold. Andi wrapped herself in a blanket as she tiptoed out of her bedroom and down the hall to

Artie's. She found him crouched on the floor, absorbed with his slinky even while writing numbers on a piece of paper next to him. The papers were a jumble, surrounding Artie from all sides. He clutched the slinky in one hand, fingers coiling through the metal rings as he wrote what looked to be equations with the other hand.

Artie looked surprised when he saw her standing in the doorway. Andi preferred to sleep as late as ten or ten thirty in the morning. He cocked his head to the side as if to ask her why she was awake so early. It was their twin language, Andi knew.

"I need to ask Jubal a few questions," she explained.

Andi felt the intensity of Artie's stare. He was obviously wondering why she needed to see Jubal so badly. She wasn't ready to answer that yet. She changed the subject.

"Are you wet?" she asked, hoping not. He'd been doing so much better lately. Grandma Bea couldn't help him unbutton his pajamas and button up a new pair anymore, so it fell to Andi to do so. Artie was patient with her on Saturdays and Sundays, knowing they were her sleep-in days. She often found him shivering in cold, wet pajamas, waiting for her to wake up.

Andi smiled back at Artie as he shook his head no, hoping the relief didn't show up on her face too much. Artie was getting older, and she wasn't going to be able to help him much in that area anymore. Even if she solved this Ms. Dugger problem, it would only be a temporary solution. Andi realized that many things were going to have to change, and this scared her.

"Pour yourself some cereal if you get hungry," Andi said, smiling. "Okay?"

He nodded, his long blond hair falling across his forehead as he turned back to his equations.

A few minutes later, Andi dashed out the door toward the village below. She'd checked in on Grandma Bea and found her asleep. Her grandmother never used to sleep so much; she used to be up before everyone else and the last one to bed. That changed when Grandma Bea started to lose her memory.

When did she start to lose her memory? Andi frowned as she tried to figure out when exactly she'd begun to see the signs. As she walked, she looked at the rocky strip of beach that stretched all the way from the base of the cliff to where the island curved inland. It'd started sometime soon after her mother disappeared; Andi knew that much.

Further down the shore where the land curved eastward was the Grey Cove harbor. A ferry brought commuters and visitors in from the mainland, from near Anacortes and Seattle. That was part of being one of the islands in the San Juan archipelago. Andi felt that the small streets leading from the ferry were touristy, fake. She felt it gave visitors what they wanted, art and seafood restaurants, but for her, this was not Grey Cove. Even the waterfront homes bordering much of the island felt unreal to her. These houses stopped just shy of the small inlet bay under her cliffside home. The many smaller boats docked in the harbor bobbed to and fro, tethered securely to shore. *Tethered.* Her grandmother was, if anything, *untethered.* As if she were a vessel come loose, bobbing along the waves and in danger of capsizing, sinking, or crashing against the rocks.

Which is what was happening now, wasn't it? Only it was she and Artie who would crash against the rocks. She admonished herself for not feeling sorrier for her grandmother. Grandma Bea deserved compassion; what she was going through was horrible. Still, Andi knew that she could not separate herself or Artie from what was happening to their grandmother. They were all tied together.

Andi followed the road that sloped toward the village below. Edge Street entered the village of Grey Cove, intersecting with the Avenue. The intersection of Edge Street and the Avenue made up what Andi considered the "touristy" part of the town. Littered with beach shops, jewelry stores, art galleries, and small health-food stores, this part of town was so *fake.* Andi rolled her eyes as she walked past.

Instead of entering the streets served by the ferry, Andi walked toward a few old and dilapidated houses that lay just hidden beneath the tourists' village. Andi lived above the village on the cliff; Jubal lived beneath it. Paint was peeling off some of the houses, while others had rooftops in need of repair or overgrown backyards. But this was real; the houses were worn by the wind that came in from the sea, from its salt air. These houses testified to what Andi thought was *real* island living. She walked toward a small gray house with black shutters that looked out onto the ocean.

Hesitantly, she knocked at the door. Andi knew that her arrival would surprise Jubal. But there was someone else she was more worried about. The black door opened inward, revealing a messy house. There were beer bottles on the table with old cigarettes smashed into ashtrays. Mrs. Smith, Jubal's mother, peered at Andi from around the door.

"Oh, it's you." Mrs. Smith sniffed. "I never see you here this early. Come in."

Andi entered the house with its strange smells of ash and stale smoke. Mrs. Smith looked nothing like her son. She was small and overweight with large, thick, round glasses. Her blonde hair looked like a bad dye job. Her white skin bore a strange pallor, like she had faded to gray from whatever color she used to be, much like her house. There was a flatness in her blue eyes, as if she had taught herself never to become excited. As if life was too disappointing — or had disappointed her too much.

Still, Andi knew Mrs. Smith was more than she appeared. At Andi's mother's memorial, while everyone had shared their regrets, Mrs. Smith had said nothing. She'd chosen to squeeze Andi's shoulder before departing the Johnston house. Andi always remembered that small touch and the comfort it had brought her. Still, Andi knew that Jubal was rarely comforted by his mother.

"In his room." Mrs. Smith cocked her head, indicating to Andi the direction she should go. Andi thanked her. Mrs. Smith shrugged and then plopped down on the couch in front of the television. Andi heard the channels change as she walked down the hall.

Andi knocked on Jubal's door. "Come in," Jubal said.

She opened the door to Jubal's room. If the house reflected Jubal's mother's personality, Jubal's room reflected *his*. Books piled on top of one another, with a computer on a desk with a ham radio on its right, binoculars on its left. Maps covered the walls. Magazine clippings of articles had been shoved into corners. Andi stepped into the room carefully.

"Smells like something died in here!" she said. She made a resolution to stay as far away as possible from Jubal's dirty socks.

"I left the socks there just for you," Jubal bantered. He was sitting in a chair peering out of the window and did not turn around to greet her. He wore a baseball cap backward, black hair curling out from under it. The front said Atoms: Building Blocks. *Typical of him not to turn around,* Andi thought.

"Did you use your foot spray?" Her voice adopted a joking tone, trying to get him to turn around.

He laughed but still didn't turn around. He pulled a yellow canister from his desk and sprayed it on his bare feet.

"Happy now?" Jubal asked.

The smell from the canister was that of chemicals, and Andi gagged. Still, she had to admit that the smell was better than his socks. "I guess," she gasped.

He continued, his voice teasing. "So the world is coming to an end."

"I'll bite," she said as she tried to clear comic books off his bed. "Why is it coming to an end?"

Jubal spun around to face Andi, a smile in his blue eyes. They were the only visible sign of his mother, although, unlike hers, his always had a mischievous glint. His dark hair and skin came from his father.

"You're here at nine o'clock in the morning on a Saturday!" He cocked an eyebrow at her. "You're wearing overalls with a stain on the left knee that has already dried. I'm guessing you wore your overalls yesterday too. Yet you criticize my smelly socks."

Andi's face flamed. "*Jubal!*"

Jubal held up his hands in a placating gesture. "Okay, okay," he said. "Andi, in God's name, what are you doing here so early? We both know you don't wake up until noon."

Before Andi could answer, Jubal's head jerked with a start, and his gaze shifted to the radio. He pressed his fingers to his lips

as he turned up the volume. A male voice filled the room. "Unusual activity was detected within the vicinity of the San Juan Islands. Whale watchers are describing whales, seals, and dolphins present in huge numbers."

The voice cut out of existence as Jubal lowered the volume, a look of excitement on his face. Her heart rose into her throat. This was part of what she'd come down to talk to Jubal about. She hadn't been sure where to begin.

"What do you think?" Jubal sounded eager to discuss this new development with her.

Andi replied cautiously. "What do *you* think of it?"

"There's going to be a meteor shower tonight," Jubal informed her, as if that explained everything.

"Um, I don't get it." Andi adopted a more petulant tone. She didn't like it when he left her in the dark. It bothered her when both Artie and Jubal shared or understood something together that she didn't. That she couldn't share in.

Jubal leaned forward in his chair. "It's going to be one of the biggest in years and quite visible." His voice quivered with excitement. "Going to be a clear night."

"Okay," Andi responded uncertainly. It sounded possible, but there was a piece missing from the puzzle Jubal was assembling. A piece that only she had.

"Andi," Jubal began. "The Pleiades show up much later in the year. It's spring. The meteor shower tonight is unprecedented. No one predicted it—at least not until yesterday afternoon—after that whole thing with the whales and dolphins. And about dolphins—well, I heard something weird yesterday. The same guy " he said, motioning toward the radio.

"A golden dolphin?" Andi asked.

Jubal looked at her sharply and then nodded.

"You've heard of it then? The guy on the radio wasn't sure. He thought maybe because of the sunset that the dolphins seemed golden, but he was really overwhelmed by what he saw ... as if they were *truly* golden ... no one would believe him anyway." He shrugged, eyeing Andi with curiosity.

So at least someone else had seen them!

"I saw them yesterday," Andi said, holding nothing back. The song, the creatures in the sea, the stars—it still all stood out clearly in her mind. "It's true. They really *are* golden. It isn't a trick of the light."

"Them? There's more than one?"

Andi adjusted the strap of her overalls and bit her fingernails. "They ..." She hesitated before starting again. "They looked like dolphins but golden. One was much bigger than the other. I think one was the mother, the other was a baby."

Jubal stared at her. "So that's why you're here so early. You want to find them."

Andi smiled. Jubal knew her so well.

"That's part of it," she said, "but not all."

Jubal nodded, not asking what the other part was.

Without knowing why, Andi knew something. "It's *me* that must find them, Jubal. *Me.* They're not going to be safe unless I do." Andi remembered the disembodied voice she heard the night before. There had to be a connection somehow with the golden dolphins. Unless the house had been creaking the night before. Maybe the cliff had been moving because of the earthquake. Had she been dreaming? What if she was wrong? Deep down Andi knew she wasn't. There was a connection. In that room in her mind.

Jubal examined her. "I guess I can understand part of that," he said. "Part of it, if they're dolphins and if they're *golden*—there'll be a lot of interest in them. Maybe not the best kind of interest."

He looked at her quizzically as if to ask, *why you? Why do you have to be the one to find them?*

Andi realized she wasn't ready to tell Jubal about the voice she'd heard the night before. Remembering was still so scary.

Remembering the sunset from the day before did something rather curious to Andi's mind. Her mind was drifting away from the conversation with Jubal. While she could still see Jubal in front of her, the sensation of swimming toward a destination took over. A destination that she would reach at a certain time. *Night*, Andi realized.

Shaking herself out of her reverie, Andi shouted, "The cave! They're going to be in the cave tonight!"

"What cave? Andi, what's going on?" Jubal's face neared hers, concerned. "How do you know that?"

Andi shook her head. "I don't know. I can't explain it. They'll be in the cave under the cliff tonight." Andi heard the reluctance in her voice.

"The cave you haven't been to since your mom ..." Jubal's voice trailed off.

"Yeah," Andi said, twisting her hair. "my mom's cave." Well, it wasn't technically her mother's but that was how Andi had come to see it over the years.

She wanted to talk about the images entering her mind from outside. They didn't scare her like the voice had the night before. It was hard talking about the cavern because of its connection with her mother. So Andi remained silent about the visions she was getting.

Jubal drew in his breath. "This is weird," he said. "The meteor shower is tonight. You're sure you want to go to the cave tonight?" There was a note of hesitation in his voice, and Andi realized her friend did not want to miss the meteor shower.

"Want to watch the meteor shower from my place?" Andi asked. "We have the best view of anywhere on the island, and we're away from the lights. You'll be able to see everything. And you could come down to the cave with me. I haven't been there since ..."

Jubal's expression was sympathetic, but Andi's face flushed with embarrassment. "Anyway," she continued, "will you come?"

Jubal's eyes sparkled. "As long as you don't give me grief about my socks."

"I don't know, Jubal," she said. "I mean, they *are* pretty god-awful."

Jubal tried to swat her on the shoulder, but Andi dodged him, jumping to her feet from the bed.

They made plans to meet that evening. He promised to bring a sleeping bag so that he could camp out in Artie's room. She did not tell him about hearing the voice the night before, nor did she talk with him about Ms. Dugger. Andi left Jubal's house feeling shaken and confused.

She was certain that, one way or another, she would begin to find answers that night.

He did not believe her. That was obvious. But he was so curious about the cave at the base of the cliff that he was willing to play along.

Andi realized that Jubal wasn't telling her everything either. Wreathing his right eye was the remnant of an old bruise. It was not the first time. She realized that was why he hadn't spun around in his chair to face her. Looking back at Jubal's house, Andi knew her best friend loved his mother and wanted to protect her. Andi found herself wishing that she could protect *him*.

As Andi hiked back up to her cliff home, she noted that the house looked still, serene as it stood on the cliff overlooking the sea. She wondered where the golden dolphins were now. Had they sent those impressions into her mind? For a moment, she felt like crying. Was she going crazy? Hearing a voice last night but knowing it was very different from the visions she was having … it felt like too much. How could she be sure? Andi went back to that first sensation when she first realized she was seeing a vision, of feeling like she was underwater with them. It hadn't scared her like the voice did, and Andi didn't know why. Should she be scared?

Try as she might, she could not find that place in her mind again. She frowned, thinking. It had been like opening a door into a room that she had never known was there. Somehow, the addition of that room changed the house entirely. But now she couldn't find the door again and was still trapped in the same old house of her mind. Andi sighed, squared her shoulders, and continued her uphill walk back toward her cliffside home.

Three

The Meteor Shower

Artie pressed his face against the glass as he stood next to Andi. She smiled at her twin's eagerness. He was looking for Jubal, who he loved as much as Andi did. Still, as she peered out the glass, she could not help but feel anxious.

Where was Jubal? He'd told her he would be there before dark, and now the first stars were already coming out. Her gaze went from Edge Street toward the ocean horizon. The golden dolphins would be here soon. Not for the last time, she found herself feeling frustrated at how she knew that.

Andi put her hands on Artie's shoulders and pulled him from the window. She looked at him, baffled again by how young he acted compared to how wise he could be sometimes. His blond hair fell into his green eyes. He was so thin, almost like a toothpick, making his eyes quite wide, wider than hers. Always the same color though. Her heart surged as she looked at him. Grandma Bea had taken Artie to doctors to find out why he was different. Diagnoses had ranged from Asperger's to autism to pure genius. No one diagnosis agreed with the other. Artie was, quite simply, Artie.

"Artie," she began. "You understand the plan for this evening?"

She'd gone over it with him many times since arriving home in time to make him lunch. He nodded reluctantly.

"You go to the cave. Then back." It was a lot for Artie to say all at once. Andi nodded.

"You don't tell Grandma Bea we're gone, if she wakes up," Andi said.

Artie's eyes flicked to the right, not meeting Andi's. Not a good sign, Andi

knew.

"Artie?" she asked gently.

Artie looked her squarely in the eyes and sighed. "Depends," he answered.

"On what?"

"How long." He adopted a stern, determined stare.

"How long what?" Andi sometimes wished Artie would talk like other people did. But then she felt guilty for becoming exasperated with him.

"For you to come back." Artie's mouth clamped up as soon as he said it. Andi knew she would not be able to sway him. *Okay. All right.* Andi breathed, trying not to panic. For all she knew, she could be going crazy. Then she

"Just give us some time, okay, Artie? Give us some time to do what we need to do. Please." Andi tried to make her voice sound as sincere as possible.

Artie stared at her for forever before he answered. "I want to go."

"No," Andi replied without even thinking about it. "You're afraid of the dark, Artie. Remember?"

Artie was quiet. "You think I can't," he said finally.

"Can't what?" Andi was impatient now. Jubal still hadn't arrived, and Artie was being difficult. "Artie, why are you doing this now? We've talked about this all afternoon, ever since I came home." There was a pleading tone in Andi's voice that she never used with Artie.

"You think I can't ... do the things you can." His voice broke her heart. Andi wanted to pull her hair out. Why was he doing this now? When he had all afternoon to do this, why now?

Before she could say anything, Artie marched off to his room and shut the door quietly yet firmly. Andi followed him to the door but found it locked. She knocked.

"Artie?" she whispered through the door. There was no response. The doorbell rang below.

Andi groaned. The timing could not be worse. Jubal was finally here. Artie, who never got mad, was now angry at her. She knocked again on Artie's door.

"Artie?" she called out. "Jubal's here. Don't you want to come see Jubal? I know he wants to see you." She hated talking to Artie like he was a baby. Other people did it to him all the time, and she did not. He was, after all, her twin. He understood her better than she herself did. She in turn understood him better than he himself did. Most of the time anyway. She gave up rapping on the door and ran downstairs to let Jubal in.

"Grandma?" Andi sang out as she opened the door. Jubal stood waiting, sleeping bag in hand and a backpack stuffed with pajamas, Andi guessed. A camera bag over his shoulder. When her grandmother did not respond, Andi motioned for Jubal to enter, which he did, not needing any explanation—something Andi was grateful for. She looked sharply at Jubal's face, at the bruise. He turned his face away from her, trying to prevent a long discussion about his eye. He succeeded. Andi had too much on her mind.

"Grandma?" Andi yelled out, walking through the house. She finally found her grandmother seated in front of the television set. Her eyes were glazed over with no sign of recognition.

Andi put her hand on her grandmother's shoulder. Grandma Bea jerked sharply, staring at Andi. Andi stared down at her grandmother, trying to figure out what she should do.

"Enjoy your program," Andi said glumly. She saw her grandmother squint her eyes at her trying to recognize her. There was so sign of recognition from her grandmother before she moved back to watch her program.

"Welcome to Saturday night at the Johnston's," Andi said to Jubal with more bitterness than she'd realized she had. She walked back up the stairs toward Artie's room. She began knocking rather hard on her twin's door. Jubal came to stand behind her.

"What are we doing this for?" He asked curiously.

Andi gritted her teeth and shook her head no, indicating to Jubal that she was not in the mood to answer his questions. She heard stirring on the other side of the door.

"Artie?" she yelled. "Artie! Please open the door."

She heard her twin walk to the door but stop before opening it.

"Artie?" Andi called hopefully. "Are you there?"

"I'm sorry," she heard him say. "Sorry."

"Oh, Artie," Andi sighed, relief flooding through her. "I'm sorry too. Can we just work this out and forget about it?"

"Not that," Artie answered.

There was a *click* as Artie unlocked the door and stuck his head out. She was about to hug him before she noticed something. His pants were soaking wet. He had a crestfallen look on his face.

"Oh, *Artie*," Andi said. "This is my fault." She pushed forward into the room with him. "This is all my fault," she repeated as she closed the door in Jubal's confused face. She would explain to him later.

"Right," Artie said. Confused, Andi looked at him. Then she understood.

"Artie, no. *No.* I never said you couldn't do things like other people. *You* said that. Not me." She made her voice as firm as she could.

Artie's shamed face told her all she needed to know. Andi swallowed, thinking. She was going to have to do her best.

"Artie, you know," she said slowly, trying to encourage him, "you're getting too old for me to do this for you. Can you take those pants off by yourself? I know you can unbutton the top button. And the zipper. You can do the zipper. You can do it just fine."

Andi made herself turn so that she wasn't looking at her twin. She whispered over her shoulder, "Just give me your clothes when they're off."

She rummaged in his drawer, grabbing a pair of sweats and

underpants. *There.* Keeping her eyes averted, she ran out of his room into the hall bathroom ... Jubal had gone downstairs. She grabbed a towel and held one half of it under the faucet while keeping the other half dry. Back in Artie's room, Andi saw that he still hadn't gotten his pants off. She knew he could put the sweats on by himself, if only he could unbutton his pants.

She waited, eyes averted again, until she heard a *snap* and knew Artie had done it. She heard him slide his pants off and throw his clothes into the corner disgustedly as he'd done many times. She sighed. She'd hoped that by taking his pants off by himself, he would feel better. Obviously not.

"Artie," she found herself talking quickly, not wanting to embarrass him, "I do have to do this thing tonight. I can't explain it to you yet, but I promise you it is important. I'm sorry I tried to leave you out of it. You can come with us if you want." She ended her speech on a more placating note.

Andi heard him pick the towel up and walk to the door.

"Jubal?" he said.

"He's downstairs," Andi said, thanking God for Jubal's quick thinking.

Artie opened the door and left the room. Breathing a sigh of relief, Andi bent down to pick up his wet clothes. She ran downstairs to the basement and threw them into the laundry. Coming back up, she found Jubal waiting for her alone.

"He hasn't come down," Jubal said, his expression sympathetic.

Andi squared her shoulders and marched upstairs again. The door wasn't locked. She found Artie seated on the floor, staring into space.

"Hey," Andi said, smiling.

Artie refused to look at her, staring at the wall or maybe past it. Andi wasn't sure.

"Artie—"

"Not going." Artie's face was still, a mask.

Andi sighed. This was going to be harder than she expected. Much harder.

"Artie, we want you to come—"

"Go!" he screamed, starting to pound on the floor with his fists, something he rarely did anymore. Andi closed his door but remained standing outside it. His pounding ceased. Andi waited until it sounded as if he had gotten up from the floor and gone to bed. There was nothing she could do. She was going to have to make it up to him later. She put her hand on Artie's door, willing all her love through it to him. It was silly and futile, she knew, but she had to do *something*. Anything.

Andi walked down the hall to the stairs. She passed by the window that Artie had pressed up against as he waited for Jubal. She wished that the conversation she'd had with her twin about his not coming with them had never happened.

Stars were falling, streaking across the sky. Their tails of fire trailed behind them right before dying just as they hit the water. Transfixed, she stared out the window a few more moments.

"Amazing, isn't it," Jubal said, appearing behind her. It was not a question.

"Do they—do they hit the water?" Andi asked. "When they land?" She blushed furiously. She hated acting the fool when she felt that Jubal was so brilliant.

His answer didn't make her feel like a fool at all, something she loved about him. "There usually isn't much left. A lot of it burns out as it enters the atmosphere. But yes, if anything's left, it hits the water." He put a hand on her shoulder.

"If we're going to do this," he said, "we should go."

Andi nodded. With one last look toward Artie's room, she went downstairs, Jubal right behind her.

Sound from the television carried from the living room to the entry hall. After grabbing a jacket, Andi investigated the living room. Grandma Bea sat fast asleep in front of the set.

So far so good. It had become a pattern for her to sneak out to the grocery store while Grandma Bea fell asleep in front of the set. Andi had banked on it happening tonight. Grandma Bea never went upstairs to check on her and Artie anymore before going to bed. As far as she knew, both she and Jubal were in the clear. That didn't help Andi's guilt though.

They walked out into the early spring chill, the stars sparkling even more in the cold. After taking a few tentative steps from the house with a flashlight beam in front of them, Jubal reached for Andi's arm. They walked several yards away from the house, further inland. Andi's eyes slowly adjusted to the darkness. She squinted into the night. Further ahead, just beyond where their property line ended, was a succession of cars, trucks, and vans. They were all parked off Edge Street. They were there to see the meteor shower. The falling stars flamed into long stripes dancing across the sky. The air was electric, dancing with the magnetism of the passing meteors as they continued their descent to earth. Tonight something important was going to happen—she just didn't know what.

Jubal was at a loss for words. Andi dragged him along as he continued staring up at the sky.

"Was it this beautiful yesterday?" he said.

Focusing on the ground in front of her, Andi frowned. "There was no meteor shower yesterday."

"No, the song. All the dolphins and the whales. Was it like this? This beautiful?" Jubal's voice was hushed and reverential.

Andi smiled. "Yes, yes, it was. In a very different way. But yes."

Andi could tell that Jubal's resistance to what she had shared earlier was starting to weaken.

They had arrived.

"This is it, Jubal," she said. "We're here."

Just as the cliff began to jut out from Edge Street, there was a small stone ridge. It ran from the cliff from the right side, serving as a path to the thin strip of rocky beach below at its base. The ridge was wide enough for one large-sized adult to walk down on. Andi was not worried about herself and Jubal being able to navigate it. He would just have to walk directly behind her.

"Stay close to the cliff wall," Andi ordered, saying it to herself as much as she was to Jubal. "As far away from the drop on the other side as you can."

Andi stepped down first onto the ridge path, clinging to the cliff wall with one hand while holding the flashlight in the other. The other side of the ridge path ended in a steep plunge down to huge and pointed boulders rising from the Salish Sea, which surrounded her beloved San Juan Islands.

"Is this where you think—" Jubal began to ask, his voice dying in the wind.

"Don't talk about it," Andi hissed through clenched teeth. She could *not* think about that. Not now. She began walking down the ridge path. She never let her hands leave the cold touch of the cliff wall as she began the descent toward the rocky beach below. Andi repeated the old words spoken to her by her mother in her mind. *Measure it out. It should be about twenty-five small, good steps down. Count every step. Remember I'm right behind you.*

Only this time, she wasn't right behind Andi. Jubal was, and he'd never been here before. She had met Jubal after her mother's death. Their friendship was a surprise that had brought a joy into her life even if it didn't lessen her grief. Andi's stomach lurched. She might be putting Jubal in danger. What would her mother say? *But she's not here to tell me anything.* For a moment, a surge of anger and bitterness welled up inside her. It gave her the confidence to take one step after another. Another. Then another.

Andi closed her eyes, determined not to open them until they were at the cliff base. Then salt spray touched her face. They were at the bottom. The meteor shower was in full glory. Instantaneous flashes of light danced down from the sky to the ocean.

"Jubal," she said. "We're here."

He put his hand on her shoulder. "Are you all right?" He looked all around them, his eyes wide. "Is this where ...?" He could not finish.

Andi nodded slowly. This was where her mother died. Grief radiated through her shoulders, her muscles like cancer. She drew in a sharp breath, trying to throw off the heaviness she felt.

"I'm sorry," Jubal said. It was nothing he hadn't said before, but the fact that he was here with her, the first person she'd shown it to, made it more real for her. She remembered seeing the jacket on top of the boulder from above with Artie. A weeping Grandma Bea pointing to it. Artie had been emotional too, in his own way. But Andi—she'd gone stone cold the moment she'd found out, seen it—three years ago. She'd studied the boulder from the cliff's top dispassionately. Examined every detail. The memory stood out too brightly in her memory.

"We'd better go," she said to Jubal. "The cave's in the other direction. We need to curve around the cliff to the other side. That's where it is."

Low tide allowed them the necessary space to walk the thin strip of rocky beach to the cavern. They stepped on any dry stone they could find, balancing themselves on it before jumping to the next stone. It did not take long. As the beach curved around to the other side of the cliff, Andi found the entrance to her mother's sea cave. At the cave mouth, the rocky beach narrowed into a thin passage entering the cavern. It barely fit one person at a time, even quite thin ones like Jubal. It widened to a quite large cave with a pool in the center of it, fed by blowholes beneath. The thin ridge encircling the pool always seemed to stay above sea level; at least, as far as Andi knew.

The roof of the cavern was high and domed. The cavern was dark, barely gray. Andi knew that the pool was quite deep since she could not see the bottom. The small ridge path surrounding the pool did not slope down into it. Rather the sides were fixed, sliding deep into the water.

She watched Jubal take in everything and smiled to herself. The cave was a secret from others. The passage into it was very hard to find and was surrounded by heather and other plants.

Suddenly Andi became detached from her body, watching herself enter the cave from underwater. *Underwater?* Why was she having this vision of herself? What was happening to her? *Looking above, she saw the huge roof of the cavern. The sheer mass of the cliff scared her. Yet it was unbroken. It would not come down crashing upon her.* Andi came to. What was she thinking? These were another person's thoughts!

All at once, she was inside herself again. She looked around. Light bounced off walls even though it was dark outside. It danced across the walls, echoing the music she'd heard the day before. *The celebration. The whales crooning their song.*

Light. She looked through the cavern entrance. A few meteors were still streaking down to earth. Otherwise it was dark. Yet the light inside the cavern grew brighter, dazzling her eyes. The water stirred. Andi blinked. Something was surfacing from deep underwater. It was the first time Andi had seen the pool so lit up. She gasped when she saw how deep it was.

An exquisite, large golden creature resembling a dolphin rose out of the water. Its mouth parted into a smile. *It must be the mother,* Andi realized. The dolphin swam around the pool of water, her head coming toward the lowest point of the ridge path. She made curious musical sounds, not the typical clicking and squeaking sounds dolphins made. This thing, while it looked and acted like a dolphin, wasn't exactly one ... or was it? It was larger and longer than a fully grown bottlenose dolphin. Andi approached the creature, kneeling on the ridge. Its eyes appeared tired, wary. But its smile seemed real.

Andi put her hands out toward the dolphin, stopping just short of her face. The creature, its mouth still parted in what looked like a smile, had a question in its eyes. Slowly, she swam forward, allowing Andi to touch her. Upon contact, Andi experienced a strange momentary shock. A door into an unknown room of her mind opened again. Andi came strangely awake, as if someone had turned a light on where there had only been darkness. Like at Jubal's when she'd heard the mother calling her, telling her to meet here ... *because ...*

Andi whirled around. "Jubal! Something's wrong! We need to do something!"

Jubal pointed. "What is that?"

A shadowy darkness twisted itself around the dolphin's torso. It was set off and made clear by the dolphin's golden sheen, allowing Andi and

Jubal to see it even though it was nighttime. The darkness seemed to contract and expand, as if it were trying to choke the dolphin. Andi put her hand out toward the dolphin, toward the blackness. Andi jumped backward, gasping. The shadow had wrapped itself around her arm and bitten on it as if it were a wolf. Andi gave a little cry as she sat back on the ridge. Her arm stopped hurting almost as soon as the darkness left the reach of her hand.

"Are you all right?" Jubal asked. He crouched behind her and began to reach out to her arm.

"I'm fine, Jubal," Andi snapped. The shadowy ... thing made her reconsider being here at all. Then Andi looked back down to the dolphin and knew she would never be able to leave. The dolphin remained motionless, her gaze never leaving Andi's.

Then Andi's consciousness exploded. She closed her eyes, and visions washed over her. Images and memories not her own but belonging to another presence. *Of a baby dolphin. Of needing to hide, of being hurt. Of herding her baby dolphin to safety. Somewhere, somewhere ...*

Andi moved through the water, vibrating, shivering, moving toward the dolphin. She was outside herself as if she were the dolphin moving downward deeper into the sea. She realized the mother was telling her something, relaying something to her mind. *Sound trembling toward curvature, edge, shape. Stone pathways. Stars shone in and out of darkness as she slid toward her destination. She reached out beyond herself with sound and movement, feeling out for a pattern. The open sea. Darkness. Deeper. Walls of stone narrowed in the sea all around her, yet she stayed her course. A tunnel. Rocky crags. Small crevices. Out. Under and out.* She realized these impressions were coming from the mother's mind to hers. She knew it was in the open water of the Salish Sea because the cliff descended directly into the water, surrounded only by a thin ridge of stone.

Andi opened her eyes. The dolphin's iridescent gold was dying out. Her skin, once so beautiful and varicolored, now resembled a pasty hue. The dolphin blinked as if in surprise and looked at Andi sadly, murmuring a faint song. Andi stretched out far enough for her hand to touch her. The dolphin rested her head against Andi's palm, her liquid eyes shining with gratitude. Seeing herself in the creature's eyes, Andi knew that the mother dolphin had glimpsed into Andi's life just as Andi had into hers. A union had transpired between the two of them. This majestic being had entrusted her with her secret. *The secret of where its child lay hidden.* All Andi could feel was the fear the mother dolphin had for its child. Andi's mother was dead, and she had only Grandma Bea and Artie. Someone had to be there for this baby calf. She would not abandon it.

Andi's hand finally left the head it cradled, allowing the dolphin to roll over on its side, dead. Andi turned around to find Jubal, his eyes bright with tears.

At least he's able to grieve. She looked at the dolphin beginning to sink into the water. She found herself wondering, rather stupidly, whether its body would wash out into the ocean. Her breath came out in short, angry gasps. Andi shuddered convulsively and realized she was trying her best not to cry.

Four

A Dive to Surface

Andi could not see the mother dolphin anymore. It had most likely sunk to the bottom of the pool and would wash out into the ocean as the tide receded. Andi scrambled out of the cavern, fell to her knees, and vomited on the rocky beach.

Jubal's hand stroked her back. She could tell he wasn't sure what to do. *Unlike her.* She knew what to do but didn't have much time to do it. Andi didn't know if she could do it at all.

Andi groped for Jubal's hand. She needed him to help her up. She was weak. Very weak. He pulled her up to her feet. Andi gasped, swallowing in the sea air.

The sheer force of her mind joining with the mother dolphin...it had overwhelmed her. It was as if she had seen the world from the mother's perspective. It changed everything. She would not abandon its child. Still breathing in the sea air, she forced herself to stand tall.

"Jubal ..." Andi said, groping for words. She could not finish.

"What happened in there?" he said. The concern did not leave his face as he looked at Andi.

Andi nodded slowly. The meteors were still sliding down into the night. *Good.*

"It's so clear," she murmured softly. "It's never this clear."

"Andi, what happened in there? It's terrible—I don't know what you want to do ..."

A memory not Andi's flickered in and out of her consciousness. Of stars and of deep passages hidden underwater. She marveled at it. It was like a compass telling her where to go. She shook her head hard, as if trying to clear cobwebs from her mind, *which was what she was doing in a way.* Andi pushed her own memories—herself—out of the way. They'd just muck up and confuse everything.

"We have to go back," she said to Jubal. "We must camp out in the backyard. We need to wait for it."

"Wait for *what?*" Jubal asked, confused. But Andi couldn't answer. It wasn't something she could express or share. She was afraid if she took time to talk about it with Jubal, the memories and impressions not belonging to her would drain out like a sieve. She couldn't afford to do that right now. Besides, Jubal might argue with her, and that would be another distraction.

Andi began walking toward the curve of rocky beach rounding around the cliff's base. She had to focus. *Concentrate,* she told herself as she started up the ridge path, her stride much quicker than when they'd come down.

"Andi? Can you tell me what we're doing?" Jubal asked, the words tumbling out at rapid speed. "What is it you have to do?"

He's nervous, Andi realized. *Nervous at the change in me.* But she couldn't explain. *Not now.* Time was going by quickly. She didn't want to miss the threshold. *Threshold. Where did I get that word?* Her mind was assigning words and meanings to the images in her head. The pictures given to her by the mother dolphin weren't really hers. *But are mine now,* Andi reflected. Her mind was processing the thoughts, senses, and impressions of another mind.

"I need to do something," she murmured, acknowledging that she'd heard him, that she was listening. "Always foggy here," she said, trying to keep her focus. "But not tonight."

For it to be so clear at night and to be witness to a meteor shower like this—it was unusual and amazing.

They reached the top of the ridge path. Most of the cars were gone. She turned to Jubal.

"I'm going to go into the backyard, where the cliff overlooks the ocean. Can you go get your sleeping bag." It was not a question. Jubal nodded and ran off toward the house. Andi strode past the huge stone house toward the backyard covered in tall grass. It was much darker there, giving her a better view of everything.

Andi sat down, letting the grasses swallow her. She hoped Jubal would be able to find her in the dark. She stared up at the sky. There were fewer meteors streaking by, allowing her to see the real stars shining in the background. Andi craned her neck, adjusting her position. *There it is*, she noted with satisfaction. *It's coming.* The stars were coming together into the correct position. They were like a map telling her when the right time was. The vision she had received needed to match the sky and the sea as well as the meteor shower.

The beam of Jubal's flashlight appeared through the tall grasses. *Good.* She waved to him. He smiled when he spotted her.

Sitting down beside her, Jubal said, "Mind telling me what we're doing here?"

Andi gave him a small smile. "I can't, Jubal. I'll be able to explain it all later. But now, I just can't."

Jubal nodded, absorbing her words. He offered her a bag of chips. She took some and popped them into her mouth, then continued to look up into the sky. Jubal's eyes were upon her. Andi sensed his curiosity as he scanned the skies with her, trying to see in the sky what was still only in her mind. This was unfair to Jubal. But she was afraid if she tried to explain her visions to him, the visions would disappear. A sacred thing had happened between Andi and the dolphin; sharing it would be a violation. Andi began to realize the mother dolphin had entrusted Andi with its baby calf because she had detected in Andi a sense of loss that matched her own. And a sense of deep love. She only hoped she could find the baby calf now. It all depended on the directions she had gotten from the mother. *It was a very strange map,*

Andi realized, scared she might not be able to follow the directive she had received.

The stars almost matched the alignment given to Andi, now stored in her mind. The meteors as they appeared in the sky right now also matched. She stood up and strode over to the cliff.

She heard Jubal behind her scream, "Andi, what are you doing?"

Andi stood on the edge of the cliff, looking up into the sky even as Jubal screamed her name again. She did not take her eyes off the swirling stars falling toward the horizon. Just held one arm out, signaling Jubal to stay back. The stars were acting as a template. She had to wait until the sky above matched the image branded onto her brain. Her mind swirled with the different thoughts and feelings the mother dolphin had given her. The waves below crashed against the cliff base.

The meteor shower spread itself across the sky, its reflections mirroring up from the ocean. Everything was happening all at once. Andi tried to gain some sort of foothold within herself. Something that would hold her up, affirm that she was not losing her sanity. But nothing came.

Even though she knew Jubal stood behind her, Andi realized just how scared she was. She was going to take care of a very strange baby calf. But she and Artie were about to lose their home. Because of Ms. Dugger. How were they going to find a solution? It was up to her to figure out a solution, and she couldn't. Jubal couldn't. Her grandmother certainly couldn't. That was why she was so alone. Yet, Andi reflected, the mother dolphin had seen into Andi's mind and still entrusted the baby calf to her. Andi would win, somehow. In some way, she would take care of the baby calf just like she took care of Artie and Grandma Bea. If they couldn't stay at their home, they would find a new one.

Andi looked down into the ocean below. Had her mother seen the same sight before

she—no, Andi wouldn't think about that. She couldn't. This was different. It had to be different. Once again the question "why?" rose from the watery depths of her mind, only for her to push it down.

A flash of gold flashed in the water, causing Andi to nearly dive into the ocean before catching herself. *Stupid, stupid.* She had to look up to the stars before diving. That was the key. The flash of gold had been a reflection from the meteor storm.

Everything was coming together. The dolphin, the meteor shower, the stars above her ... these things were coming together. Fitting together like pieces of a puzzle. But it was only the border. She'd matched up the pieces with even lines, tracing out a frame but no picture inside.

What she couldn't see was the center of the puzzle. All Andi knew for certain was that she was also at its center, with whatever was waiting for her on the other side.

The stars finally locked themselves into the position corresponding to the image in her

mind. Andi gracefully spread her arms apart before bringing them together over her head in a diver's posture. Jubal's screams rang in her ears. It occurred to her that she should feel guilty for putting him through this, for not explaining. But how could she explain when she didn't even understand it herself?

She pushed herself off the cliff.

All she knew was one single overriding feeling as she flew down, the air rushing by her ears, before she hit the water. *She was not alone. She would never be alone again.*

For a split second, Andi floated over the sea. Deep down, a part of her asked how she had jumped out so far from the cliffside. She'd shot far beyond the rocky beach below. Diving straight into the sea—*a surprisingly deep part of it considering how close it is to shore*, the little voice in her said. Andi suddenly was afraid. What if this was all a mistake?

The dive from such a high altitude propelled her to the bottom of the ocean floor. It had to be there. Fear rushed up into her stomach, making Andi cry for air. It was pitch black, yet Andi could see. The water was not paralyzing cold as it should have been. Andi realized she had received a special dispensation from the mother dolphin to help her do this. But it would not last forever. She had to hurry. The opening loomed right up in front of her. *An underwater grotto.* Her mother had told Andi about these underwater caves. It matched up with the vision, and for several seconds, her fear began to ease.

Through her dive, Andi had gained enough speed to shoot straight down into the grotto. Inside the watery passage, Andi's hands groped, searching. She found the sides, forming some sort of tunnel. She pushed on, her lungs starting to burn. *No.* She couldn't die here. What would Grandma Bea do? Artie? She wanted to pull out of the cavern. *This wasn't worth it. It wasn't.*

Andi couldn't turn around, finding herself trapped. Her lungs were going to burst. She pulled herself through the passageway, persuaded she was going to die. The walls of the passage were smooth as if hollowed out by someone—or something. Its smoothness allowed Andi to pull herself through the passage even faster. The passage curved downward and was narrow enough for Andi to swim through, using the walls to push herself along. After it curved down, the passageway curved upward, like a U. *Down, under, then up.* Andi had no choice but to keep pushing herself through, feeling panic in every vein. She was going to die.

Her lungs close to exploding, Andi pushed off the bottom of the passage as it began to slope up. Her head emerged from the water into a tiny open space. Her lungs exploded as she sucked in the hot, heavy air trapped in that small part of the passage. Her lungs hurt, burning, but she was alive! Alive. Her panic began to subside. Should she continue? Andi was barely able to raise her head out of the water into the small pocket of air in the passage. But she was able to breathe. With the panic beginning to subside, Andi remembered the urgency of the mother dolphin's message. Yes, everything matched. She'd even somehow allowed Andi to know where this trapped pocket of air was.

Could she make it to the next step? Could she hold her breath again for such a long time? To the underwater cavern whose passage only opened when the stars were aligned just so?

Her hands guided her through the next part of the dark passage. There was a slight difference in the texture of the wall. While still smooth, there were indentations, as if someone had carved pictures or symbols into the surface. Digging her fingers into the indentations, Andi pushed herself along the passage.

Panic rose as her lungs began to burn again. Her fear was starting to obstruct her ability to recall the directions given to her by the mother dolphin. It wasn't remembering—these were not her memories. They were someone else's. She willed herself to calm down. She could not die. *What was she doing, putting herself in jeopardy like this?*

Andi knew why. The mother dolphin had left its child here, hoping to protect it. Its fear had been for its child's safety.

This was the encouragement she needed to keep going, to not give up. She surged forward with a powerful stroke that propelled further her down the tunnel, curving up toward a large opening above her. The tunnel continued beyond the opening to somewhere else, but the opening above—this was it. Her destination. Andi was sure of it. She swam frantically to the surface.

Light flooded through the water as Andi rose to the surface. *It must be from the baby calf.* Gasping for breath, she tread water for a moment, looking around the cavern. She looked for the baby calf. Although the cavern was lit with a golden light, she could not see the calf. It was hiding, Andi realized. It was scared. The cavern ceiling was covered in stalactites. It spread far back to where the rocky surface disappeared in darkness. After swimming to shore, Andi realized it was not a pond; it was more of a lake. She frowned. Somehow, she got the feeling that this cavern was *not* beneath the cliff. The passage only opened when the stars were aligned in a certain position. *Could this be somewhere else? Another place?* What had happened so far was supernatural; could the passage be supernatural too?

Andi pulled herself up onto the rocky soil and then to a standing position. She was so relieved. When the mother dolphin had impressed part of its own mind and emotions into her mind, Andi had not been herself. But now that she was here, she was whole again. The blurry series of visions guiding her here had stopped. She was on her own.

Andi looked around the cavern. It stretched back forever, the farthest part completely in darkness. A pang of fear began to rise, but Andi pushed herself to explore, measuring each breath against every step she took. She walked toward the other end of the cavern, maneuvering around large rocks along the way.

Her fear worsened when she reached the opposite edge. In front of her was a huge pile of rocks that rose slightly above her head. Was something buried under the rubble? Andi reached toward the raised mound. A rock slipped from the pile, revealing something that looked like a large, raised stone bier.

As if she had awakened someone, Andi sensed a presence. Familiar. It was the same presence from the night before, the voice that spoke to her in her home. Had it been only the night before? Andi took a step backward. Something was moving under the rubble, under the enclosed bier. As if someone were trying to get out.

"Help me," a chilling voice wailed.

Andi fell backward, hitting her head. She massaged her head, choosing to crawl instead of walking back to the lake. She did not want to be near that *thing*—whatever it was. Desperately, she made herself forget everything else in the world except for reaching the water. Even the possibility of drowning didn't scare her.

A movement in the lake caught her eye. All the feelings, thoughts and impressions given to her mind came rushing together into a single picture come to life in front of her as it burst out of the lake. If it had been giving off light before, Andi thought, it fairly glowed now. Andi gave out a little laugh of relief.

"You're so bright," she said to the creature in front of her. "Let me *see* you."

As if it had understood her, the pulsating golden light dimmed. It revealed a beautiful dolphin. A baby dolphin. Andi was breathless. *A calf. My calf.* She held her hand out toward the glimmering creature. She was surprised; it was large, more than half the size and length of a large bottlenose, about five feet in length and heavier looking.

The baby dolphin was *standing* on its fins in the water! He—Andi knew it was he—smiled broadly at her. Certain that it was a true smile, she smiled back at him. Her head rang with resonating emotions—happiness and joy. The secret, hidden room in her mind came alive again.

He was curious about her. Andi realized that he was probing, trying to find out more about her. He made curious musical noises, sounds like his mother had made. The music was asking her a question. Without knowing how, Andi understood what he was asking. *Where was its mother?* She pushed herself up from her knees and stood before him.

Slow. She had to take it slow. Andi smiled encouragingly as she moved closer to him. He watched her with a curious astonishment, his liquid eyes wide in wonder.

Then he moved closer, propelling the whole of his body forward with his fins still dancing on top of the water. Andi laughed. He was trying to *walk* to her! He was somehow levitating! His mind bubbled laughter back, delighted at her joy. Then a question with no words formed itself in her mind. Andi's face became sober. The baby dolphin's smile did not disappear, but something in his eyes stilled.

She spoke hesitatingly to him. "Your, your mother is dead." Andi remembered her mother who had disappeared. At least this creature would know that his mother had wanted him to be safe and loved, that her final moments had focused all on him. She looked back at him and realized the same thoughts that had been running through her mind had been running through his. He regarded her in a frozen silence and then let out an anguished cry and dove in.

Andi dove after him. As she chased him down into the depths, he changed his skin from fiery gold to a more muted gold that was easily hidden the deeper he swam. She couldn't catch up with him so shouted out at him with her mind, *Wait!* He slowed enough for her to swim alongside him. He stared at her, and Andi's heart began to beat with his as if the two became one. She pointed at him. *You.* She pointed to herself. *Me.* Then Andi brought her two hands together, clasping them. *Together.*

Andi became sleepy as she began to lose her breath. She shrugged it off, knowing that the baby calf needed to feel safe with her. She would do anything to make that happen. She felt him under her, propelling her to the surface.

After breaking through the water, Andi pulled herself out of the underground lake, gasping. Her breathing finally became normal. The little calf swam quite close to her, its eyes anxious. Then as if reassured that she was all right, it did a little flip back into the water before returning to her. He appeared shy, but he nudged her with his nose, nuzzling her. In her head, she heard the word come from him, haltingly but surely. *Andi. And-ee.*

Andi smiled and responded, *That's me.*

Five

A Whole World Set Spinning

Andi scanned the illuminated tunnel as she and her golden dolphin glided underwater back toward the open sea. The indentations on the walls of the tunnel were now clear. They would put old cave drawings to shame. They told a story—but *what*, Andi couldn't tell. The pictures whizzed by as she and her dolphin moved toward the ocean.

Andi's dolphin swam much faster than she had been able to; holding her breath this time was a snap. She held on to him just under his flippers, which kept her secure as he swam ahead, pulling her through the cavern.

Adoration swelled out from the dolphin toward *her*—her! The same devotion rose within her toward her small dolphin. *If it is a dolphin*, she wondered uneasily, bothered by the fact she did not have an answer for this. She had received no information from the mother other than the feelings and directions impressed upon her mind.

Andi felt her way around the new room in her mind. Through it, she was able to exercise the same communication with the baby calf that she had with its mother. It was a space where their minds could meet and speak to each other.

As Andi probed, she came to understand something. He was just a baby. His thoughts were just beginning to form themselves into concrete ideas. He knew who she was, that he belonged to her and she to him. But even though she discovered a few memories of his mother, Andi still couldn't find out what they were, these beautiful golden dolphins.

Andi gave a start. They were now deep underwater. She had not noticed, being so absorbed in the dolphin and who—or what—he was. It was not paralyzingly cold. It must have been because she was with him. *But the calf was not rising to the surface!*

Slow down, slow down! Andi screamed silently at the dolphin. The dolphin stopped swimming, motionless at the bottom of the ocean floor. *Up! Up!* Andi formed a thought in her mind, hoping the dolphin would understand it. Her lungs were about to burst. Suddenly she was shooting upward. Her head shot out of the water.

Gasping, she tried to catch her breath while looking around her. A high wind blew spray into her face. The dolphin had swum too far out from the cliff. They had to turn around. Jubal would be frantic with worry over what had happened to her. She beckoned to her dolphin in her mind, pointing the way to the cliff. She slid her hands under his flippers.

As they swam back, she wondered, where was she going to hide him? He couldn't come up to the house with her, could he? *The cave. Mom's cave,* she realized. The one she had taken Jubal to so he could meet her little calf's mother might be a place where it—she didn't want to say *it*—could stay. Just until she figured something else out. Unlike the underwater grotto she'd had to dive out and swim underwater to, the cave inlet was accessible and a place she could visit often.

"Turn around!" Andi said aloud, sending a mental image of the cavern and where it lay.

She gave the dolphin an image of the cliff. Just how fast could he swim? Andi marveled. He spun around, pulling her toward the cliff. Andi had wondered if he would dive underwater again, but this time he stayed afloat. She squinted toward the top of the cliff, hoping for a sign from Jubal. If Jubal had gone in and woken Artie and Grandma Bea, she would never forgive herself.

The meteor shower had ended. She marveled once again at how clear the evening had been, allowing her an unobstructed view of the stars.

Andi heard a shout from the top of the cliff as they neared the cavern. She could not see Jubal but spotted the beam of a flashlight waving back and forth. *Poor Jubal.* She'd put him through so much by not explaining what she was going to do. Still, Andi had never had an experience like that before. Images pouring into her mind from someone else. She had not wanted to lose those. She'd known how important this was as soon as she stumbled out of the cave after the mother dolphin's death. She was, for the most part, something like a mother to this baby dolphin now. Its real mother and she had bonded because of this beautiful golden baby calf. She wanted to hold on to that bond for as long as she could.

Her dolphin trembled slightly as she remembered his mother's death. Andi winced. *I shouldn't have recalled the incident.* He could read her mind. Refocusing her mind on the cavern, the dolphin relaxed as he understood that she was telling him where to go. He slowed down as he curved toward the cavern. After entering through the watery passage, they arrived in the cave.

Andi's mouth opened in surprise. Jubal sat on the ridge, trembling. He stared as she and the dolphin swam closer to the ridge, but he said nothing. Mentally telling her dolphin to stay where he was, Andi pulled herself out of the water. She knelt before the still-shaking Jubal.

"How did you get here so fast?" she asked.

"I don't know," Jubal chattered, his eyes half-crazed.

"Did you run down here?" She was ready to be angry if he had. Her mother died walking that ridge.

"N-no," Jubal whispered, trying to control his shaking. "I told you. I don't know what happened."

Still not understanding, Andi pressed on. "You woke Artie. It was him waving the flashlight?"

Jubal grabbed her hand. "No, Andi," he said emphatically. "That was *me.*"

"Then how ..."

"I don't know!" Jubal yelled. "I was there—then I was here. *I don't know.*"

Andi looked back at the dolphin. He was gazing at them with curiosity. She entered the new room in her mind where he could access her mind.

After a moment, her dolphin began singing to her. She nodded and then turned to Jubal. Cocking her head over to the dolphin in the water, Andi said, "I think he brought you here. He knew I wanted to see you, so ... he just brought you here." She looked at the dolphin. "He has ... he has," she repeated nervously. "He has *powers.*"

"He can do that?" Jubal was incredulous. "*Teleport?*"

Andi's baby dolphin chimed in with his musical voice as if giving affirmation. He continued to stare at Andi and Jubal. Andi could sense his confusion. *Hadn't he done as she wanted?*

Andi turned back to Jubal. "I was worried that you'd wake up Artie and Grandma Bea. He can read my mind, and I can read his. So I guess he was helping us out."

Jubal stared at her, as if trying to make sense of what she'd just shared. Finally, he grinned and then crawled over to the edge of the ridge and reached out with his arm to stroke the dolphin. Andi smiled as her baby dolphin began to respond to Jubal. It—*he*—leaped up out of the water just to have Jubal's hand stroke him. Andi could sense its—his—feelings. The baby calf was thrilled to meet Jubal.

"His skin changes as I rub it," Jubal marveled. He was right. The dolphin gave a golden and fiery sheen. As Jubal touched his skin, the area became a darker orange. There were so many things Andi had to find out. She looked around the cavern, biting her lip. Could she really leave him here alone? Was he still nursing? How would he eat? Even if she came here every night after dinner, that would leave him by himself for most of the day. What would happen to him if she weren't there to see him, watch over him?

Watch over him. Andi remembered Artie. How late was it? He always woke up during the night. If he found she wasn't home, he would be upset.

"Jubal," Andi said, trying to keep her voice as light as possible. "What time is it?" Her hands shook. She could not imagine leaving her dolphin but knew she had to go back to the house. She waited for Jubal to answer.

It took him more than a minute to look at his watch. He lifted it to his eyes. "It's two in the morning," he said, sounding alarmed.

In dismay, Andi looked at her dolphin, who stared back at her, his eyes wide in adoration. She remembered the feeling when coming off her grandfather's sailboat after spending a few hours on it. She'd wobbled forever. She knew that the sea under her would never stop moving now. That was how much her life had changed.

Suddenly, Andi went cold. Her baby dolphin had become less golden! With terror in her heart, she ran toward the baby calf, remembering the dun color its mother had faded to as she died. She lay on her chest and reached out to the dolphin, who gave her another *chirrup*. He moved in the water, laughing at her surprise.

"How did you do that?" Andi yelled, not caring how she sounded. She held her hands out toward the dolphin as it swam around the cavern pool. "How did you do that?" she repeated, more calmly this time. There was still gold and fire dancing on his skin but nowhere near as brightly as before. No one would detect him hiding in the cave from outside based on the light he gave off now.

An image entered her mind of a golden dolphin surrounded by menacing figures, shapes, and shadows. They all wanted to hurt the dolphin—*her* dolphin, she realized. The silhouettes slowly closed in on her dolphin, and his color faded as he dove deep down into the small lake.

Andi understood. Her dolphin had seen into her fear and had come up with a solution.

He had figured out how to hide. Andi's eyes were wet as she realized he had read in her mind the many possible scenarios of what might have happened to his mother.

"He did it for you," Jubal whispered, at her side. "He knows you can't watch him all the time, even if you want to."

As if the dolphin had understood Jubal, it leapt up, its beak touching Andi's mouth. A kiss, Andi realized. As if telling her not to worry. As his body slid back into the lake, his face nuzzled her cheek. Andi recognized it as another sign of encouragement.

Andi finally understood the expression *her heart in her throat* as she said good-bye to the dolphin. She pictured herself returning to him every day. Andi implanted the joy she knew she would feel in seeing him each time so that he would know how loved he was. The same joy returned to her multiplied several times over. He would wait for her, Andi realized.

As she and Jubal trudged up toward her home, on the thin ridge on the side of the cliff, Andi could not help but feel the weight thrust upon her. Artie, Grandma, and now this dolphin—this otherworldly creature. How was she going to protect him while also trying to figure out what to do to keep herself and Artie together? Already overwhelmed by responsibility, she wondered if she was strong enough to save them all.

Six

Like A Whirlwind

Artie barely spoke to her the next day, Sunday. Andi had slept quite late, even for her. She tried to speak to him when she got up, but he refused to look her in the eyes. After an hour, she finally decided to go to the cavern to check on the little dolphin. She had so much fun playing with him that she completely overlooked the fact that night had fallen. When she did finally get up to the house, she found Artie's door shut. Grandma had looked up once from the television as she'd entered the house. She had gone back to watching whatever it was that left her hypnotized in front of the screen.

Monday morning dawned somewhat gloomy. A heavy blanket of gray cloud covered the island. As she dressed in her customary overalls, Andi's pain about how distant Artie was from her began to consume her. Something had sprung up between them that she did not seem able to fix. At breakfast, she finally broke the cold silence between them in a most unceremonious way. As she poured milk into Artie's cereal, something inside her snapped.

"Don't be so angry with me because you wet your pants," she said coldly.

Artie looked up at her, a momentary expression of shock crossing his face. Andi never shamed him. *Never.* She could see the hurt and humiliation on her twin's face before he finally got up from the table and walked upstairs. She followed him to the bottom of the stairs but didn't call out after him. *Why should she?* He was the one with the problem, not her. She returned to the table to find Grandma Bea hovering over it, unsure of what to eat. Andi made her a bowl of cereal before grabbing her backpack and marching out the door to school.

Trudging down Edge Street, Andi finally figured out what was bothering Artie so much. She'd doubted him. The other night before going to find her little dolphin, she'd hinted to him that it was better for her to handle it without him. The fact that she'd come home so late and then left one hour after waking up had confused him deeply. They were twins, after all. Artie knew something momentous had happened to her.

Andi looked out to the bay that curved inland toward the island as she walked. She vowed to make things right with Artie that night. When she reached the gravel playground, Andi groaned, remembering. *Gaby.* She was pretty sure that somewhere, somehow, Gaby lay in wait to take her revenge. Feeling even more dejected than she already was, Andi trudged into the school and into her classroom.

An hour before lunch, Ms. Dugger called her up to her desk. "I've had a disturbing letter from Gaby's mother, Andi," Ms. Dugger began. "It talks about a fight that you initiated on Friday after school." Andi's teacher's brown eyes framed behind thick glasses did not appear sympathetic. She had never been sympathetic to Andi, the girl realized. Not a hair of her woven bun was out of place. *No exceptions to the rules*, the hairstyle said. *No exceptions for you* was the feeling Andi got.

"Normally, I wouldn't put any stock into it," Ms. Dugger continued. "But I do realize that the fight took place after our discussion, which gives me pause. I could imagine that I might have upset you." Her teacher gazed at Andi, her pen tapping her desk as she held the letter from Gaby's mother in her other hand. *Tap-tap-tap.* Andi closed her eyes, trying to think of some way to respond.

Yes, you upset me because of our discussion in which you said my grandmother is mentally incompetent. That she was unable to take care of Artie and me. That you've already called a social worker to investigate the situation. Then when Gaby tried to call my brother a retard, what other choice did I have but to defend him? He's my brother!

Andi knew Gaby was looking at her from behind as she sat at her desk. She knew the girl was smirking behind her back. She wished something horrible would happen to Gaby. Something that would get her out of having to answer these questions. Andi opened her eyes and began to respond to Ms. Dugger, who was still tapping the pen on her desk, waiting.

Before Andi could respond, a loud crash came from one side of the room. The classroom window facing the sea had shattered into a million pieces. A strong wind blew through the empty hole, coiling itself into a small funnel reaching from the floor to the ceiling. It wound itself between the desks of the students, scattering papers and books off its surfaces. Andi's classmates screamed as the whirlwind neared.

The wind followed a path toward Gaby's desk. Desks fell over. Gaby's cold blue eyes were frozen in fear as the funnel of wind came toward her. Her blond braid whipped around her neck as the whirlwind spun around her old-fashioned tablet desk. The desk slowly lifted into the air—and took Gaby with it. Gaby let out a piercing scream as she put her head down on the desk, her fingers grasping its edges out of desperation. The desk floated in the air, Gaby's head nearly hitting the ceiling.

Without knowing how she knew, Andi realized with a sinking feeling that this whirlwind was because of her somehow. She ran toward the hole left by the window. Staring out toward the water, Andi screamed one word: "Stop!"

Gaby's desk spun around in the middle of the room. Then it crashed down to the floor. Gaby tried to stand up so quickly that her legs got stuck under the desk as she tried to get out, making the desk topple over to its side. Trying to grab something for support even as she fell with the desk, Gaby's hand flailed for the desk next to her. Instead of holding her up, the tablet desk next to her fell over as well, hitting the desk next to it and so on! *Like dominoes.*

Ms. Dugger hurried in her high heels toward Gaby, trying to wrest her out from under her desk. Gaby, still half-seated in the desk on its side, was paralyzed with fear. Ms. Dugger's heel broke off as she pulled Gaby out, and she fell on her backside.

It was then that students and teachers from other classrooms burst through the door. All were screaming. Ms. Dugger slowly rose to her feet, trying to lift Gaby's desk so that the girl could finally wrangle out of it. She began talking to one of the other teachers, but Andi could not hear her over the din.

Gaby sobbed as Ms. Dugger helped her up and then led her to the door. Ms. Dugger hobbled, not having bothered to remove her shoes. The two of them made quite a sight as they walked unevenly out of the classroom. Neither was injured, Andi realized, exhaling slowly.

Andi looked back to the hole in the window, her heart pounding. What had just happened? But she knew. The dolphin was protecting her. He'd sent the wind into the room directly toward Gaby because Andi had been mad at her. Despite her shock and panic, Andi smiled. A tendril of warmth wound itself around her heart.

Confusion filled the classroom and school after the incident. Shocked parents herded their children out of the school for the day. Andi snuck out on her own. Once on Edge Street, Andi began running up the slope leading to the cliff and its ridge path as fast as she could. Her backpack bounced against her as she ran. She needed to get to the cavern. She wished Jubal were here. Jubal was back on the mainland, attending a magnet school for gifted children. He stayed at a small dorm during the week with a few other boys his age. He'd told Andi that it was hard there. He found school on the island harder, because while he had friends, they weren't like Andi. Or Artie.

The cavern lit up as soon as she entered. Andi recognized the lighting up as a sign of her little dolphin's excitement. She strode around the tiny outcropping of stone that circled the lake inside the cavern.

"Was that you?" she demanded. "Did you do that?"

Andi heard a hum of pleasure echo in her mind at the fact she knew it was him. She knelt by the water's edge and said as emphatically as she could, "You must never do that again! Never. Do you understand me?"

To herself, Andi muttered, "Thank God no one was hurt." Other than Gaby's horrible experience, everyone had emerged unscathed. Scared but unscathed. Andi giggled as she remembered Ms. Dugger tearing her heel off.

Andi sensed a hurt and sense of puzzlement coming from the baby calf. *Baby* calf. *This dolphin could be dangerous*, she realized. He had powers Andi didn't understand, and no one would teach him how to control it. Andi tried to think of something she could show him to make him understand.

"How did you do that?" she demanded.

Slowly the image of a funnel emerged in her mind. It was somewhere far away. Her mind's eye looked with astonishment as the funnel disappeared and emerged right in front of her classroom window. Andi realized that he had *teleported* it, as he had teleported Jubal two nights before.

Andi suddenly felt very helpless. She put her head into her hands. "Please don't do anything like that again. People could have been hurt. Really hurt. Gaby could have been killed."

Then Andi faced the dolphin in the eyes. "Can you show Gaby to me?" she asked. "Listen ... I don't know how you found that funnel ... but you saw it before you teleported it. Do you understand that word? Teleport? It's moving something from one place to another, only ... um, without picking it up yourself and moving it. You're able to move it from one far place to another. Without worrying about the distance." Andi sighed. She was not explaining this very well. Jubal would be able to explain it so much better. As would Artie.

"Look," Andi began again. "The person you wanted to hurt ... Gaby ... can you picture in your mind where she is now?"

A wave of assent came from the dolphin.

"Can you picture her where she is right now without teleporting her?"

Again, a wave of assent.

"Can you show her to me? Is she by the water?" As much as she hated it, Andi needed to make sure Gaby was all right. At least okay.

He had been protecting her by scaring Gaby. He was so in tune with her that he could feel what she was feeling, see what she was thinking. *How did he figure out to do this?* She wondered what the school was going to do about the incident. If they couldn't say what the cause was, they would need to investigate it. Would that mean school would shut down for a while, or ...?

He showed her what she wanted to see. Closing her eyes, a few houses appeared on the eastern shore of the island. Dilapidated houses with peeling paint and broken shutters hanging at odd angles from the windows. In even worse conditions than Jubal's.

Andi frowned. Gaby was from *there*? Gaby who always wore dresses to school and whose haughty attitude made her seem that she lived at the top of the world? Andi began to see how that had been a mask for Gaby. Gaby, Andi realized, hid a lot behind the smile she conjured up for the other sixth-grade girls and teachers.

A tiny house appeared in the vision the dolphin was showing her. It was in even worse shape than the others. It looked as if it used to have a yellow color. The front porch had caved in, the wood collapsed on the ground. The path leading up to the porch had a smaller path leading from it to another part of the house. Andi guessed this path had been trod into being by many repeated trips. The porch had been like this for a long time. Andi suddenly was sad. The nice houses were on the southern part of the island, near the ferry rides. This part was much poorer.

Look, her mind spoke out toward the dolphin. *Find her.* In that new room in her mind, Andi saw inside the house, the dolphin probing. She marveled that it—she *had* to give him a name—was able to do this. A woman with an unhealthy pallor was smoking in front of a television. Her glazed eyes never left the television as she flicked the ash from her cigarette into an ashtray next to the chair. Many cigarettes filled the ashtray. There were several ashtrays!

The carpet was coming apart in many different places in the house.

A huge pile of unwashed dishes lay stacked on one another in the kitchen, smelling like trash. How the dolphin was able to sense its smell was a mystery, Andi marveled as she drew in a breath of fresh air from inside the cave.

Finally, Gaby emerged. Through the dolphin's mind, the girl sat on the edge of her bed, crying her heart out. She looked nothing like the girl in class. Here, she appeared vulnerable and afraid. There were many drawings and magazine photos of pretty flowers and gardens filling the walls of Gaby's bedroom. Despite herself, Andi had to admire her. Gaby was creating her own world inside that depressing house.

The attempted beauty of the room came apart as a tall, heavyset, and unshaven man entered her room. Without knowing how, Andi heard the bellow of "Shut up!" from the man to Gaby. Gaby sat up quickly from the edge of her bed, trying to muffle her crying. Gaby moved from the bed, her mouth moving, forming words. Andi realized she was trying to tell this man about what happened at school today. The man slapped her hard across the face, and Gaby fell to the ground. The man approached her again, pulling his belt off, holding it in his hands.

That did it. Fury rose in Andi. Questions began coming from her dolphin. *Do it!* Her mind screamed. Anger rose in the dolphin, joining in with her own. The roof over the man's head disappeared. The man stood ashen faced and trembling, staring at where the ceiling used to be. Gaby fell to her knees and clung to the man, trembling. He shook her off, leaving the room. Andi felt bad. Had she just made the situation worse or...? No. The man was leaving the house. Gaby was OK. At least for now.

Remembering what had happened at school, Andi whispered to the dolphin, "Do you understand? We can't do things to people. We don't know what their lives are like. We just don't know why they do the things they do," the realization hitting her as hard as the whirlwind had hit the classroom. "We have to be careful," she finished. It was so painful to feel the indignation rising in her dolphin, to feel him beginning to understand that this was the way the world was. She jumped into the water and wrapped her arms around his torso, never wanting to let go.

Seven

A Nighttime Swim

A quiet and thoughtful Andi walked down the ridge path the next evening. She was still disturbed about Gaby and the scene she'd seen in Gaby's home the day before. Andi wished she could help. She was pretty sure Gaby would be humiliated if she knew that Andi had seen anything. But she hadn't seen Gaby that day. Tuesday had been a day off for the school to assess the damage done by the whirlwind.

Artie had stayed in his room all day. Andi had gone in to apologize, but he hadn't looked up at her; he'd just played silently with his slinky while she told him how sorry she was. The rigidity of his posture as he sat on the floor had relaxed a bit afterward though. She hoped this was a sign that he had accepted her apology, even if it took him a while to return to normal.

Andi's subdued mood began to change into anticipation as she neared the little inlet cave. She could not wait to see her little dolphin again. When she entered the cavern, his golden and fiery sheen blazed off the walls as he swam from one side of the inlet toward her. Andi's heart soared. He burst through the water, his nose coming up straight toward her, his eyes showing his pleasure at seeing her. A song broke out from him. Andi smiled.

Stroking the dolphin while resting on her knees, Andi looked at her reflection in the water. The water stilled for a minute, startling Andi with the image reflected at her. For a moment, she did not recognize herself. Then Andi realized that she looked *happy*.

Guilt consumed Andi. When was the last time she experienced joy with her grandmother, with her brother, or even Jubal? Jubal had brought her a steadiness, a comfort, been a constant. With her grandmother the way she was, Andi realized, her own anxiety had just kept growing. As if she were holding her breath, waiting. *Waiting for what?* She wondered. For Artie to help her? For her grandmother to come to and realize what her forgetfulness was doing to the whole family?

Andi started to cry. All the feelings and fears she'd hidden inside herself finally came out as she cried. The odd thing was these feelings were all mixed up with a feeling of joy she could not describe.

Then it happened. The voice spoke into her mind clearly. *What wrong?* She stared at the dolphin, uncomprehendingly at first, and then said aloud, "Are you talking? Saying something other than my name?"

Learn, the dolphin responded. Andi stared at the baby calf, and he stared back, eyes sparkling with mischief as if he were laughing at her. Then he jumped out of the water, did a backward flip, dove in, and jumped out of the water again in delight. Andi sat watching him open-mouthed, laughing unexpectedly. She reached out toward him with her mind. *When? I mean, how did you—*

Listen. Hear you. From outside, he responded. *Learn how.* His head emerged out of the water again, his eyes still glinting with mischief. *Want surprise Andi.*

"Surprise me?" Andi laughed. "Yes, you did."

Delight shone in his eyes. He hopped up on his fins, attempting to use them as legs, using them to propel himself forward, closer to her. As he tried to balance himself on the water, dancing around on top of its surface, his head came to the same height as hers. Moved by the moment, Andi put her hands around him and pulled him to her, kissing him on top of the head.

He stopped trying to propel himself on his fins and sank back into the water. The glint of mischief in his eyes was gone, replaced by curiosity. His voice rang in her head. *Why do that?*

Andi hesitated. How did she explain? Or did she even have to try? If he had eavesdropped on her, her mind all day before, having figured out as much as he had, then he should be able to understand. She shrugged. "I am happy. Happy to be with you, so that is why I kissed you. To, um, to *show* you."

He was silent. Slowly he began to stretch himself out and to swim around the inlet pool. The entire bottom of the pool was lit by his glow. Andi smiled. His excitement was palpable. She found herself wondering what he remembered about his mother. She was sure he had questions—*just like she did about her own mother.*

Suddenly, Andi realized she would have to be careful with her little dolphin. He could hear her thoughts.

But it was too late. His voice spoke into her mind again. *New made.*

"New made?" Andi frowned. Then an image appeared in her mind— his mother dolphin in a different place, happy and whole. There was something different about the mother dolphin, but in what way, Andi couldn't say. She was certain it was the same dolphin who had entrusted its baby calf to her though. The image faded from her mind, leaving a feeling of sadness yet contentment. The baby dolphin was with her now, and he had closure. *Closure,* Andi realized bitterly. She was not jealous of her dolphin, but oh, how she wanted to feel that certainty.

I—I want stay. You. His shyness, his excitement at being with her, at somehow being a part of her just as she was a part of him was obvious. His sadness tempered by his excitement at being a part of her life. Another question came to her. *Love? Artie? Grandma Bea?* Andi realized he'd eavesdropped on her, Grandma Bea, and Artie.

"Love is—love is many things," Andi responded, confused, and touched. The dolphin had referred to her grandma as Grandma. Not exactly as his grandma but as belonging to him as Grandma did to her.

A word whispered out toward her from the young calf. *Belong?*

Andi responded. "Yes, to belong." She hesitated and added, "But not own. To belong but not own."

The little calf's mind fell silent, thinking. She realized that the dolphin did not know what the word *own* meant. And she wasn't sure how to explain that to him. Andi disengaged herself from feeling his emotions. She would remain true to her word. They might belong together, but she did not own him. His mind was his own unless he cared to share it. It was a good reminder for her, she reflected. And maybe for him as well.

He reached out to her again. *Name? Want name.* Andi's face reddened. The responsibility of naming this extraordinary creature was on her. Strangely humbled, Andi had a name to offer. She hoped that he would like it. She started. "What about ..." she stumbled. Starting again, she spoke to the dolphin. "What about Lux? It's Latin. It means bright. It's from one of my grandfather's favorite songs. He meant the world to my grandmother. And to us," she added.

The question floated up to her. *Why?*

Andi was ready for this question. "Grandpa Tomas was a kid at heart. He loved dolphins more than anything. He worked at the wharf. I don't think he ever swam with dolphins. I just know he loved them. It just seems perfect for you."

Belong more. Name make belong more. Andi nodded, understanding. The name tied them together even more in ways she couldn't explain yet. The warmth Andi experienced from him echoed his pleasure at their bond.

"You're speaking much better already."

Rules. Many. His confusion at the nuances of their language, Andi's language, was obvious. She heard his voice again. *Learn. Again and again.*

Andi laughed at this, which drew a puzzled response not defined in words. She grinned at Lux, relishing the moment of acknowledging him as such. "Lux," she said, the name rolling naturally off her tongue.

Lux dove to the bottom of the pond and then shot straight up in the air to the top of the cavern, flipping as he dove back down again. Andi gasped. She did not know how he had managed to jump that high, but it was beautiful to watch. The whole ceiling illumined by his glow.

Lux spoke to her. *Who I?* Andi understood.

"I don't know, Lux," she said. "I've never seen or heard of anything—or anyone—like you before." His confusion rose in her mind as she said this. "The only time was when I met your mother. That's it, Lux. I wish I knew more. I'm sorry."

Want know, he told her, swimming around the inlet pool furiously. Andi understood. He was restless, trying to figure things out. His head popped out of the water again. *Together. Under water. Seek.*

"Seek?" Andi said. "For answers? How?"

Idea. Have idea.

Andi hesitated. It was nighttime. Late. She answered him mentally in one word, a question. *Breathing?*

His response came. *I fix. Be fine.*

What if someone sees us? Like they did with your mother? Andi would not risk any harm to Lux.

Andi sensed Lux pause in his thinking. His world was enlarging all the time, Andi marveled, new rules and things to consider at every moment.

Swim too high, too close, he answered. *Us deep.* A pause. He probed inside her mind, reaching for something. Then it came. *Dare!* He laughed. She looked at him with a reproving yet teasing stare, and instead of feeling abashed, she got a wink from him in return. She smiled. The name Lux *did* fit.

"You'll keep me warm, like this afternoon?" she said.

Yes. Lux sounded confident.

"Oh, all right," Andi responded, adding a slight teasing note of exasperation. She jumped into the deep pool and wrapped her arms securely around Lux. He shot forward out of the cavern, pulling her deep into the water. Andi's first reaction was to panic. He was glowing too brightly. Someone would see him. But then Andi realized how deep they were. They needed to be bright. She wasn't sure how much he could see when his light dimmed, but she wouldn't be able to see anything. Andi knew she wouldn't like that.

As they swam, Andi felt the same warmth she had experienced before. Suddenly Andi felt herself slowly merging with the dolphin.

Her body was still on top of it, distinct from it but part of it at the same time. Her hands, her arms were all *golden*. She realized she was able to breathe oxygen as they swam underwater.

Lux, how? She asked in wonder.

Only you, the dolphin replied. *No one else.*

Andi understood. He could only do this for her. That was as far as his powers extended. Because they were *bonded.* This was something she had understood from the mother dolphin—that if she rescued her child, they would be bonded. Because she was the first human Lux had ever encountered. This made Andi feel bad. What if there was someone more deserving, someone who *knew* what to do for Lux?

She felt Lux's love for her swelling from the inside of her body. He was glad it had been her.

Andi reached one golden hand out into the sea. It sifted through seaweed, touching upon rocks and broken shells on the ocean floor. Sand on the bottom of the ocean shifted in Lux's wake yet never blurred her vision. Fish began to appear, moving out of the dolphin's path, startled by the dolphin's light and even more startled by Andi.

She realized that Lux was using a form of echolocation that she'd heard other dolphins had. What was interesting about this was he seemed able to share this echolocation with her through their connection. She found herself sensing things ahead of them like high rocks. What was more interesting was the many kinds of underwater life that lived below. They could feel schools of fish, things embedded in the sea, porpoises and the like. Andi had never felt so *aware,* and it frightened her a little bit. The reaching out through echolocation came naturally to Lux; it did not come naturally to her. She realized that even though their minds were connected, they both retained their uniqueness and differences. Just being able to see marine life with Lux at the bottom of the sea was enough! Very politely, she asked Lux if he could somehow not share with her his sense of echolocation. When he realized how overwhelmed Andi was, he stopped that part of their connection. Andi felt very relieved. She realized her mind was not built for that.

Two otters swam alongside them as they glided farther out from the islands and into the deep of the ocean. Andi stretched a hand toward them. They nuzzled her hand, blinking curiously. They moved ahead, swimming parallel to Lux. Lux's voice broke through Andi's amazement.

Strong current they say. Know. Dangerous? It was a question from him.

Don't go there, she told him silently.

They separated from the otters. Soon they approached what appeared to be giant shadows that were not illumined by Lux's light. Andi found herself taken aback when an eye opened in the darkness. Orca whales, Andi realized with a start. Touching upon Lux's mind, Andi sensed he was asking the whales a series of questions but was not satisfied with the answers.

Had they ever seen anything like him? The answer was a vague and confused no. Lux pressed on, asking about his mother and the hidden cavern and whether they'd seen any dolphins at all. They had no helpful answers. Lux drew from the whales and the otters a collective memory of celebration that revolved around his birth. Beyond that, there was nothing. Their minds were haphazard and different from humans'. Lux was able to sort through these impressions and feelings, but Andi was not. Lux's disappointment weighed hard upon her.

He might have had closure interns of his mother being newly made, but Lux wanted to know who—and what—he was.

Suddenly Lux swam away from the orcas, further into the inky blackness. The light around them revealed nothing but themselves. Empty darkness surrounded them, and as they continued to dive, Lux's frustration grew. The light of his skin began to blaze an increasingly bright golden, to the point where Andi had to close her eyes. Her own skin was blazing, and she suddenly felt very, very hot instead of merely warm. Lux swam faster and faster. And became scared.

Andi shouted out toward Lux with her mind: *Stop!* He stopped, his anger tempered by her fear. Feeling his remorse, Andi reached out to tell him not to worry, that she understood that he was looking for answers but that he had scared her.

He asked her again. *Who I?*

Special, Andi replied firmly. As she told him this, she became aware of light shining down on them from high above, from the water's surface. The light was purplish in nature and shone much like the sun. She frowned. It was nighttime. What could be the source of that light? And how could any light penetrate this deep in the ocean? Andi told Lux to rise toward the surface and to be careful while doing so. Somehow, Andi could not imagine such a bright light coming from a ship or lighthouse.

Lux swam up and up until they rose from the water. Andi gasped. Against a lavender sky, a sun of both silver and purple sank toward the horizon. Lavender rays washed across an endless sea, darkening Andi's hands to a purplish color. Lux's golden skin shone against the purple, standing out against it.

Oh my God, she thought. *Oh my God.* Where were they? She began to shake. The golden light in her arm had settled into a warm, soft light. Somehow, when Lux had been angry, they had *moved* here. Like Lux had *moved* Jubal. *Teleportation,* she realized with a growing panic.

"Lux," she said to the dolphin out loud. "Can you take us home?" She was trying to remain calm.

He did not answer her but gave her a general feeling of exhaustion. He had used so much power by accident, and now he was worn out. Andi tried to calm herself down by reassuring Lux that he didn't have to do anything *right now* but maybe soon.

After placating Lux, Andi turned around. There was nothing in the water save for two tall mountain peaks rising above it. They were a distance away. They rose out of the water with no shoreline, just two huge mountain peaks rising out of the water opposite each other. Their sides met in a perfect point like a triangle. *Conical,* she realized. *Two upside-down cones.*

With no word uttered between Andi and Lux, the two swam closer to the mountains. As they approached, a small sliver of sea appeared before them, running between the two bodies of land. The mountainous cones rose on either side of it. The passage between the mountains was quite tiny, but Andi was sure that Lux would be able to fit through.

One mountain was done colored while the second was slate. Both slopes were smooth and free of crags and rocks. There was an enormous seat carved out on one the side of the dun-colored mountain. Sitting on it was a giant wooden statue of a man wearing a strange triangular hat. He had eyes and a nose but no mouth. His arms were at his sides as he sat with a spear in his right hand. He fit perfectly in the seat carved out of the mountain.

There was something between the two mountains, on the water. The object was immobile, as if trapped on unmoving glass. It did not look as if it was floating. No waves bobbed around it. It was a dark color and reminded Andi of a ship.

Only...it *was* a ship! Andi gaped. It looked very old yet regal in its curves and lines, something out of mythology. Its sails were high and triangular. The odd thing about it was that large cylindrical tubes ran over all parts of the ship. The tubes ran along the ship's decks, disappearing into one porthole only to emerge through another. They ran along its bottom, above and beneath the water. The tubes bent smoothly around the sharp contours of the ship.

What sent a chill up Andi's spine was that the people on the ship were immobile, as if they were toys. Life-sized toys. There was a tall and fat man that was in the middle of giving orders, his arms pointing in two directions. Crewmen were frozen in the middle of carrying out those orders.

As Lux began to approach the ship, Andi looked up at the slate-colored mountain to their right. There was another giant seat carved out of the mountain much like the first. Again with a giant statue, differing only from the first in its slate. It shared the same cap, the same seated position, and the same spear, only it was in its left hand. Andi looked back to the first statue, its eyes closed. She then looked ahead to the second statue. Its eyes, too, appeared closed. With the spears in their hands, the carved men appeared to be guarding the immobile ship.

Shrugging, she spoke to Lux to guide them to the lifeless ship. The water was still as glass as they neared it. Putting her hand on the ship, it suddenly bobbed to life on the water, responding to her touch. Startled, she looked up at the sails of the ship. Different patterns on the sails had appeared. More importantly, these shapes were *moving*. On the sails! Raising her eyes even further, Andi found she still couldn't make out what the patterns were or what they meant.

Suddenly, the statue ahead of her opened its eyes and leapt to life. Turning around, Andi saw that the first statue from behind had leapt up as well, its eyes open. Both statues twisted their torsos and threw their spears at Lux—and at her.

As the spears sped toward them, Lux's fear rose in her, merging with hers. The sudden tension in his muscles spurred Andi to duck even as Lux submerged himself into the water. *Teleport us! Teleport us!* Andi screamed. She felt his exhaustion. He had reacted out of fear and was trying to disappear, take them home. It was not going to be quick enough.

A spear went through her shoulder. Instead of feeling the pain though, Andi was more aware of the fact that Lux had dived down to the bottom of the ocean. Blood streamed from her shoulder as she reached toward him with her mind.

Lux! Lux! My shoulder! Blood gushed all around her. Andi stared at her own goldenness and how it shone through the dark mass of blood coming out of her shoulder. Lux's glow kept brightening as he plummeted the bottomless depths of the sea. The light from above disappeared, the darkness folding itself around Lux. There was no light above them, no purplish light from that strange sun they had found themselves swimming under. And the light that came from Lux was pulsating in panic. Andi sent one word toward Lux: *Home! Home!*

Blinded by the lights dancing and changing around her, Andi closed her eyes and huddled against Lux.

Andi's eyes opened. Lux rose toward the surface slowly. Breaking through, Andi was relieved. She knew that they were home. A familiar light shone from a house on top of a cliff face—her home. She did not have to remind Lux to be careful. He navigated the way back to the inlet cave.

Entering the mouth of the cavern, a great shock of devastation entered her mind from her dolphin. Dismayed at his allowing this to happen to them, shame ate at the baby dolphin for allowing them to be so exposed.

"Lux," she murmured, "it's okay. It's all right. We're home." Confused herself, Andi began to ask questions. "Lux, why did we go there? Why did you take us there?"

Do not know, the dolphin replied. *Wanted search. Find out who I? Then we there.*

Lux was upset. He could not continue. He allowed her to slide off his back and swam to the inner ridge inside the cave. Pulling herself up, Andi realized that the spear had penetrated through her shoulder. The arrow was sticking out just above her chest. She suddenly realized she was in pain. A great deal of pain. Her heart began to beat quickly. Dizzy, she put her hand to her forehead. As she passed out, she saw Lux in the pool. Fright was in his eyes, as if he could see something she didn't.

Eight

The Starry In-Between

Andi opened her eyes to stars. Millions of them. They were not only above her; they were beside her and below her. She floated, nearly flying among the stars. She laughed. The stars moved with her, caressing her, lifting her up. She pushed herself up as if she were getting out of bed, even though she couldn't see anything concrete under her body. She extended a foot in front of her, touching upon something that was not ground or solid but that still bore her weight. Mischievously, she jumped off from it. Now she was flying. Yet the stars flew with her even as she flew through the stars. Andi knew she did not understand something, but she also knew she did not have to understand. She just was.

Andi slowed to a steady floating position. The stars swirled in front of her, around her, each one glimmering as if in accordance with music. She heard a song that broke her heart, cracking it into pieces, only to mend it again with its beauty. It was as if her nature had been set to starry music, revealing to her layers she had not known existed before. She longed to hold on to it. She even then kind of knew the beauty lay in never being able to hold on to that feeling, only able to know it in one fleeting moment.

Andi opened her eyes and decided to look at just one star in the vast dancing universe of lights. She chose a tiny reddish star spiraling around her. As Andi focused her entire attention on it, the star began to grow. Andi grew steadily smaller in comparison to it. She looked around her. The other stars had not increased in size. They enveloped her, swirling around her, each star calling out to her with its individual song.

She knew somehow she was supposed to be in pain but felt none. She relinquished control, allowing her body to float through the heavens. All the while, her eyes remained on the one red star. It continued growing and growing. Nor were the other stars growing larger. It was the red star that were healing her, Andi realized.

Andi was alive. She would be alive. She would live again. She lived, and the darkness had not won. Clarion. *Glory. Sorrow. Grief. Courage. Failure. Striving.* The last word hung on to her heart, and that was when it beat again. *Striving.* The red sun that was her heart throbbed in harmony with the starry host wrapping her in its embrace. *Live.* Her heart pounded in her ears, the stars closing in on her. *Live!* The red star pumped energy in and out into her, pressing down on her. She held her arms above her, holding the red sun at bay. The stars danced around her wildly in a glorious circle. Andi looked up above her. As if she were surfacing out of water, the red sun, powerful, now stood as a monolith, ready to drop down on her.

Golden. Fiery. Artie. Grandma. Her eyes closed. *Golden.* An ugly metal undertone began to shake her. The stars were beginning to disappear. She couldn't become afraid and knew that was why the red sun had not dropped on her. She had to remain unafraid. That was it. She closed her eyes again. *Golden.* She jerked up, seeing a thread of energy stretching from her to the red sun. *Lux!* Fear shivered through her. The red sun burst into a fiery frenzy, alive, gloriously alive. Andi whispered, "Lux."

She woke to a hand on her shoulder. It was Artie. His touch was urgent, insistent. Andi realized she was in her bed, covered in sweat. Artie's eyes were wide, focused on her. Andi's body was convulsing, shaking. Tears streamed from her eyes. It had been so beautiful. She wanted to go back. She reached her hand out not toward Artie but toward the reality she knew she had just been in. Yet, the red sun ... Andi stopped trembling. The place she had been in ... was ... beyond. The only word she could think of—*beyond*. She swallowed.

"Yes, Artie?" she managed to say.

Artie continued to look at her. Finally he shook his head and stood up as if he were ready to leave the room. Instead, he closed the door and then came back to sit by her.

"Forgive you," he said, his voice firm.

Andi could only nod. Wordlessly, she stared at her twin brother. He spoke again. "What?" Andi knew he was asking what happened to her.

Andi nodded again. "I'll tell you everything. But ... Artie, it's something I can only show you. I can't tell you. It's something you need to see for yourself. Okay?"

He considered that at length. Finally he nodded.

"Artie," Andi said, "how—how long have I been here?"

He hunched his shoulders and sat forward so that his face was only a few inches away from hers. "You appeared." He indicated the bed. "You were not in your bed, but then you were."

Andi swallowed, absorbing this information. This was a lot of talk from Artie. He must have been really upset. Then a memory impelled her to touch her right shoulder underneath her shirt. There was nothing ... wait, there was a thin scar. It hadn't been a dream.

"Artie," she began, "I think I did. Appear out of nowhere, I mean." The effort to say it was exhausting. "Please, Artie. Be patient. I'll show you everything. You won't be able to believe it." She finished with a wan smile.

In a way so unlike him, Artie leaned over and kissed her on the forehead. He then squeezed her hand.

This gesture of affection brought tears to Andi's eyes. He smiled at her and finally got up to leave. She stopped him with one last question.

"What made you check up on me?"

He turned around. "Earthquake." He spoke in a hushed voice as if he were afraid that by speaking he would cause another earthquake to happen. He held his arms far apart as if to tell her how big the earth-quake had been.

Andi forced herself up into a seating position, surprised at how weak she was. *Another earthquake?* Andi turned back to Artie. Wearily she answered his puzzled expression. "Artie ... I'll talk to you more tomorrow. I'm just so tired."

After Artie left the room, Andi slid down into her bed, putting her head on the pillow. The music from that starry place was fading away, and she stilled herself to see if she could hear it. Instead, she heard something else.

Andi?

Oh, Lux. Is that you? I don't know what happened to me, to us. It's all so strange. There was so much more Andi wanted to say, but she stopped herself.

Better? The love and concern came through to her. Lux was still upset.

I'm great, Lux. I'm all fixed up. Lux, where was I?

The answer came back to her. *Far away.*

She responded. *Lux? Can I—can I ever go back?*

He answered. *Too dangerous. You will want to stay forever. Needed to heal. Why I sent you over there.*

Lux? She asked. There was silence. How had he known about that place? There was no answer from him. Andi sighed. Lux had gotten his answer; she was well, and that was all she was going to know for now. Suddenly she realized something. Lux's language was improving! This made her smile and helped her relax a little bit. Just a little bit. She didn't think he would ever talk normally—he was too different. His mind didn't work like hers did. Or anyone else's.

The music was no longer there as she closed her eyes. Another certainty intruded upon her as she traced her finger on the large scar right above her right lung. She could have died.

She shivered, pushed the thought out of her mind, and slept a deeply troubled sleep.

Nine

Aftershocks

The phone rang several times the next morning, waking Andi. She wandered out of her bedroom in a blur, surprised that Artie was not awake yet. He always woke up first in the mornings, way before she or Grandma Bea did. The light outside told her that it was late.

Yet no one had woken her up for school. No one usually had to, but on the rare day she overslept, Grandma Bea or Artie had always come to her rescue. Did they have more days off? She wondered if the earthquake the night before related to it. *What about what happened with the window and the whirlwind?* She wondered. She hoped Gaby was doing better. Even though it was just a few days ago, the whirlwind incident felt like an eternity ago. With what had happened with her during the evening swim with Lux and that starry, far-off place. Andi closed her eyes. *Better not to think about it.*

Grandma Bea sat in the kitchen talking on the phone, her face tight and drawn. She nodded rather curtly at Andi. *Grandma Bea is with it today,* Andi noted. *So far.* Was her grandmother angry with her? While pouring herself cereal, Andi listened to her grandmother's side of the conversation.

"Yes, I do understand your concern," Andi's grandmother was saying.

"Our house is a little far out from everyone else on the island ... Tom's ancestors were one of the first to settle on the island, you know. We've always taken pride in this house and being out here ... what? Yes, I do agree, it is a glorious view." Grandma Bea's voice trailed off as Andi ate her cereal. So. Someone was showing concern about their house being so far away from everyone else. It wasn't that *far*.

Its isolation was one thing Andi had liked about it ever since her mother first brought her there when she was little. Everything that mattered to Andi situated around the house and the cliff. And Jubal too, she realized.

"How *unusual*," her grandmother said. "Yes, yes, I can understand how there would have to be an inspection—" By now, she was quite certain that Grandma Bea was on the telephone with someone from the school.

Just the surprise of the earthquake the night before and how high the water had come in could put everyone on edge. That on top of what happened to Gaby. Andi sighed. Somehow, Lux was at the center of it all. *Even her experience with the stars.* Lux had sent her there. She was sure of it. To heal, somehow.

She closed her eyes. The stars were a fleeting memory. At moments Andi could hear a strain of the music that had floated her among those celestial lights. When she turned the whole of her attention on it, the sound disappeared. It could only sneak up on her when she wasn't looking for it. Her head throbbed with the knowledge of the other day's events. She knew she was avoiding it. She didn't want to think about the other world. Where those figures had tried to attack her and Lux. Where they'd seen that ship.

The phone slamming against the receiver interrupted Andi's reverie.

Her grandmother faced her, trembling. Her nostrils were flaring, too. Not good. That usually meant that either Andi or Artie was in trouble, and Andi sensed this went beyond that.

"Your—your *teacher* is coming here with a *social worker* to check our situation. Do you hear me, Andi? What are you telling this woman about us? About me? Are you not happy with me, Andi? Do you want to break up this family even more? Because *that* is *what* is happening here."

Andi's eyes stung with tears. The discussion with Ms. Dugger from that last Friday came roaring back, and Andi came undone. It was too much. She rose over her grandmother, full of fury. In some small corner of her mind, Andi realized just how diminutive her grandmother had become. It didn't stop her.

"How *dare* you speak to me that way?" Andi screamed. Ignoring her grandmother's shocked look, she went on. "*I'm* the one who takes care of things around here. Not you. *Me!* I'm the one who takes you upstairs and puts you to bed when you're having one of your spells. I'm the one who cooks dinner most of the time. I'm the one who helps Artie get dressed and makes sure he goes to the bathroom before I go to school for the day. I'm the one who helps him change when I get back. I make lunches for myself and Artie so that you won't do it. I'm the one who does all this! Me! I go to the grocery store for us all the time! You don't know that because you've either forgotten it or don't want to admit it."

Andi towered over her grandmother. Something inside her told her she was crossing a line, but she didn't care.

"Why would I tell Ms. Dugger what goes on here? *Why?* My mother's dead! I'm only twelve years old! Do you think I want something to happen to you? We don't have anyone else! Do you think I want us separated? They're not going to take the two of us! I'm *not* going to lose Artie. I've lost too much already! We can't even find Mom's body. If we could, then we could bury her and be able to visit her grave—" With a sob, Andi broke off and started running toward her bedroom.

She crashed into Artie on the stairs, blinded by her tears. He stared down at her openmouthed. How much had Artie overheard? *All of it,* she realized hopelessly.

Artie's mouth was wide open, but what was worse was that tears flowed down his cheeks. Andi put her hand to her mouth. Artie never cried. *Never.* She'd said things to Grandma Bea that she'd never dream of telling him to his face. Andi turned around to see Grandma Bea at the foot of the stairs. Bright tears stood in her grandmother's eyes too, but she did not cry. She ran her fingers through her white hair, fiddling with her glasses. Andi wondered how long her grandmother would remain lucid. Long enough for her to fix the damage? Or would it be better if her grandmother forgot about what had just happened? But no. Even if Grandma Bea forgot, Andi would not.

Andi waited. She could not move. Out of the corner of her eye, she realized that Artie was wet. She groaned inwardly. For the second time in less than a week, she'd upset her twin so horribly to the point of him wetting his pants. Artie hadn't been able to talk about it—their mother's disappearance. He had instead withdrawn even further into his world of toys and ideas. Grandma had told Andi back then that perhaps in his own way Artie was acting out and expressing his grief. Hearing all that Andi had said had been too much for him.

Andi turned to her grandmother, begging for help. Grandma Bea nodded slowly then folded her arms across her chest. She cleared her throat. "Is this true, Artie?" she said. "What Andi said to me?"

Andi tensed. Grandma was pulling Artie into this, asking him to take part in something Andi wasn't sure he was ready for. She was treating him like a young adult. Artie blinked, unsure of what his grandmother was asking of him. He shook his head indicating that he didn't understand.

Grandma Bea drew in her breath. She cocked her head toward Andi before looking at Artie again, asking, "What Andi said. Is it true?" Her grandmother might as well have turned into stone. Her face was un-readable. Andi braced herself for whatever Artie's answer might be.

Artie looked down to his pajama shirt and started fiddling with the buttons. He began to rock himself on the balls of his feet before starting to sway with his hips. He said one word, not looking at either Andi or Grandma Bea as he said it. "Yes."

Grandma Bea let out a deep sigh. Andi could not get over how *tired* her grandmother looked. *What had Andi done to her family?* She began to walk downstairs toward her grandmother, but Artie caught her from behind. She turned around, and he pulled her into an embrace.

"Don't leave me. Don't."

Andi's heart ripped in half. Having heard her what she said, her brother was afraid that she might leave him. Her gut twisted inside her. She pulled out from Artie's hug but drew his face closer to hers, their eyes locking.

"I will do everything I can to keep us together," Andi replied, "*everything.*"

"Maybe we should find Dad." Artie's face was the most expressive Andi had ever seen it, which wasn't saying much.

Andi sighed. Not their *father* again. It was something Artie brought up again and again. He did not seem to understand how much it irritated her. Their father had abandoned them, and she was not going to look for him.

"We are not going to do that, Artie." She felt quite strong as she said it. Slowly, Artie nodded. She smiled at him one last time before walking down toward her grandmother. She put her hand into her grandmother's, squeezing it. Her grandmother squeezed back, much to Andi's relief.

Grandma Bea looked at her. "I must really be far gone if I'm so *unaware.*" She paused. "I had no idea, Andi. If I had, I wouldn't have said what I—" She stopped.

"You were right to say what you did, Andi." Grandma Bea squeezed her hand one more time. "Who knows? If your mother had always spoken to me that way, we might've had a better relationship." She sighed. "We never knew how to talk to one another."

"Andi, you have a real way of saying how you feel and getting your point across. What hurts me the most is that you were driven to that point where you said what you did." She shrugged sadly. "But isn't that my fault?"

Andi whispered, "I just lost it when you said I had been telling Ms. Dugger about you, about us." She shook her head. "I would *never* do that. *Never.*"

Her grandmother responded. "What bothers me the most about this is ... I know that. And I said it anyway." She looked down at her feet.

"I think it's starting to become more than just forgetting for me, Andi. I'm believing things that aren't real. I'm becoming ..." She trailed off with a small, ironic grin. "Unhinged. That's it. I'm losing myself."

Untethered, Andi remembered. Her grandmother was coming undone. She looked so small and frail standing right there in front of her that it hurt. *Grandma Bea was—no, is—*Andi reminded herself, *the strongest person I know.* To see her become something less hurt her deeply, violated something fundamental to her. That's when Andi realized a startling fact. She was surer of who Grandma Bea was than of who her mother was. What was it Grandma Bea had said? *If she had spoken to me that way, we might have had a better relationship.*

"Grandma," Andi said after, making sure that Artie was out of earshot. He'd gone upstairs; she hoped that he was changing out of his wet pajamas. "Why weren't you close to Mom?"

"Just because she came here to live with me after your father left didn't mean that it was because we were so close." Grandma Bea smiled bitterly. "Our relationship wasn't like that. She came here because she had nowhere else to go."

Grandma sat down on the couch opposite the fireplace and stared at the ash from the fire the night before. Andi wondered if Lux was listening in on their conversation and if he even understood what they were talking about. Before sitting next to her grandmother, she searched that space in her mind where she and Lux connected. She knew his awareness lay deep in the background. It retreated even deeper when she probed though, as if he didn't want to intrude.

Her grandmother began, speaking so quietly that Andi had to lean over to hear her. "Your mother believed that your father left because he couldn't handle Artie. There are men who rise to the occasion when they have a special-needs child, but your father—he just couldn't. So when he left, your mother came here, I think in part because she had nowhere else to go. She knew that I would love you two just as much as she did. She knew that I would fight for you like she had and that nothing could make me love Artie or you any less." She paused, gathering her breath. "It must have been hard for her to come home. I didn't want her to marry him, and she did anyway. So for her, coming back was the same as admitting that I had been right. I didn't want to be right." Her shoulders shook. "I wasn't right. If you and Artie weren't here now, I can't imagine, I can't imagine …" She trailed off, her face in her hands.

"Grandma," Andi said, "do you know where my father is now?"

"Joseph?" Grandma answered, startled. "No, no. I don't, no. He wrote a letter to me after your mother died. There was no return address. Only the postmark. It was from somewhere back east. I can't even remember where. It was sad. He wrote how much he loved your mother and how sorry he was at how everything turned out. He asked after you …"

Just not Artie, Andi realized. And even after he'd known their mother was gone, he hadn't come looking for them. He was so afraid of her brother that he hadn't come to find out who his children were. How they were doing. Andi became bitter.

"Every time I'm hard on your father," Grandma Bea said, "I think about how I objected to your mother marrying him. Maybe he has reason to be hard on me." She said it without anger, without bitterness. "Don't you for one second think he didn't miss out. He missed out on so much. *So much.*"

She stared off in the distance, again lost in her own world. Maybe she was floating between a jumble of confused memories, unsure of which scrap she could hold on to. Grandma had told the truth about her father; of that Andi was certain.

Andi felt overwhelmed. Overwhelmed at the tragedy of her life. She had lost her mother, would lose her grandmother, and would probably Artie. Not to mention Lux. She decided to lie down on the couch, pulling a heavy blanket off the couch and wrapping it around herself. She put her legs on Grandma Bea's lap. She knew her grandmother wouldn't object. A tear slid down her face. Andi knew that she'd better enjoy it all now while she could.

Andi looked out the window from the couch and noticed how high the sun was. Frowning, she asked her grandmother why neither she nor Artie had woken Andi up for school.

Grandma replied, "Artie told me you were sick, that I shouldn't wake you up." She sighed. "That was why your teacher called. Then it led—to *that*." She paused, frowning, as if she were trying to remember. "The school has closed for an indefinite period. They need to check the structure of the school because of what happened two days ago. Especially after another earthquake. They can't take any chances."

Andi nodded and rubbed her shoulder, not even thinking about the scar until her fingers traced its line running across her arm. An idea entered her head that was so alien to her that she stared stupidly out of the window with her mouth open. She was thunderstruck with the enormity of it. It might work, and all three of them could stay together. *Could Grandma Bea be healed?* That starry far-off place?

Her grandmother's mouth had gone slack; she was gone. Andi stroked her shoulder as way of farewell, then rose from the couch and hurried upstairs to her room to change.

Minutes later, Andi ran out the front door. She hurried down the ridge toward the base of the cliff, then edged along the thin strip of beach toward the inlet cave.

As Andi arrived, the mouth of the cavern lit up with golden fire. Lux knew she was coming, and his excitement showed. Focused though she was, Andi's joyful excitement rose within her as well. As she entered, he was swimming around the small inlet pond in excitement.

To her great surprise, he flipped out of the pool toward her, his bottlenose touching her lips as if in a welcoming kiss. *You are Andi,* he said.

"Yes, I'm Andi," she responded confusedly. Just what did Lux mean? Doing another backflip, Lux brushed his nose against her arm, near her scar. "Oh." She understood. Healed, fully herself again. *Is that what you mean?* She voiced the question silently to him. A series of musical notes crowded into her head, each note adding to the next in a happy cacophony. While not the same music from the starry in-between, it was a representation of Lux's joy, of how much she loved her.

Was my mistake, Lux voiced into her mind, *Was wrong, wrong, wrong. Accident that we were there.* Lux became angry. *Then we were there.*

Andi could only exclaim, "No, Lux! No. It wasn't you. It was … it was just what it was." She frowned and asked, "Lux, where were we exactly yesterday? What was that place with the mountains? It wasn't here."

Distant. Far. Worlds away.

"*How* did we get there? I mean, how? We were swimming underwater and"—she gesticulated wildly around her—"and we were there! In that place. How, Lux? *How?*"

Father. The word echoed in Andi's mind. *Your father is gone. Yours.*

"Yes, my father is gone," she answered him rather rudely, not wanting to remember. "What does that have to do with where we were last night?" She wished Lux would answer her question.

Answers. Lux looks for answers. Lux is here, alone but not alone. You are mine. Andi's heart wrenched at this last statement, but he continued. *Lux belongs to who? Lux belongs to where? Searching only to disappear. Disappear to the other world.*

Andi wanted to be sure she understood. "You're saying that you were trying to figure out why you're here, who you are, why you are who you are, and then we ended up there?"

Andi became hurt. Your spirit was fading. It is why Lux sent you there. The healing place.

"Lux." Andi knelt on the edge, her hands on top of his head. "You didn't even mean to go there, did you?"

No.

"You can teleport. It's a word Jubal uses sometimes," Andi said. "And you can speak into my mind." She finished wonderingly.

Teleport?

"Move from one place to another in a jiffy," Andi explained awkwardly. "Can you speak into other people's minds?" she asked, somewhat jealously.

No. Hard to explain.

Andi felt ashamed of her jealousy, so she changed the subject. "Maybe ..." She groped for words. "Maybe ... that place is where you need to go. To find out who you are. Maybe you need to get past those two ... statue-looking people. Those things." She shuddered, remembering how still they had been before they jumped to life. How fast their spears whistled through the air.

Not going back. The answer was firm.

"Lux ..." She trailed off, thinking. "Maybe you're not supposed to go back right now. Maybe it's the wrong time. Still, it doesn't mean you can't ever go back."

Do not want to.

Andi nodded, showing Lux she understood. She held her hands up in front of him, signaling that she would leave it be for now. His—not remorse exactly but more—anger at what had happened to her touched her. Anger mixed with fear. Not for himself. For her. He was not going back to that *world*. He was not leaving her.

"Lux," she said desperately, "I don't want to ask you this, but I have to."

Fading. Lux cannot stop it.

"What do you mean, *fading?*"

Grandma fading. Becoming new. Other side. Cannot stop.

"She's dying," Andi answered in a sudden flash of recognition.

Yes. Disappearing from this side, here. Other side. Will be new.

"There's nothing you can do to stop it?"

His voice was sad as it whispered the answer in her mind. *No.*

Andi began linking things together quite rapidly. She did not know what to do. Ms. Dugger would come and find out that her grandmother was dying, and then she and Artie would go their separate ways. And there was Lux. What would happen to Lux if she went far away? What if she was inland? Where there was no sea, no way for him to reach her. It was too much. She fingered the gravel beneath her knees. Time. She needed time. She needed to plan.

"How much time does Grandma have?" She held up her thumb and finger to show size. "A little bit? Or more time?" The gap between her thumb and finger widened.

Lux gazed at her for a minute, not saying anything. Suddenly, Andi's attention jerked to the entrance of the cavern. The light outside was fading. Andi rushed to the mouth of the cave entrance. It was pure blackness, and it wasn't even night. She turned back to Lux in alarm.

The water had become still, black. While Lux remained his golden fiery hue, it did not extend into the water or reflect off the walls. He was able to draw all the light into himself, so that none of it emanated into the cavern.

A small point of light began to form in the small inlet lake. It grew steadily until Andi realized that it was the sun. The reflection moved from the right of the lake toward the left, disappearing only to appear again at the right. Andi took this in, not quite understanding. The sun moved slowly across the surface of the water, disappearing toward the edge of the right. It did this several times.

The last time, the sun arrived just short of the right side of the lake. Then as suddenly as it had appeared, the sun went out. Light filled the sky outside. There was no sign that anything out of the ordinary had occurred. Andi returned to the water's edge, where Lux's head emerged above the surface. Light from his skin once again bounced off the cavern walls.

"Around and around several times," Andi murmured. Then she understood. Sunrise and sunset several times. She looked at Lux in dismay. "A few days."

To which his sad eyes could only respond with a mournful *yes*.

The Memory Game

A few days. Andi repeated the words to herself as she climbed the ridge path. *A few days.* A few days until her grandmother was dead and she and Artie were all alone in the world. Her shadow followed her up the ridge path, the sun past its median point. Soon it would be night, and Ms. Dugger would arrive with the social worker. *The social worker.* Andi clenched her teeth. Entrusting their fate to a person they didn't even know made her so angry.

She was so lost in herself that as she walked up the path toward her home, Andi did not see Artie standing on the top waiting, his eyes worried. As Andi joined him on the top, he spoke one word: "Gone."

"Gone?" Andi asked.

"In the kitchen then wasn't" was his reply. His eyebrows rose, questioning.

Andi understood. Grandma Bea had disappeared. With a furtive look back to the bottom of the cliff, she pulled Artie with her toward the house. Artie looked down to the bottom of the cliff then back at Andi. She knew he was suspicious.

Lux? Andi asked.

Instead of answering in words, she heard the dolphin smile into her mind. Andi ran into the house, Artie close behind. She looked in the kitchen. Grandma Bea was not there. But then Andi heard footsteps. Grandma Bea entered the kitchen. Andi's heart dropped as her grandmother entered. Grandma Bea's eyes, dazed and unfocused, suggested her dementia had returned.

What Grandma Bea said next changed everything. "I haven't heard music like that, I don't think ... *ever*," she murmured.

"Music?" Andi repeated back.

"Oh ... I guess I lost it for a bit," Grandma Bea answered. "I heard this wonderful, heavenly music right after it hit, but it must have been my imagination." She bit her lip.

"What do you mean, 'after it hit?'" Andi asked.

"Didn't you feel it?" Grandma's eyes were on her, sharp.

Artie looked up from where he now sat at the table. "Another earthquake," he said.

An earthquake? Andi hadn't felt an earthquake, had she?

"It's odd," Grandma Bea commented. "Several earthquakes in almost as many days. That hasn't happened around these islands in the longest time." She looked at Andi somewhat critically. "I can't believe you didn't feel it while you were outside."

There was no way to answer this. Andi had been with her dolphin. Lux had done something. Earthquakes followed whenever Lux did something *big*. A faint hope rose in Andi's heart.

After a long silence, Grandma Bea looked at her grandchildren. "Do you feel like brownies?" she asked.

Andi blinked. *Brownies*. Grandma hadn't made brownies in two years. That part of her grandmother had faded.

Andi sat next to Artie at the kitchen table. "Sure," Andi replied happily.

Soon, Grandma Bea deposited two brownies on the table for her and Artie. Andi took one, savoring its delectable aroma.

"Grandma," she began, "you said you didn't have a recipe for brownies. That you kept it in your head. That's why you couldn't make them anymore."

"Fancy you are remembering that!" Her grandmother had a huge smile on her face. "How on earth could I have forgotten anything with you here to remember it all for me?" She kissed Andi tenderly on the forehead before putting her hands on her hips. "It's the strangest thing. After that earthquake, it was as if I just remembered, out of the blue. Maybe the earthquake knocked some mothballs out of the attic." As if to show her point, Grandma Bea pointed to her head, rolling her eyes self-deprecatingly.

After that earthquake. Andi's head jerked up. *Music.* Everything came flooding together. The wound on her arm last night. The starry in-between. The earthquake happening right before she woke up in bed. She understood now. Grandma could remember. Lux had sent her grandmother to the starry in-between. *Every time there was an earthquake, it was Lux using his powers!*

Andi got up and hugged Grandma Bea.

"Goodness, Andi! Why are you crying?"

"Am I?" Andi asked. She realized Grandma was right. She was crying. She wiped at her eyes. With Grandma looking at her for an explanation, Andi had to look away, out of the window. "I'm just glad you can remember how to make those brownies," she gulped. It was not the whole truth, but it would have to do.

Grandma Bea sighed. "You carry way too much, Andi," she murmured. "I'm to blame for that ..."

"None of us asked for this," Andi said. " It's just the way it is. I'd rather carry a lot and us be together than to not worry and not have you ..." She bit her lip, forcing herself to still look out of the window. *A few days.* Lux had healed Grandma Bea of her dementia, but she still only had a few days left.

Grandma Bea beckoned to both Andi and Artie to come to her. They did, and she wrapped her arms around them. "I am very, very loved," she began. Overcome, she could not finish. Her eyes were very blue and very bright.

***

That evening, Grandma Bea, dressed in an old but regal dress, opened the door to their fates. Ms. Dugger and the social worker, Jan Harlow, stood before them.

Andi was silent. She stood with shampooed hair, alongside Artie who, surprisingly, did not play with anything. Instead, he absorbed himself in studying every feature of Ms. Dugger's face. Ms. Dugger's irritated looks in Artie's direction showed how uncomfortable this made her. Artie's gaze remained bland, as if without malice. Andi knew that he was studying Ms. Dugger for a weakness, a point of instability to expose.

Jan Harlow, a sallow-faced woman, began the proceedings with a direct comment.

"I must confess," Jan Harlow said directly to Ms. Dugger, "at being baffled at your concerns." Jan glanced all around her. "This house is warm, large, and comfortable."

Ms. Dugger looked none too pleased to have her concerns dismissed so early in the evening. Ms. Dugger did seem to feel comfortable enough to stretch her hand toward the brownie plate for the fourth time.

Even as she munched on the brownie, Ms. Dugger offered testimonials from several of the villagers testifying to Grandma Bea's state of mind. Andi didn't recognize any of the names. She wondered crazily if Ms. Dugger had made the names up. Before she could think any more, Grandma Bea interrupted.

"Ms. Harlow, Ms. Dugger ... I feel the need to clarify something with the two of you." Grandma Bea spoke in a tone of steel. "These names that you are reciting ... they are names of people who worked with my husband more than ten years ago. We haven't had any contact with them since."

Grandma Bea paused. "There was an accident aboard my husband's boat one night about fourteen years ago. We lived in the village then. An accident my husband was found innocent of only after a long investigation. A great deal of pain was inflicted upon us by those who were grieving." She paused. "It was finally chalked up to negligence by a ..." Grandma paused, as if trying to remember. Andi's heart sank.

"A man named Greg Fielding," Grandma continued. "It is true that the boat exploded and that several people died, either through the explosion or by drowning. What is also true is that my husband saved all those who survived," she ended, her eyes blazing.

Andi looked at her grandmother. She had heard this story before but only in bits and snippets. The villagers and even her classmates had talked about it but never directly to Andi. This was the first she'd heard her grandmother speak of it.

Grandma continued to speak. "Many survivors held my husband responsible for what happened. Instead of thanking him for putting their needs before his own, they decided to try to sue us for all the money they could get. It was a long and painful trial." Grandma's eyes settled upon Andi and Artie. If her resolve faltered in the face of their discovery of the facts, she did not show it.

"The evidence finally showed that Tom was innocent. Instead, the ship's mate, Greg Fielding, was the one found responsible. We ended up paying nothing. Still, the damage was already done."

"Because of this large house, people think that we ought to have paid some sort of compensation. Compensation to those my husband *risked his life for*." Her emphasis was hard. "This is his family's ancestral home. I didn't always love it here, and I would rather have left Grey Cove completely than to come live here." Looking at Artie and Andi again, she shrugged. "But things change, and we became comfortable here after moving up thirteen years ago."

Thirteen years ago? Andi wondered. *Yes.* Her mother had grown up in the village. She remembered her mother saying once to Grandma Bea how happy she was that her children were growing up here instead of in the village. It was a very old, distant memory.

Grandma Bea turned to Ms. Dugger, her eyes flashing. "And if you don't mind my saying so, it is people like you that make me happy we live so far away from the rest of the village!"

Ms. Dugger's face paled and then went a deep shade of red as she listened. Judging from her expression, Ms. Dugger was about to make a sharp retort to these comments when Grandma Bea held up her hand.

"I'm sorry," Grandma Bea paused, "but your last name is *Dugger?* *Dug-ger?*"

Panic rose in Andi's chest. She remembered the day she came home from school, after seeing Lux and his mother in the ocean the first time. She'd arrived home and tried to explain to Grandma Bea what was going on. Her grandmother had faded out, saying the word Dugger in the same way she was now. Was her grandmother fading out? *Please, not now.*

Grandma Bea continued, her gaze level with Ms. Dugger's. "If I recall, Greg Fielding left the islands quickly after the trial. He was never held responsible for his crimes. I seem to recall hearing that a few years later, his wife left him. As I recall, the wife returned to using her maiden name, which was *Dugger.* They had a girl my daughter's age at the time. I'm assuming that's you."

Grandma Bea's eyes were flashing as she said this. She turned toward Jan Harlow again. "So, there you have it. A little island history. I'm sorry you had to come all this way to hear it. I do hope that Ms. *Dugger* will make up for any trouble she's caused." She turned to Andi. "Say good-bye to your teacher. You won't be seeing her again. We will have to make other arrangements for your education."

Jan Harlow was already packing things into her handbag, apologizing profusely to Grandma Bea. "You could make a complaint about her to the board—" But Grandma cut her off.

"I don't think we want to pursue this matter any further, do we, Ms. Dugger?" Grandma answered coolly.

This was the final straw for Ms. Dugger. She stood up from the couch. "I want to make it clear that my family's history has nothing to do with why I am trying to intervene on Andi and Artie's behalf," she said hotly. Little beads of sweat stood out on her forehead. "It is not healthy for Artie to be educated by you alone here. It is not healthy for any of you to live so far from where people can reach you, in case of emergency." There was a note of insincerity in her voice. Jan Harlow detected it too.

"Time for us to go," the social worker said firmly. "This is the stupidest case I've ever had. All because of a personal vendetta that shouldn't be a vendetta at all. Let's go, Kathy." Andi had never heard her teacher called by her first name before.

"*Wait!*" Kathy Dugger's voice was desperate. "There is a treasure in this house, a treasure that belongs rightfully to me and my family!" Andi looked at her teacher, stunned. Never had she seen a person's true motives revealed so grotesquely. Kathy Dugger pointed a finger at Grandma Bea even as Jan Harlow moved to stop her.

"Your husband told my father about the treasure in this house. After what happened, after how my father's name was vilified, I deserve my share!" Her hands trembled. "My mother left my father because he never got over being pinned as the villain of the explosion and sinking. I deserve *a share!*"

Grandma stared at her openmouthed, not knowing what to say. Finally, she replied, "*What treasure?*"

"The treasure that's hidden here!" Kathy Dugger responded, her face contorted in rage.

For a few moments, Grandma appeared to be completely baffled. Then she covered her face with her hands. She had begun to giggle. Jan Harlow looked from Grandma Bea to Andi's teacher. Ms. Dugger's face filled with a rage she could not contain.

"Dear old Tomas!" Grandma gasped. "Dear old Tomas!" She laughed so loudly that Andi became nervous. Would Jan Harlow begin to believe Ms. Dugger's claim about Grandma's rationality?

Grandma looked around at the group, wiping tears from her eyes, still trying to suppress the giggles she could not contain. "Tomas loved how this house overlooks many of the creatures of the sea." Andi's ears pricked up as Grandma Bea continued. "Porpoises, otters, the like. He said it was the treasure of this house. The treasure of Grey Cove. It's what finally persuaded me to stay here." Then she burst out into yet another gale of laughter.

Kathy Dugger walked straight toward Grandma Bea. She pressed her finger against Grandma's chest. Grandma looked at her as if to say, *what the hey?* Andi stood up, pulling Artie up alongside her. Jan reached for Kathy Dugger.

"So," Grandma Bea said, becoming angry, standing up, pushing Ms. Dugger's pointed finger out of the way, "you wanted Artie and Andi out of here. You wanted me out of here. So that you could get into this house. So that you could search it for this *treasure*." Grandma Bea was angry now. She poked Ms. Dugger in the chest as she confronted her. "You didn't care what happened to us, did you?" Kathy Dugger's face was white, livid with rage.

The earthquake hit like a thunderclap. The movement was so violent it was as if the cliff had wrenched itself to one side. Grandma fell while Andi stumbled forward. Artie caught both and then pulled them to the floor, covering them protectively. The earthquake increased in its intensity, the house shaking. *It was angry,* Andi realized. Lux was doing this somehow. She saw water spume from the ocean far below, hitting the window. *It was Lux. Jan Harlow* tripped, grabbing at Kathy Dugger's arm to steady herself. At the same moment, Ms. Dugger fell straight off her feet, and sailed backward in a slow floating motion. Then her head hit the wall. She lay on the floor, knocked out.

Lux? Andi's mind reached out to her little dolphin. *Lux?* She sensed him but could not reach him. Lux was fiercely angry, no question about it. An anger directed at Kathy Dugger. *Lux?* There was no response, only that feeling of great, incredible rage.

Andi crawled out from under Artie's protective grip, flashing a look of gratefulness at him. She stood at the window, looking out, unaware that she was speaking out loud. "Lux?" Her voice was small, afraid. Not afraid for herself, maybe, but for him. "Lux?"

Andi could not define the feeling unfurling from inside her. Something had happened. Something irreversible. Something frightening. She looked down to her grandmother, still covered by Artie's arm. Grandma Bea smiled a weak, dazed smile up to her granddaughter. Her eyes retained the same clarity they'd had since that afternoon. Nothing had changed in that respect.

Andi watched as her grandmother picked herself up and walked to Kathleen Dugger. Grandma Bea stroked the cheek of Ms. Dugger, a look of sad pity in her face. Shaking her head, Grandma Bea turned to Jan Harlow. "She's knocked out, but she's alive. We should call an ambulance from the village though."

Jan Harlow had picked herself up and was now shaking her head. Looking at Andi, she raised her eyebrows as if to say *what an evening,* but all she said was "The house withstood that earthquake. I can't imagine many new houses being able to withstand that kind of earthquake half as well." Her voice was approving yet strained. Andi got the feeling that Jan Harlow was focusing on the present rather than on the events of the evening.

Jan answered Grandma Bea. "Yes, we need an ambulance. Go on please, telephone down to the village."

Grandma Bea nodded, rising. She limped slowly toward the kitchen.

The ambulance would be coming then. Andi frowned. The tension in her stomach had not resolved itself. She was still waiting for something to happen. Andi knew her sixth sense came from her connection with Lux.

Andi walked over to her teacher's side. *Her former teacher,* Andi now realized, knowing there was no going back for either one of them. There was a small gash on Ms. Dugger's head, but it did not look serious. Looking at her face, Kathy Dugger still looked angry and demanding. Andi surprised herself by the pity in her heart toward Ms. Dugger.

Still, it was hard to forgive Ms. Dugger. Andi's grandmother was going to be dead in a few days. She trusted Lux. If Lux could tell she was dying, then she was truly going to be gone soon. No matter if Ms. Dugger succeeded or not, Andi and Artie's world would never be the same. She wondered for a moment if Lux could keep the two of them hidden. She shook her head. It would be a charade that not even Lux could carry off for a long time.

It was a quiet evening, and the ambulance broke through the quiet in its short journey toward the house, sirens blazing. Both Grandma Bea and Jan Harlow walked toward the door, ready to let the paramedics in. Jan shot Andi a sympathetic look as if to say *I'm sorry for this whole stupid mess* before answering the door. Then Jan stopped in the hall even as Grandma Bea opened the door.

"We're going to see what can be done about your teacher." Jan inclined her head to Kathy Dugger's still-unconscious body on the floor. "For bringing us here under false pretenses."

Jan's face was now serious as she looked at Andi.

Suddenly, Andi knew she had to run upstairs to her bedroom window. Something was happening. She could feel it through her connection with Lux.

A huge, magnificent, ancient-looking ship sailed on the water in the bay right in front of the house. Its sails swirled with moving pictures— some looked like comets while others were stars. It was the ship from the other world. Andi gasped. The ship was dark, but Andi could still make it out against the night. It swayed dangerously from side to side, as if caught in a violent storm. Andi stepped back from the window. The thing was *immense*. People were running to and fro on the ship's deck, frantically pulling at ropes and adjusting the sails. All the crewmen were moving around the ship very quickly. Andi guessed that they were in shock.

As Andi watched, the bow of the ship began to vanish, as if disappearing through an unseen gate. Several of the crew were rushing to the side, throwing something off the ship, something that hit the water. Then, just as suddenly as it had appeared, the ship was gone.

Eleven

Survivors and Refugees

"What do you mean, a *ship* sailed by in the middle of the night?" Jubal sounded as if the limits of what he could absorb were at a breaking point.

Andi gripped the phone. "Well, it sure looked like a ship, yeah. I mean—it disappeared quickly."

"But not all at once. You said it disappeared bit by bit as it moved." He paused. "Right?"

That was the part Andi did not like remembering. The way the crew moved in such panic as they threw something overboard—something or someone—as if though their lives depended on it.

"Have you, you know, asked Lux? All these weird things, they all have something to do with him. They're all connected somehow." Jubal's voice sounded baffled.

"Yeah," Andi heard herself say. "I know."

She had been so shaken up by what she had seen that she had chosen not to see Lux that morning. She heard his mind press against hers. She responded with an *all is okay*, summoning all the love she could muster and relaying to it him until Lux relaxed.

Andi ran her fingers through her hair. She hadn't had time to tell Jubal about Ms. Dugger. Kathy Dugger was now at the hospital.

Grandma Bea had found out she had regained consciousness that morning. So Jubal knew about the ship, and only the ship, which is what they were discussing right now.

Andi hung up soon after. Jubal was right. She would have to ask Lux and begin to unravel this knot in front of her. Grandma Bea had just a few days left to live. Andi didn't want to spend any time on anything else, just Grandma Bea. Of course, she'd have to start thinking about what to do after. *After.* The finality of it hit Andi like a huge wave. Then she had an idea.

Andi jumped off the couch and ran toward the front door, grabbing a pullover sweater to wear. The screen door banged against the wall as she ran toward the cliff path.

Walking around the thin strip of rock bordering the cliff base, Andi pushed out with her mind. *Lux?* Again. *Lux?* She sensed him faintly. He was aware she was coming but was not awash with joy as he had been on her previous visits. Something was going on. Whatever it was, Andi hoped it wouldn't interfere with what she had to ask him. Her stomach was wound into a knot.

Arriving at the mouth of the cave, she peered inside. The light reflecting off the walls had muted itself, as if Lux had toned down its intensity. She entered the dimly lit cavern. Lux floated at the opposite end of the small lake. While he gleamed golden fire, it reflected off the walls in a slanted and angular fashion. It left the far corner completely wrapped in darkness. Lux's head was out of the water, his attention aimed toward the darkened corner.

Andi called out. "Lux? I wanted to talk to you about the earthquakes."

He did not answer at first, just kept looking into the far corner of the cavern. Then he dove down, sliding along the walls and the bottom of the lake. He emerged out of the water splashing happily, but Andi was able to detect an undercurrent of concern.

He spoke into her mind. *Come,* he said.

She walked along the thin ridge bordering the water, using Lux's light as a guide. Circling around to the other end, Andi peered into the corner. She could not see at first. The light reflecting off the walls blinded her temporarily as she tried to look beyond it. Then with a slow intake of breath, she realized someone was crouched in the corner. Someone had found them. Hesitatingly, Andi stepped forward.

For a moment, her heart skipped a beat. Had someone discovered them, found them out? As she neared, her heart relaxed because she realized that Lux had found this person instead of the other way around. She gasped at the beauty of the figure that crouched before her. It was a boy, the most beautiful boy Andi had ever seen. He had bright, red hair; part of it fell around his shoulders, the rest of it tied back into a ponytail with rope. His hair was his most unusual feature; it was the color of ripe strawberries. His face was milky white with a proud aristocratic nose, and he had the greenest eyes Andi had ever seen. And *freckles*. He had a scattering of freckles on his cheeks and nose. She guessed his age to be around ten or eleven, but she could not be sure. He was wearing a white tunic with black pants made from unfamiliar material. It looked as if his clothes had begun to dry. He wore tattered sandals, again out of a material Andi did not recognize.

Andi turned toward Lux, who looked up at her. She pushed the question, *who is he?*

Lux answered. *It is only your mind that I can read. Not his.* Andi understood that Lux was telling her that he could only communicate with her mind. This was interesting to her. She and Lux hadn't figured out the extent—or limits—of his powers yet.

Andi realized that this boy was what she had seen thrown over the side of the ship the night before. Lux had found him swimming and prodded the boy into following him into the cave. He had tried to make the boy as comfortable as possible.

Andi lowered herself to her knees and crept closer to the boy. She spoke to him softly. "I'm Andi. What's your name?"

The boy's eyebrows furrowed in puzzlement. He answered her in a language Andi could not understand. The language was nearly musical in nature, with cadences and a lilt that Andi had never heard before.

She shook her head from side to side, indicating that she could not understand him. Rather than seeming frustrated, he looked relieved. He appeared less afraid, as if he had understood her.

He had been hugging himself, but now he pulled his hands free. He held them up in front of Andi and then drew his hands inward, closer to himself. "Donalys," he said.

To be sure she had understood, Andi pointed at him. "Donalys," she repeated. The boy flashed a quick, shy smile at her, making him seem even more beautiful to Andi. He reached out and stroked the back of Andi's hand. Andi stared at him, smiling while at the same time trying to take everything in. She turned to Lux, a question on her mind.

How old is he? Ten?

Andi sensed a hesitation from Lux, as if he were unsure about something. Andi understood. He could tell things about another person only if she, Andi, was engaged with that person. What did the boy think of the glowing baby calf?

He is millions of years.

"What?" Andi said aloud to Lux. "What do you mean, millions of years?"

Millions of cycles and rotations.

Andi gasped, starting to get an inkling of what Lux was saying. She turned to Donalys even while she spoke to Lux. "Are you telling me he's *much older* than he looks?"

Yes.

Andi read Lux's mind. What she saw astonished her.

"The stars weren't in the positions they are now when he was born. It was that long ago."

Yes.

The ship. Andi remembered how ancient it was in its lines and contours. Immensely beautiful and sophisticated, yet its design harkened back to another time, another age. She began to question Lux, but he interrupted her.

The mind is not aged millions of years.

Andi responded. "Can you read his mind?"

No. You only.

"Then how do you know?"

Lux sent a picture into Andi's mind. Impressions rolled off Donalys like rays of sunshine. Andi understood. Lux was like a detective. He could analyze these impressions while her mind could not.

Understand? He asked.

Yes, she answered.

Young. His mind is young. Lux returned to the subject. The boy was looking at both she and Lux oddly, transfixed by something he could not understand.

Andi puzzled over this. Just what did Lux mean? Before she could ask for clarification, her young dolphin interjected.

Many upon many, but the mind, no.

Andi frowned. She asked aloud, "Do you understand why he's here? How he happens to be here?" She relayed an image of the ship to Lux, of the vision she'd experienced the night before. Lux answered with surprise and bewilderment.

In water. The winds blew. He floated, but then waves covered him. Made earthquake because I was angry with Dugger. Then the ship appears. I swam and found him in the water.

Andi nodded. This confirmed what she had already figured out.

Talk. Andi frowned. Then she heard Lux again. *Talk. To him.*

Sighing, knowing that it was useless, Andi began talking to Donalys. "Donalys," she began, "I don't know how to make you understand, but we just want to help. We don't want to hurt you."

Andi held out a placating hand toward Donalys. The boy stared at her hesitantly then stepped forward and took her hand in his. Then, to Andi's great surprise, Donalys lifted her hand to his and kissed it. Then he looked up at her and smiled shyly.

Andi thought about what to do next. Then she jumped into the pool of water coming up next to Lux. She put both hands around Lux, to show Donalys that he didn't have to fear the dolphin. She realized too late that maybe Donalys wasn't scared of Lux since the dolphin was the one who saved him.

Still, it worked. Donalys smiled down at Lux. But then he did something else. He leaned down into the pool of water and grabbed Andi's hand. The boy pointed to himself and nodded. Then he pointed to Lux and shook his head no. Andi suddenly blushed. The boy wanted her all to himself. She heard Lux laugh internally.

Andi climbed out of the pool, now soaking. She was beginning to shiver. She started rubbing her hands together vigorously. Looking up at Donalys and seeing the pleased expression on his face made Andi realize that he was a little spoiled. *Maybe he doesn't know any better,* she thought.

I will teach him! Andi heard the dolphin speak into her mind too late.

Andi turned toward the dolphin. "No, Lux!" She screamed. "No!" But of course this only made Donalys turn and stare at the dolphin. Lux stared at the boy from the pond and then dove underwater. He came up on the other end, near Andi and Donalys. He rose out of the water until he was nearly standing on his fins in the water. Donalys, his face a mixture of pride, haughtiness, and fear, met the dolphin's gaze. Andi wondered what Lux was feeling but then realized Lux was laughing inside. He was laughing at Donalys. Andi had to cover her smile in fear of upsetting the boy.

Lux squirted a huge plume of water through his blowhole toward Donalys, soaking him completely. The boy, surprised, leapt to his feet in outrage, his face a mask of anger, nostrils flaring. Lux laughed as his eyes met Donalys'. Lux continued laughing, as he flipped backwards into the water, the sound of laughter trailing after him as he swam away.

Twelve

Artie's Quest

Andi rehearsed what she would tell her grandmother and Artie about her newest discovery, Donalys. She had concluded on her walk home that he could not stay in the cavern with Lux. He'd catch cold, and besides, he didn't seem too fond of her dolphin. *My dolphin*, she repeated, smiling to herself. Had it only been a few days since she'd seen him bursting from the water with his mother in the sunset? So much had happened.

Gathering all her courage and willpower, she walked to Artie's room. His door was ajar. She opened it, unsure if she was disturbing him in one of his periodic rituals. As it was, he sat on his bed bent over his slinky. Unlike other times, though, his head rose as he heard her enter. He smiled his slow smile, the one Andi recognized as reserved only for her. He had missed her. Guilt overcame her. She'd missed him too—more than she'd realized.

He put down his slinky as she sat next to him on his bed. His eyes were alert. He was waiting to hear everything. So she told him. She told him about the song of the whales, dolphins, and porpoises in sunset. She told him about Lux's mother, about how she entrusted Lux to her. She told him about Lux. She shuddered as she recalled the excursion into that other world, remembering how those two lifeless statues leapt to their feet, how they threw their spears at her. She showed him the scar on her shoulder. She explained about the earthquakes, Ms. Dugger. She told him about Grandma Bea's memory returning, something that made his eyes light up. Seeing his joy, Andi found that she could not bring herself to tell him about their grandmother's impending death. Her voice broke as she spoke to him, but she did not say why.

Then she told him about the ship and about finding Donalys. She finished, out of breath, waiting for him to say something.

Artie's blue eyes had flickered once during her spiel but other than that had never wavered. He nodded quietly, absorbing the information. He stared down at his slinky for a long time before speaking.

"You told Jubal before you told me." It was not a question. Andi swallowed and nodded. Just as she was about to respond, he continued. "Because of Dugger." He glanced at her. "You didn't want me to know. To worry." He waited for confirmation. Andi stared at him levelly and nodded. She could not lie to him without looking away, and Artie knew this. He nodded, satisfied.

Andi slid her hand into his. "Were you hurt by that?" More than anything, she wanted to take away his pain. She wondered if he knew how much he meant to her, how far she would go to keep them together.

Artie nodded before shaking his head. "For one moment." He squeezed her hand as if in reassurance.

Artie stood up. He put the slinky in his pocket carefully. "Can we go see him?"

Andi stared at him, slightly taken aback. She'd expected Artie to go with her to the inlet cave the next day to help her with Donalys. Not now. She looked out the window. It was getting dark. Artie's fear of the dark as a child was so great to the point of his going into hysterics. For him to propose going to the inlet cave to see Lux so straightforwardly startled her. Andi was uneasy but could not say why.

"Yes," she began. "Yes, we can. Why?"

Artie spoke with a heaviness that spoke of something deeper.

"I want to ask a question."

They reached the mouth of their mom's cave with little trouble. The light emanating from her dolphin did not reach the entrance like it had. This pleased Andi. It had dimmed to the point where you didn't see the light until you ventured inside several feet. Lux must have been swimming near the bottom of the inlet pool. Donalys slept huddled in a corner, his arms wrapped around himself to stay warm. The picture of this lost little boy made her heart ache. Andi sighed, exasperated with herself. Was she going to let everyone break her heart?

Artie fidgeted as they went through the dark passage. He trembled slightly as they reached the cave itself but not as badly as he would have before. Andi suspected that it was Lux's soft golden light that put Artie at ease.

Andi saw Lux surface. The surprise in his eyes was evident; she never returned to see him after having left for the evening. Artie moved to the edge of the rim, near the pool. His face was unreadable. Lux's pleasure at finally meeting her twin echoed in Andi's mind and heart. He deviated slightly, propping himself up on his fins to meet Artie properly. Lux was mastering his powers. Andi wondered if he had mastered them completely or if he was still finding out what he could do, what his limits were.

Artie spoke to the dolphin as he balanced himself on his fins on the top of the water, his head coming up to Artie's belly. "Can you take me to see my father?" Artie asked with an intensity that surprised even Andi.

And there it is. Andi breathed in the realization of her brother's request. *Of course that would be what he wanted.* Always straightforward. Artie rarely showed emotion or amazement over anything. She had privately been hoping that this time would be the exception, that he would show appreciation for the wonder of Lux. It wasn't. There was no gasp of amazement, no dropped jaw, nothing. He asked Lux a question, wasting no time getting to the point.

When was Artie going to understand about their father? Andi wasn't going to explain to Artie that he was one of the reasons Dad left. *But not the only one,* Andi thought guiltily. She knew there had been more reasons. Just what, she didn't know.

Lux's confusion lasted only momentarily. She understood. Her dolphin had no reason to think that Artie would behave like herself or others. *If only other people were like that,* she wished bitterly. No one judging her brother on rules of behavior they had internalized and couldn't even put to words. Still ... wasn't she the same as those people she claimed to despise? She'd hoped for some reaction from Artie when he met Lux, disappointed when there hadn't been much.

Water. That was Lux's answer, echoing in her mind. She understood and turned to Artie, placing her hand on his shoulder.

"Artie ... he's ... Lux is saying that if you want to see Dad, he needs to be somewhere near the water. If he's on land, solid land, he can't get there."

"He is." The answer stunned her. Artie sounded so sure and confident of himself. Her twin who never asserted himself was making his desires well known now.

"And how do you know that?" she asked.

He closed his eyes. "Grandma wrote him a letter when Mom disappeared. The address. I've never forgotten it."

Andi was surprised. Grandma Bea had *lied* to her. But then she instantly forgave Grandma Bea. She might've forgotten. Or maybe her grandmother did not want any more possible tragedy for her grandchildren. Their conversation several days ago had opened Andi's eyes to Grandma Bea's remorse at her memory loss, at what her grandchildren were facing.

Artie opened his eyes and looked at Lux. "He lives on Rhode Island. That's where he is."

Andi responded, "Artie ... I'm really bad at geography. Can you ... can you create a picture in your mind of where we are and then ... *which* barrier island Dad is on? You have to kind of bring that picture to the front of your mind. Push it out toward me," she finished lamely. She was sure that Artie had no inkling of what she meant. The impressions from Artie would roll off him like very bright rays.

Andi's tone of voice must have risen because Donalys shuddered in his sleep, opened his eyes, and began to rouse himself. He blinked at them sleepily, smiling upon seeing Andi, his smile changing into a scowl as the dolphin neared. He noticed Artie but said nothing as he rose to his feet.

He came over to where she and Artie were standing and made a little bow to Artie with his hands folded together. Artie stared past him rather than meeting his gaze. Andi's skin prickled; she had a bad feeling that Artie's failure to look Donalys in the eyes would not be good. And so it was. Donalys' face flushed angrily, his skin matching the wild red of his hair. *What a temper.*

Artie's attention had returned to the dolphin. His eyes were now closed, his face screwed tightly, concentrating. Andi realized that he was doing what she told him to—telling Lux where their father was. Their dad. She heard him say, "Rhode Island."

Was she really going to see her father? After all these years? Andi forced herself not to think of the ramifications. OK. Whatever was going to happen was going to happen. She turned to Donalys, who, while somewhat calmer, was staring at Artie coldly. Andi put her arm on the smaller boy's shoulder, making him meet her gaze. She smiled, shook her head at him. She waved her hand back and forth to tell him that the perceived slight Donalys had received from Artie was no slight at all. She smiled reassuringly at him. The tension left Donalys' shoulders. The anger in his eyes faded into something that was not anger but something that was not acceptance either. It was as if Donalys was saying to her, *Okay, I'll wait, but this isn't the last you've heard about this.*

Still, Andi took Donalys' temporary acquiescence for what it was. It was an agreement to go along with whatever was going to happen. Her stomach lurched, remembering what had happened the last time she and Lux had traveled. Her scar burned at the memory. Lux looked at her. She spoke aloud to him, trying to sound confident. "It's not as if we're going to another planet. Are we?" Yet her stomach heaved as if it were such a trip, and in a way she realized that it was.

She heard his voice in her mind.

Come.

Andi translated. "He wants us to get into the water with him. I'll hold on to him, while the two of you hold on to me." She looked warily at Donalys, hoping that he had forgiven Lux from before. Even as she said it, she wondered how it could work. Lux was not that big, and she wasn't either. Still, he was bigger than most baby calves this stage of their growth. About 9 feet? Maybe he could bear all three of them after all. She jumped into the pool, surprised as always at how warm the water was whenever she swam with Lux. She hoped it would be the same for the two boys. Both jumped in without saying anything. Artie's eyes were intent, as if he were finally seeing the finish line of a long race rise before him. Andi supposed that in a way it was.

Andi held on to Lux's trunk. She did not take on Lux's golden sheen this time. Lux was going to swim on top of the water because the boys were not bonded to him the way she was. He would not be able to take them underwater and protect them.

But what if someone sees you? Your brightness? Andi was worried.

Lux reassured her. *Very short. Do not worry.*

Both boys swam to opposite sides of her. Both enfolded one arm around her back, holding on to her stomach, something that made Andi blush. Artie was to her right while Donalys was to her left. Donalys was respectful of her space, looking at Andi to make sure that what he was doing was all right. Andi nodded at him. She could not focus on Donalys right now. She needed to focus on seeing their father. What would she say to him? *Oh hi, Dad, we need your help because we have nowhere else to turn?*

Stop. Lux's anger was evident. Andi understood that he was angry at her father for making her feel this way. Andi smiled to herself. Lux did not understand relationships yet. His only relationship was with Andi.

I have you after all, Lux, she projected good-naturedly to the dolphin. His pleasure echoed within her at this statement. Who knows? Maybe Lux understood relationships better than any of them did. He was trying to help them despite how young he was. Wasn't that what she wanted from him? Help? Andi remembered the two questions she had for Lux and tried to shield them from him. She didn't want him figuring them out while Artie was with them. Because one of the questions was about Artie. Andi hoped she was helping Lux—that Lux was bene-fitting from her help—because she needed his help more than ever.

Lux shot out of the inlet cavern with a speed that astonished Andi. He was carrying three human passengers, all at the same time! But Artie and Donalys were holding on more to her than they were to Lux while she was holding on to the dolphin. And they were not going underwater! She hoped it was safe but so far, so good. She tried to compliment Lux on how well he was doing, but even as she tried to do so, a wave rose in Lux's mind. Andi felt a small wave, surging toward the island through a small touch of his echolocation. Extracting herself from his mind, she saw the same wave loom in front of them. They were about to pass through it. Right then, something extraordinary occurred. The wave froze for a moment, not moving. Andi followed the wave's line across the sea. As she did, she noticed with astonishment that they were not swimming off the coast of Grey Cove anymore. The island next to them was much bigger, with swampy marshland along the shore. Lux kept swimming. They were moving from the ocean to-ward a series of islands. They continued to move with a speed Andi was sure that no boat could keep up with. There were several islands in the vicinity. She looked over to Artie, who nodded, his brow furrowed.

"It is up ahead," he confirmed. *How did he know that? Was he so in need of their dad that he knew all this already?* Andi guessed the answer was *yes*.

Lux moved toward the island Artie was pointing to. There were few houses on the shore; Andi could detect about four houses all spaced wide apart from each other. Most of the houses had large windows allowing them to see out toward the water. Their lights shone brightly in the darkness. Andi frowned. It was darker here than it was at home. *Duh*, she realized, *three hours' difference.* Lux looked up at her, scolding her for being hard on herself. He did not like it when she criticized herself.

This is new. For you. His voice sounded in her head.

I know. I know. I'm not smart like Artie and Jubal are, Lux. Andi paused. *God, I'm so nervous. My father.*

The question entered her head, demanding an answer. *Why? Love. You are shaking like water.*

I haven't seen him since I was three, Andi responded. They were now in water shallow enough that they could walk up to shore. Artie was already standing, his hand extended to help Andi off Lux. Donalys was behind her, his hand on her back for support.

Why? Lux asked.

Andi swayed, resulting in Donalys falling backward into the water. Andi turned, sure he would lose his temper. But he was laughing as he grasped her hand, pulling himself up. He shrugged as her eyes met his, smiling. Andi realized that wherever—or whatever—he had come from, he was happy to be there with them, no matter how confused he was.

Lux's voice entered her head again.

Why?

Andi found herself on her knees in the mud, her face in her hands. The question undid her. Donalys' hand was on her arm, trying to pull her up. Lux's worry hit her as he swam toward her. But it was Artie she needed. Then she heard his voice.

"Andi. Up. Up now."

She responded. "No. I can't. Artie, why are we doing this?"

"Andi. Up, up." His hand was on her cheek, and she looked up at him, tears running down her face.

"This is too much, Artie. It's way too much. I can't—I can't do it."

For a moment, Artie hesitated, and then that same focused look reentered his eyes.

"I need to see." He was resolute.

"But why, Artie? Why? It's been so long."

Then he was down on his knees, next to her.

"Because you almost died." There was a quaver in his voice.

"What? What are you talking about?"

He touched the large scar just above her lung. She understood.

She was silent. Then she began, "But you have ..." She was going to say *Grandma,* but the words died before ever reaching her lips. In just a few days, Grandma would be gone. And she had not told Artie yet. Who did Artie have other than her? The guilt rose in her, ripping her apart even as it gave her renewed strength. She rose to her feet.

"Come on," she said to him. "Let's go." She turned to Donalys. "Let's go."

She looked at Lux, who was swimming in circles. "Which one?" She pointed to the houses. "Which one?"

Lux's head beckoned to the one just before the last one on the right. *That.*

How can you tell? Andi asked.

Your father. The connection you have with him. It is like the one you have with Grandma but much weaker. Andi received an image in her mind of a golden cord, thin, but stretching from her to the house. Lux was able to receive impressions through his bond with her that she could not understand.

Andi grabbed Artie's hand, leading the way to her father's house. She could scarcely believe it, and yet here they were. She wondered what Donalys thought about all this. That is, if he even understood what she and Artie had been discussing. Probably not. She walked toward the house with a determined gait, all the while holding Artie's hand. *It isn't fair.*

It wasn't fair that they were on this island, looking for their father! Why on earth were they in this situation? The last time she remembered her father was when she was young. He'd been bouncing her on her shoulders. She remembered hearing yelling and doors slamming and her mother sobbing.

Was this the place he had disappeared to the same morning her mother had packed Andi, Artie, and herself off to Grey Cove? The same day when her mother whispered into her ear, "We'd have had to return anyway, darling girl ... you'll see why in time." But Andi hadn't listened. All she knew was that her father wasn't there with them, and she was playing with Artie. Because somehow even then she'd known it was about Artie, and she wasn't going to let him get hurt.

Andi came to. They'd made it to the house Lux had steered them toward.

"We'll look in the windows and then figure out what to do after that. We'll figure out if we should knock or what. Okay?" Andi said.

Artie nodded. She sensed his relief at her renewed resolve. He needed her. He was more afraid than she was. But why would he be? *Because he knows Grandma is getting worse. Because he knows I almost died. This is his fallback plan. For himself.* They walked up a sandy hill, with clumps of beach grass scattered about.

Large windows rose before them as they approached the house. The light inside was warm and inviting. There was a large wraparound porch outside the windows. A door between the windows opened out onto it. Andi pulled Artie alongside her onto the porch and down into a kneeling position. Donalys took a spot behind them. Inside was a large and beautiful family room and stairs leading up to the second floor. Behind the family room was a kitchen that they could see only just a bit of.

Music began to echo faintly from inside the house. Andi squinted, her eyes still adjusting to the light after the deep darkness surrounding them. There was a piano in the middle of the family room. A man sat at it. A man with Artie's beautiful white-blond hair. Andi and Artie's father sat behind the piano playing one of the saddest songs she had ever heard. She strained to hear the words, yet the tune carried with it deep sadness and longing. The same feelings began to rise within her. She looked at Artie. It was the same for him.

Their father—for it was their father—his hands moved across the keys. For a moment, Andi wanted to knock at the porch door so that this man could discover her, perhaps quieting the sadness inside both.

Artie squeezed her hand tightly, hurting her. She turned to him, shaking her head no, before realizing he was pointing at something. He pointed to the top of the piano, to the many photographs framed on top of it. There was a framed picture of her on the piano. She was much younger, but it was definitely her, with the brown hair coming down around her shoulders. Her teeth shone through a crooked smile, her green eyes sparkling. Her heart sank. There was no picture of Artie. Andi caught her breath. She felt Lux catch his breath too.

She kept scanning the piano hoping to find Artie among the photos but there were none. Andi couldn't bring herself to look at her twin. She didn't have to. Lux was questioning her inside because he felt the change and swirling of her emotions. His confusion demanded answers, and yet she could not bring herself to answer them. Now she looked over at Artie. The look of hunger and devastation playing across his face ripped her heart to shreds.

But there was more. Movement at top of the stairs caught Andi's eye. She looked to the top of the stairs. A tiny dark-haired boy that looked so much like Artie was walking down the stairs. The same eyes as her brother's. The same as hers. Reaching the bottom, he skipped toward his father, who did not see or appear to hear him, and enfolded him in a hug from behind. A shuddering croak rose from Artie's throat. Andi released his hand, tried to reach for him so that she could hug him. She wanted to hug him so hard and so deeply that the pain he felt would squeeze itself out, banished into oblivion.

But Artie shook her off. Andi fell backward on her seat. Her brother kept looking through the window, a naked look of longing on his face. Their father turned toward the boy. Andi gasped at what came next. He gesticulated at the boy, pointing upstairs. The little dark-haired boy shook his head no. He did not want to return to bed. He came closer to the piano, pressing his fingers into the keys. Their father did nothing. The boy pointed up to the sheet music.

As he was pointing to the notes, the boy climbed onto the piano seat next to his father. Andi could see their father's exasperation. The little boy raised his hands toward the piano notes but knocked over his father's wineglass by accident. Artie gasped as the wine splattered onto the floor.

Suddenly, the man's face contorted itself into one of rage as he shook the boy he now held in his arms on the piano bench. The boy's mouth parted into a small o as his father shook him angrily, telling him to go to bed. The boy pushed himself away from his father and ran up the stairs.

Andi did not have to hear it to know that the boy had slammed the door hard behind him. She looked at her father, who stood dismayed at the bottom of the stairs, his head slumped. He stared up the stairs for a long time, uncertain if he should pursue his son up the stairs. Finally, he walked toward the piano, leaned against it, staring over their heads toward the ocean.

Oddly enough, whenever she remembered that incident, the thing that came to her mind the most was how quiet Donalys was. He knelt behind them in silence, watching the scene unfold. Andi always remembered Donalys placing his hand on Artie's shoulder. Artie had nodded, acknowledging his touch even if he didn't say anything. Artie continued to stare through the window into the now-darkened room, as if in shock. Andi feared that he was. She put her hands on both sides of his face, moving it until his eyes met hers.

"We are going to go," she heard herself say, "and we are going to forget that this ever happened. Okay?" It was as if someone else was speaking. She was sure the incident had not hurt her as much as it had Artie. *She knew he had dreamed of their father and of meeting him much more than she had. And to see that their father had a third child all along—a virtual clone of Artie, who wasn't different the way Artie was.*

"We are never going to come back here again, and we are not going to let anyone else know that we were here." Her voice had a commanding tone to it, although she knew Artie would see it as nothing but love. "We are going to get up. And we are going to go. *Now.*" Her hands did not leave his face as she rose. She had a faint awareness of Donalys moving aside for them. She and Artie held each other as they trudged toward where Lux was waiting.

Andi remembered seeing Lux rise from the water, lit by his inner glow. She recalled how he was crying in her mind, his light shining all around them. Entering the water with Artie, Lux swam through the small space between their bodies. He caressed Artie, circling around again to caress Andi. She watched the dullness of Artie's eyes begin to fade as the desire for his father began to disappear. Artie for the first time began to discover her little dolphin. She watched as his hand rested on Lux as the dolphin moved around them, between them, his love for them as deep and as brilliant as his glow. His mouth began to pick up at the corners, perhaps beginning to smile at the miracle of this little dolphin.

For the first time since she'd met her little dolphin, her focus was on her twin rather than Lux. Yet Andi knew that Lux understood. He loved Artie just as she did, because Lux loved her, just as she loved her little dolphin. This love united them as they swam out to the ocean. Even Donalys. He had maintained a respectful distance, joined in with them through Lux. The immense hurt they carried within them began to float outside of them to the dolphin, whose light burned more because of it. He partook in their pain, and they took his love in. For a moment, the universe was lit brilliantly with the shared experience of it all.

Thirteen

The Two Questions

Donalys appreciated the complexity of their situation when it came to explaining him to Grandma Bea. Andi and Artie finally agreed on putting Donalys in the basement. Grandma Bea seldom went down there, perhaps because she wanted to avoid the memories that lay hidden in her boxes of mementos and photographs. Andi announced to Grandma Bea that she was going to do some research. She wanted to find out what happened with her grandfather and the sinking of his boat all those years ago. It was an excuse Grandma Bea accepted, given the revelations during Ms. Dugger's visit. Andi went down to the basement only twice a day, so as not to arouse Grandma's suspicions. Andi knew that Donalys must be terribly bored, which was why she took many of her and Artie's old picture books downstairs in the hopes that if he could not read, he could at least enjoy the illustrations. She always took enough food and rations to last Donalys well beyond the day and night. Donalys had several blankets and pillows and was comfortable, grinning from ear to ear when presented with his bedding. Andi watched as he fell asleep, finally comfortable, oblivious to the world. *He must have been so cold in the cave,* Andi thought fondly.

Andi could not get over Donalys' bemusement over the food he ate—his shock at the idea of eating meat. His red hair flew all around as he shook his head no at the piece of chicken Andi held out to him. She finally had to resort to biting into it and making "mmmm" sounds for him to believe it was edible. He took a bite with reluctance. The second bite that followed was anything but reluctant, to Andi's great amusement. He preferred vegetables and fruits and even nuts but became more open to trying whatever she brought. Conversation was still limited to gestures and pointing between Donalys and his hosts.

Andi took time every day to sit with Artie in his room. If her time with Lux became more limited because of her new focus on Donalys and her need to check up on Artie, Lux did not complain. He murmured to her in her mind every now and then, reassuring her that he understood. She missed him horribly but knew she needed to make sure that her family and Donalys were all right. As for Artie, he had not spoken about the incident since it happened, choosing instead to focus on the miracle of Lux. Every time Andi entered Artie's room to check on him, Artie was poring over huge pieces of paper, drawing. He always held his slinky in his right hand though. Oftentimes, Artie stopped in the middle of his drawing to stare intently at the slinky.

When Andi finally asked Artie what he was doing, Artie replied, "Teleporting. Lux got us there from here." He held up the slinky and showed her a reverberating rhythm from one end of the slinky to another. Then he folded the coils of the slinky together. Andi understood. Lux had traveled a long distance in a very short time because a large tunnel between Grey Cove and her father's home had been compressed, making the distance between its opposite points very short.

So it was several days later, on a quite stormy day, when Andi finally pulled Artie from his drawing to sit on his bed. She made him talk about what had happened with their father. "So," she began brightly, realizing at the same time how nonsensical it was to act all positive and happy. "We should talk about the other night."

Artie stared at her, or rather past her. His eyes never quite met hers when they talked about emotional things. It was always as if he were looking just past her to the wall or whatever was behind her. Yet Andi knew he was trying to listen to what she was saying. It was just that the emotion of the moment was too much for him.

"Artie," she said, nudging him.

"That boy," he began.

Andi waited. "Yeah?"

"He—he's *related* to us." It was not a question.

Andi sighed. Not being sure how to answer him, all she said was "Sure looks like it."

"He looks exactly like me." A silence. "Except for the hair."

There. Andi nodded. Artie had finally said it. Exactly like him but at the same time nothing like him. Of that she was certain.

She folded her hands in her lap, looked over at Artie, and began talking about what had been on her mind from several nights ago. "Artie, I never realized how much you looked like Dad. I guess—I guess when we left, we were still so young. What were we, three—four? I kind of forgot what he looked like."

Artie nodded, agreeing as he gazed at his slinky. She continued.

"You know, when you're a kid, you don't make those connections." Andi smiled. "I didn't, anyway. Not until Dad and"—she hesitated—"that boy." She looked at Artie for a reaction. There was nothing, but she was sure there was a war going on underneath. "That boy looks so much like you, Artie. He looks exactly like Dad, just like you look like Dad. You're just, just"—she groped for words, finally settling on—"just different ages. He's much younger than you are." This was not going the way she wanted it to. She added one word. "Duh."

It worked. Artie half-smiled, one corner of his mouth lifting while the other stayed the same. Then he spoke. "Should we do something for him?"

Andi, a little confused, responded. "You mean the little boy?"

"Yes, our half-brother."

There. He'd said it. Their half-brother. Their little brother. Feelings swirled around inside Andi, feelings of shock, warmth, and worry all mixed into one.

"Help him how, Artie? We don't know who he is. We don't know his life. He has a mother of his own that we know nothing about. It's out of our hands." She paused and then did something she hadn't done in a long time. She ruffled her brother's hair. "You're worried about him, even though you're hurting. It's just like you." Her heart broke again right there as she said it.

"He left because of me." It was not a question.

"Artie. You don't know that."

In a flat, unemotional voice, he answered, "I do know. There were no pictures of me there. There was one of you. There were many of the boy. None of me." He looked at her, and his stare hurt her so much because of the pain within. "I remember that year we had those pictures taken. You had yours taken, and so did I. Then we had photos taken together." Andi's head bent low, touching upon Artie's shoulder. She remembered the same thing. She shut her eyes, her head still on his shoulder, her hand still in his hair even though she wasn't ruffling it anymore. There was nothing she could say.

It was at this moment the light shone through the window. The sun had broken through the storm clouds. Andi looked at the ray of sunlight shining through the clouds onto the sea below. It was like her life. The ray of light was Artie, the one who kept her steady while everything else was uncertain, up in the air. The ray of light was Lux, loving her and caring for her the way he did. But for how long? How long could all this last? The ray of light disappeared even as Andi began to ask herself questions. What was going to happen? How long could she keep this up? Then she realized something: she couldn't.

That's when she decided to say it. She lifted her head from her brother's shoulder. "Artie," she said, "Grandma is dying." He turned to face her, his eyes questioning. "Lux told me," she answered. "He healed her. That's why she can remember. He healed her for the meeting with Dugger. So that she would seem okay. But he can't help her get better so that she can go on living. She's going to die, Artie. And soon," she finished helplessly.

Artie's eyes remained fixed on hers. Finally he spoke. "Will you tell her?"

"I don't know, Artie," Andi answered helplessly. "So much has happened. I can't even think about tomorrow."

"More to tell me?" Artie was still staring at her.

"No," she answered. "No, Artie. That's it. I promise. That's it. I would've told you the other night, but you were so determined to see Dad. And I couldn't bring myself to tell you right after."

He nodded, sliding down to the floor, pushing aside his drawings, instead choosing to play with his slinky. He began to hum and sway slightly, a sign that the conversation was over. Andi stood up. He wasn't angry with her. Overwhelmed and overloaded, he needed time alone. Then he would come to her. Her heart ached for him, but now her conscience was clear. There were no more secrets.

Closing the door to Artie's room behind her, Andi began to cry. She was thankful Grandma Bea was upstairs so that she would not have to explain to her why she was crying. Walking downstairs into the living room, she looked out the large window to the ocean. The storm raged on. Andi's mind began to drift back to before Artie met Lux; before Donalys' rescue. She remembered. She ran to the hall closet, pulled her raincoat on, and dashed outside. The rain was coming down hard. She looked down the top of the cliff, from her home to Jubal's house.

Guiltily, she realized that she hadn't checked in with Jubal over the weekend while he was visiting home. She promised herself she would make it up to him when he got back. He wouldn't believe all that she had to tell him. She wondered what Jubal would think of Donalys. Then she found herself wondering what Donalys would think of Jubal. She shrugged off these questions and her feelings of guilt as she stepped upon the small ridge path.

The rain beat down even harder on her as she navigated the path. Andi was nervous. The questions she had to ask Lux weren't going to be easy. She heard thunder. Lightning was going to hit soon. She hurried around the thin strip of rocky beach under the cliff toward the little inlet cave. The sound of thunder grew closer as Andi hurried into the cavern.

Lux's joy resonated within Andi as she entered the cavern, but for the first time, it didn't quite echo within her. She was too keyed up about the questions she had to ask. She hugged her little dolphin as he stood up on the water. Andi let Lux swim around the small pool a few minutes out of his joy at seeing her. Again, the guilt rose in her. *Was she asking too much of Lux? First Grandma Bea and now this?*

He swam toward her, his head now just out of the water. He spoke to her mind. *Ask.* His was more serious now. And he respected her enough not to intrude further in on her mind, which she appreciated. Andi looked out toward the mouth of the cave. It was darker than when she first entered.

"Lux, you know how we went to see my dad and how all that turned out?"

Yes. A surge of anger came from him. At her father, not herself, Andi understood. Powerful waves of sympathy and love and … not quite understanding but something close to it emanated from him. It echoed around in her brain. Buried under the anger, she sensed an undercurrent of curiosity.

Putting aside her nervousness, Andi finally asked the question that had haunted her for so long. It had hidden itself secretly in her mind, even when she hadn't always been aware of it.

"Lux, you said your mother was in the—in the *other* place." Lux's definition of dead was different from hers, Andi realized. To Lux, his mother was in a place that he could not reach yet but would be able to someday. To her, death signaled a horrible finality that spoke of night without stars, an end of self that terrified her. She imagined death to be total blackness that came after hitting a brick wall.

"Can you feel other people there? In the other place?" At this, she stretched toward him palms upward in a sign of vulnerability, showing him how hard this was for her—to even ask.

Lux swam the span of the pool before coming back. He jumped up onto the water, balancing himself precariously on his tail fluke, as he often did. Approaching her, he held out his left pectoral flipper to her head. Andi closed her eyes as his shimmering golden flipper touched her forehead.

Clouds rose in front of her mind—heavy, thick clouds like the ones outside the cavern, although not as dark. These clouds were gray, as gray as the rocky promontory circling the island. For a moment, she was outside of herself as she had in the starry in-between. But this was different. A hand stretched forth from her, and Andi realized it was her hand, and yet at the same time it was not. Her hand was glowing with the same golden radiance Lux exuded. The glowing hand reached out into the gray cloudy mass and parted it slightly in the middle. Beyond, a great body of water stretched as far as the eye could see, with a night sky. But this night sky had different cast to it. It was bright even though there was no sun. The sky was decorated with multicolored stars, some of which were close.

Lux whispered from within Andi. *Think about them.* A pause. When she did not respond, he followed up with, *Think of them. Those who are here.*

What is here? Where is here? Andi asked, disoriented. The clouds framed the vision of the vast ocean with the amazing night sky. Andi could not tell where she stood, the vantage point from which she was taking this all in. Seeing her hand the same golden hue as Lux's frightened her.

Tomas. His voice spoke to her again from within. *Your grandfather.* Andi allowed herself to remember her grandfather, and suddenly he was standing in front of her, framed by the clouds in that other world. The ocean stretched back behind him, and the stars shone above him. Andi blinked. Her grandfather Tomas looked at her, his eyes shining with love. He looked exactly as she remembered him. Except ... no. He did not look exactly as she remembered him. There were strange, subtle differences. He still had white hair, but the wrinkles and sagging eyelids were gone. His blue eyes shone, lending him a vigor that Andi did not remember from his last days. There was no trace of the former sadness her grandfather carried within him like a heavy weight. Andi knew now that heavy weight was the result of the boat accident and drowning that he had been falsely blamed of. The man before her now was so *light*. Her grandpa Tomas had always been loving and mischievous, even when sad. There was a quality present now that he hadn't possessed before. A sense of freedom.

Now think, Lux's voice whispered inside. *Now you understand.*

Andi willed herself to think of her mother. She made herself remember her in ways that she hadn't dared before. She had feared feeling her loss so much that she might never be able to come up from the depths of her grief again. But she did so now. Andi pictured her mother moving before her, laughing, playing with her and Artie on Grandma Bea's side lawn. A clear sun shone down on them with a cold wind blowing. The image was so vivid, so deep and so real that Andi knew her mother had to be there standing in front of her.

She opened her eyes. Her grandfather had disappeared, and in his place was no one. No mother was there. No one was there. The ocean stretched far away. Mysteriously lit waters moving slowly and calmly. The stars and planets and constellations continued to spin in the sky, uncaring and oblivious to her pain. It was too much. She'd seen her grandfather, who she knew was dead. She'd expected to see her mother. All the pain from the last few days came to the surface.

"Stop, stop, *stop!*" Andi screamed. "Stop this right now! I don't want to see any more! I've had enough!"

The vision faded immediately. Still screaming, Andi collapsed onto the cavern's rocky edge. She cried for so long and so hard that she did not realize Lux had pushed himself out of the pool. His beak (yes it was a beak, not a nose—she'd looked it up) prodded her shoulder. Her face covered with tears, she looked up and laughed. The dolphin's head was even with hers, and he was looking at her with such love and concern that it stilled Andi's crying.

"'S' okay," Andi muttered, rising to a sitting position. She stroked Lux's head even while shooing him back into the water. The dolphin eased himself back in with a dive but raised his head out of the water a moment later, meeting her eyes with concern. Andi moved closer to the pool and let her hand trail down to his head. Being close to him comforted her.

Andi nodded, still stroking his head. "It was weird." She stopped for a minute, feeling as if she might cry. "Lux, I want to find out what happened to my mother. We never got any answers."

Lux's head moved imperceptibly under her hand, as if he were saying yes. She continued.

"Why isn't she there? In that place?"

Do not know, the dolphin answered.

"Shouldn't she be in there?" Andi asked helplessly. "Are there other places like that?"

I do not know. Lux sounded as helpless as she was.

The pain building inside her broke loose, much like the storm that raged outside. Andi was numb, angry, furious, devastated, and wondering.

"I'll never find out then," she said. For a moment, she had allowed herself to think that she might be able to see her mother, have some of her questions answered. That would have been something. Something to make up for being in this situation, for having to take care of Grandma Bea. Something to make up for worrying about Artie and wondering what to do with Lux.

I have no knowledge of how to do what you wish. With this admission, Lux's unhappiness at being unable to help her came flooding inside her mind. It was more than she could bear.

"You can't find her?" Andi asked, a little angry. "You can do that kind of thing, but you can't find my mother? You can't find another one of those places?"

No.

Andi stood up, her anger surging. She was angrier than she had been in her whole life. "You can take us to the other side of the US just like that to see my father, and you show me my grandfather, but you can't show me my mother?"

Lux's fear became worse, rising in her. *I am connected to your mind only. Others ... it depends on impressions from them. Depends on how close you are to them. Teleporting is how I opened portal. I cannot do more.*

"Lux," she said, "I'm sorry. I didn't mean to scare you."

Angry.

Andi sighed. "Yes, I'm angry. But I'm not angry at you." How to explain to a dolphin about her mother who had been there for her whole life and then just disappeared? How to explain to a dolphin about her father who left when she was young? Lux's confusion and fear made her feel impatient and sorry.

Ask the other question. His voice rang in her head with a hint of desperation. Andi closed her eyes. All he wanted to do was please her, but she was battling undercurrents of emotions that threatened to rise and consume her.

"Lux, I'm sorry," Andi said. "But I need to know. You healed me and Grandma Bea, but you can't stop her from dying. You can see into the other place, but you can't find my mother? You found my grandfather so easily. Just *what* can you do?" There was a note of exasperation in her voice, brought to the surface by her hurt.

Bonded together. In your mind.

"I know that," Andi replied more irritably than she meant to sound. "I know that we're bonded."

No. Only you and me.

"You really can't read anyone else's minds? Just mine?" Andi asked.

Yes.

"Like the other night with Donalys ... you read impressions he was giving off. Much better than I could. But you weren't reading his mind. Then you did the same with Artie."

Yes.

"And you can teleport," Andi stated. It was not a question. "You can move from one place to another."

I can move to places.

The dolphin made no response, just swam away, and began circling the pool. Not once did he flip out of the water, as he usually did. Instead he plunged deep into the water returning to the surface only to circle around the pool once more, agitated.

You and I are bonded. You, Grandma Bea are close. More work to move her if it was not you. The closer you are close to others, it may be possible. Very difficult. Easy with you. Andi blinked. Lux had really struggled to describe what he could do.

"So," she started, "you can read my mind and speak into it but not into the minds of others. And you can teleport places with me. You can send me places. Depending on how *close* I am to another person, you can send them places. Like Jubal, when we first came here. He's my best friend, and you were able to teleport him. Just like you were able to teleport Grandma Bea to the starry place. Is that right? Is that what you can do with your powers?"

Yes.

"You can send people away to be healed?"

Yes, no, depends.

Andi quivered with excitement. Lux was going to be able to help her. It was going to more than make up for not seeing her mother in that faraway realm. She plunged into the second question.

"Lux," she said to her little dolphin. "Can you heal Artie?" The moment the words left her mouth, a crash of thunder echoed throughout the cave. Shame rose in Andi, filling her. What she had said was wrong. *Very* wrong. Her stomach constricted with guilt. If Artie found out what she'd said, she would never forgive herself.

Lux rose out of the water, again floating on top, balancing on his fins. He propelled himself toward her from the opposite end of the pool, his eyes never leaving hers. His dismay at her frustration with her mother was gone, replaced by something she didn't quite understand. He stopped just short of her face.

Nothing wrong with him.

That did it. Andi lost her temper. "Nothing wrong with him!" she screamed. "Of *course* nothing's wrong with him! You saw what happened to him the other night! If you *fixed* him, then he wouldn't be so hurt anymore. It wouldn't be so hard for him anymore. It wouldn't be so hard for *me* to watch him suffer!"

Is not about you. Is about him. Not you.

Lux's disappointment hit her hard, squarely in the stomach. To herself, she suddenly looked like her father from the other night. Artie no longer resembled him. *She* instead resembled him.

Andi cried, "I'm sorry," before running out of the cavern, stumbling as she went. Her tears blinded her. Rain beat against her face. She shielded her face from it as she ran, rocks slipping from under her feet.

Andi! Lux screamed in her mind, dismayed.

She knew he was swimming rapidly out of the cavern toward her. Refusing to look behind her, Andi ran up the cliff path, looking up toward the top.

Andi! Andi! His voice screamed into her brain. She could barely concentrate. She stayed close to the cliff wall, feeling its side with her right hand as she kept running. She tripped just before arriving up on top of the cliff. Out of the corner of her eye, she could see his golden figure trailing along the ridge path in the water, his screams still rising to her. Irrationally, Andi covered her ears with her hands, even though she knew his voice was inside her mind.

That was when Andi slipped, twisting her line of vision toward the beach. Her mouth gaped open. Lux's screams had *not* been pleas for her to stay but rather cries for help. The large ship with moving objects on its sails had come out from somewhere. It was chasing her beloved dolphin around the curve of the island where both disappeared beyond her line of sight. Lux's screams for help slowly faded out of her mind until she could no longer sense his presence.

Fourteen

Bathtubs and Pocket Universes

That following Saturday, Andi and Artie took Jubal into the basement to meet Donalys and to discuss ways of finding Lux. With Lux's whereabouts a mystery, Andi had tried to busy herself with taking care of her grandmother and Artie. And now Donalys. It didn't keep her from worrying about Lux or blaming herself for his disappearance. Still, she knew that keeping herself busy was one way to keep her from running all over the island in search of Lux. She could not even sense him. The bond between them had broken, which in turn left Andi in anguish. A part of herself was missing.

Earlier, Andi had turned her attention to Donalys' personal hygiene, trying to distract herself. But this new project had turned out to be a disaster. Andi had decided that Donalys needed a bath or shower. She had decided with a firm determination that he would not deter her efforts. After descending the stairs, she met Donalys' face with a firm look. She resolved to herself that Donalys would not wriggle his way out of this with either his charm or his temper as he already had. She motioned to him with her finger, and he jumped to his feet, coming over to her. She held up a pair of Artie's old PJs, indicating that they would fit Donalys. She led him by the hand to the bathroom door, opened it, and turned the shower on. She put the bar of soap in his hand.

Something odd happened when Andi turned the shower on. Donalys' face paled as the water rushed out of the shower head. He pointed to the water gushing out and shook his head no. He did not look resolute, angry, or rebellious; he was scared. It was then that Andi understood. He had been thrown overboard. Even though he could swim, of course he would be nervous around water. For right now anyway.

Donalys was looking at her with a pleading look. He put his hands around his throat and made a gagging noise. Andi sighed. The water from the shower head was coming down so fast that Donalys was afraid that he would not be able to breathe. How to explain to a boy of… around ten who did not understand her language? She looked at her watch, sighed, then held her finger up to Donalys as if to say *wait*.

Andi ended up making Donalys wait until eleven thirty at night. That was when she was finally able to sneak him up with Artie's help to the upstairs bathroom that had a bath. Andi had filled it up with water, and she indicated to Donalys that was all the water he would have to get into. No more, no less. Donalys eyed the bathtub with suspicion but did not shake his head no. Nodding her head one last time toward the bathtub, Andi closed the door to the bathroom. Then she asked Artie to go and stay in her bedroom instead of his. She had a plan. She hoped Grandma Bea wouldn't wake up, but just in case, she had a contingency plan.

Grandma Bea did indeed wake up and come downstairs from the second floor to check on Andi and Artie. Andi tried to look as sleepy as possible. She had chosen to sit on the small chair they had in the hall past the living room.

"Hey, Grandma," she said, making her voice as nonchalant as possible. "Artie had an accident, so he's taking a bath now. I am *tired*," she ended with a yawn. That much, at least, wasn't a lie.

Grandma looked at her in concern. "That's strange. That hasn't happened to Artie in a while. Not this early in the night anyway." She looked thoughtful. "Andi, why is Artie taking a bath *downstairs*? Why not upstairs closer to his bedroom?"

"Oh, um, I don't think he wanted to wake you up."

Andi bit her lip and shrugged, trying to look sleepy.

Grandma smiled down at Andi. "You're a good sister," she said. "Just turn off the lights when he's done."

Andi yawned again, a real yawn. She nodded, not wanting to lie any more than she already had.

As her grandmother started up the stairs toward her bedroom, she looked old and frail, which made Andi's heart implode inside. Impulsively, she ran to the foot of the stairs. Hearing her footsteps, Grandma Bea stopped and turned. Andi looked up at her grandmother.

"Grandma, I ... I have a lot to tell you. I want to talk soon. Okay?"

Her grandmother looked at her, not saying anything. Finally she spoke. "You and Artie have been so tight-lipped, tiptoeing around me all the time, always going out. Did you really think I hadn't noticed?" She paused. "I know you kids are getting older. You don't share as much with us old folks when you're this age. But I hope you know you can count on me."

For a moment, Andi couldn't speak. Then she answered. "Grandma, I've always known that." That was not a lie.

Grandma smiled. She started back up the stairs.

"Definitely," Andi answered with a sinking feeling in the pit of her stomach. Their talk would have to happen soon, or it wouldn't happen at all. She watched her grandmother ascend the stairs, turning into her bedroom and closing the door. A minute later, she heard Artie step out of her bedroom. He stood at her side.

Andi turned to her twin, happy he knew all that she did. "It's too much," she told him. "This ... is all too much." Part of Artie's face fell in the shadow of night, but the other part showed her that he understood.

They walked back into the downstairs hall, and Artie knocked on the door as quietly as he could muster. He did not want to wake Grandma Bea. Donalys came out of the bathroom in Artie's PJs, looking much cleaner and somehow shy. Andi sighed in relief and motioned for Donalys to follow her down the stairs to the basement. Donalys walked downstairs with her, looking rather pleased with himself. He curled up in his corner bed of blankets and began to nod off. She smiled and walked upstairs toward her bedroom, ready to go to sleep for the entire evening. The last thing she remembered was falling into her bed.

"ANDI JOHNSTON! ARTIE JOHNSTON! You both get up RIGHT now!" Andi awoke to Grandma Bea screaming from downstairs. Looking at her clock, which said 9:17 a.m., Andi arose from the bed and dashed downstairs. Artie came walking down quickly, no daydream look on his face, signaling his agitation.

Grandma Bea stood in the hallway, an odd mixture of surprise and disbelief on her face. She pointed into the bathroom. "Could you two ... *please* ... explain this?" Andi realized in dismay that she had not remembered to get Donalys' clothes out of the bathroom. Was this why Grandma Bea was so angry? She walked into the bathroom, and despite herself, she gasped. Artie drew in his breath with surprise.

All the towels hanging on the racks, all the washcloths, bathmats, and Donalys' clothes were in a bathtub filled to the brim with water. *Jammed* in the bathtub was more like it, Andi realized in dismay. Donalys must have put all the towels and clothes in the bathtub. He had been trying to wash them! Andi pulled one towel out of the bathtub, shocked by how heavy it was, sodden with water. *This must be how they did it on the ship, where Donalys came from.* She could imagine the crew of a ship putting all their bedding and clothes in one big pile. Donalys was trying to be a good guest. Just that... he *wasn't*. She drew in her breath carefully, knowing that Grandma Bea was measuring her and Artie's reactions.

Andi turned around to face her grandmother, and so did Artie. Her grandmother walked up to Artie. Grandma Bea said, "Artie, what were you *thinking*?" Artie's face went ashen. He looked at Andi, waiting for her to say something.

Andi walked to her grandmother and put both of her hands on Grandma Bea's shoulders from behind. "Grandma," she began, "this is what I was talking to you about last night. We need to talk. But," she concluded somewhat clumsily, "that time isn't now. We will need to talk later. I will clean up this mess, and I will pay for new towels out of my allowance. I can't tell you right now. *I can't.* Please don't make me lie to you."

Grandma Bea stared hard at both Andi and Artie for a minute before rolling her eyes in exasperation. She turned to Andi. "Your mother was never as honest with me at the same age as you're being right now," she said. "That's the only reason ... the only reason why I am going to let this go." She drew in a deep breath and walked toward the kitchen, shaking her head.

Artie looked dismayed. He turned to Andi. "She's mad at me," he said.

"No, Artie, she isn't." Andi sighed, her arms folded across her chest. "She knows something is up, and we're not telling her. She's just confused, that's all, and she doesn't know what to do about it."

Tears came to Artie's eyes. "I don't want her mad at me before ..." He could not finish.

Andi hugged Artie. "She won't be. I'll make sure of it. Even if we still don't know where Lux is, I'll make sure of it. That she knows everything. *Everything,*" she said with finality.

Now it was Saturday, and she still had not told Grandma Bea anything. She was sure there was only a day or two left. Andi let herself think about this for one minute, shuddering. If she told her grandmother, she'd have to tell her in front of Artie. And she was afraid of dealing with the fallout of both their emotions. She couldn't predict how Artie would react even though he already knew everything. And if Grandma Bea knew, wouldn't she act differently? Be different with them? Andi knew she would not be able to handle that. And she was so worried about Lux. She couldn't sleep at night for thinking about him, where he was, what that ship might do to him if they caught him.

Andi had called Jubal Friday evening as soon as he arrived from the mainland, asking him to come over the following morning. She had lamely explained about Donalys, seeing her father, and Lux's disappearance. But no one in the world was ever going to know what she'd asked Lux to do for Artie. No one could know. Andi's heart skipped a beat whenever she remembered her shameful request. No one could *ever* know.

Now, Jubal peered closely at Donalys, muttering under his breath as if to say, *what now?* Donalys did not like Jubal's expression. He had immediately jumped up and inserted himself between Jubal and Andi. Jubal was tall for his age, and while a peace-loving and kind boy, he could get into a fight if provoked. Since Donalys was shorter than she was, Andi didn't think it would be much of a contest.

Jubal was staring at Donalys, which made Andi nervous. More importantly, she could see it was agitating Donalys. Jubal started to snap his fingers and pointed to Donalys.

"He can't speak our language, but he can draw." Jubal's serious expression transformed into a smile. "That's it! Andi, where are your crayons, coloring pens, all that?" He smiled at Donalys, who, confused by the change in expression, smiled back uncertainly. Donalys looked at Andi, questioning her about Jubal.

"Upstairs in my room," Andi answered. She could have sworn an argument or worse was about to explode between the two boys, but Jubal had been thinking this whole time. Jubal grinned at her and ran upstairs. They heard the footfalls fading as he reached her room. In just a few moments, he was back, his arms full of crayons, coloring pencils, and paper. He spilled them onto the small table next to Andi.

"Andi, draw the ship the best way you remember it. Then show it to him." To Andi's momentary hesitation, he replied, "You're an artist. You can do this. He'll respond to what you saw—you just need to draw it."

Andi knew it was a good idea. Artie nodded at her from the opposite end of the room, where he sat hunched over. He was about to go into a swaying motion, like he did when he became overly anxious. Andi grabbed the paper and, after putting it on top of one of the picture books Donalys had rejected, sat in a corner of the basement. Jubal was right; she was an okay artist. She began to draw.

Andi drew the ship in as much detail as she could. She drew the sails with the patterns on them. She could not quite recreate it on paper the way she remembered it. After finishing, she looked at the drawing critically. There was no mistaking the fact that it was the ship she'd seen even if it wasn't perfectly accurate. She gave it to Jubal, who held it up for Donalys to see.

Donalys' expression, which had been sullen because of his confusion, underwent a dramatic change. He paled and then nodded. He pointed to the drawing and then to himself as if to say *yes, I'm from there* or *yes, I know what you're talking about.* Andi wasn't sure which. She took the paper back from Donalys and drew Lux swimming in front of the ship. She was trying to convey the fact that the ship was chasing the dolphin.

She drew a frown on Lux to show Donalys that Lux was unhappy with the fact that the ship was chasing him. She held it up to Donalys again. This time she pointed to herself, then to her eyes, then to the ship in the water chasing Lux. She hoped Donalys understood that she was trying to say that she had seen this occur.

Jubal started pacing around the room, which made Artie so nervous that he started rocking back and forth. Donalys stared at the picture for a long time, his eyes narrowed into thin slits. Jubal watched Donalys stare at the drawing and said to Andi, "Something about the picture is new to him, I think. He's figuring out what it means."

Donalys exclaimed in surprise, forming a word in his language that Andi did not know. He grabbed another piece of paper, pulled all the crayons and coloring pencils off the table. He then lay down on the floor and began to draw in a fevered manner. Andi and Jubal both moved closer to see what he was creating.

The drawing was much more rudimentary than Andi's but still clear. Donalys drew the ship and then drew a purple background. Squinting her eyes, Andi tried to understand it but could not. Donalys finished, throwing a crayon on the ground, and jumping up to his feet as if to say, "There!"

Andi and Jubal studied the image. She smiled to herself as she looked more closely. Donalys was not an artist, but he had tried his best. He had drawn several stick figures on the ship, but there were two that stood out from the rest. Donalys had drawn himself as a small redheaded stick figure standing next to an extremely tall, large, and fat man. He had the same long hair Donalys had, complete with a thick red mustache and eyebrows as thick as the mustache he wore. Andi realized this was the same large figure she had seen on the ship's deck when with Lux.

Donalys had drawn himself as not smiling but not sad either. All the faces on the ship wore level expressions, neither smiling nor frowning. It was as if their faces were blank, Andi realized, devoid of emotion. She looked up from Donalys' drawing and looked at him trying to wrestle Artie to the ground. Artie was allowing it, which surprised her; he usually didn't enjoy physical contact. To be true, Artie wasn't wrestling Donalys; he was just allowing Donalys to pull him down from behind.

Andi looked back to Donalys' drawing. There was one thing she was curious about. The tower she'd seen on the ship. Donalys had traced out the same tube-like cylindrical shape running in different directions throughout the ship. It was both horizontal and vertical, running in and out of portholes but rising vertically through openings on the different decks of the ship. The design was *fascinating*. Donalys had drawn the steering wheel of the ship just behind the cylindrical structure. The large structure spread itself all over the ship, connected to the steering wheel. But this was where the drawing had become strange. Donalys had drawn a person *inside* the cylindrical apparatus. Andi frowned, trying to figure it all out. So much didn't make sense.

"I don't understand it," she said finally, mystified.

"I don't either, but ..." Jubal trailed off, a frown on his face. He looked up to the ceiling of the basement, lost in thought. "I wonder if we're trying to understand it too much," he said finally. "What if it *is* what it looks like?"

"What does it look like? It looks like the ship is floating in some sort of—some sort of *nothing*."

"Exactly!" Jubal replied.

Jubal gave the drawing back to Donalys and began to do some sort of mime act. He stepped forward and put his hands on an unseen wall, opening his mouth in a look of dismay as if he were stuck inside. He widened his eyes in terror and kept feeling the wall as if looking for a way to escape. Jubal was so comical that Andi began to giggle, but then she looked at Donalys. His face was rapt. He kept nodding vigorously, as if Jubal were making all the sense in the world. Andi stifled her laughter as best as she could.

Now Jubal fell flat to the ground. He put his feet together much like Lux's flukes, positioning his arms so that they looked like his dorsal fins. He made swimming motions. Then he jumped back onto his feet feeling for the wall. He acted as if he expected the wall to be present but smiled exaggeratedly, displaying to Donalys that the wall was gone. Then he brought his hands together in a scooping motion, indicating that the boat was sailing. Donalys nodded at Jubal, smiling broadly, his eyes affirming what Jubal was showing him. Then Donalys looked at Andi with wide-eyed excitement. Then he did something unexpected: he hugged her. Andi hugged him back. Artie had come out of his reverie, so Donalys went over to him, his arms outstretched. Artie clasped him on the back, which surprised Andi.

Andi walked to Jubal. "That whole act—what did you just do?"

Jubal pointed to the drawing. He motioned to Donalys and then pointed to the ship in the drawing. "They were stuck in that purple place you told me about—and don't ask me what it is. But wherever they were, Lux somehow got them out. Without meaning to," he ended.

"So why would the ship be after him?" Andi tried to hide her impatience.

"Andi, I can't be sure. Look at the way you drew that ship. They're not from here, not from this time anyway. I think if he got them out of that place—then those people think he can get them *back* to wherever they came from." He frowned. "Or wherever they *want* to go."

Jubal beckoned Donalys over to them. Jubal put his finger on the drawing and pointed to Donalys' face, indicating the lack of a smile. Jubal started his mime act again. He went from his trademark goofy grin to a serious countenance, neither smiling nor frowning in a frozen posture. Donalys looked at him, then to the drawing, then nodded his head before going one step further. Donalys imitated Jubal's pose. He stiffened, not moving, appearing to be stuck. He did not even close his eyes. His stare became faraway and vacant, frozen.

"They couldn't move," Jubal blurted, unfreezing himself. Pointing to the drawing, he continued. "That—wherever they were, they were stuck. They couldn't move." He smiled at Andi. "Until you upset the applecart, that is."

Andi stared down at the picture. She nodded. It would explain the frozen, blank stares of everyone on the ship that she had seen in the purple world with Lux. One of the stick figures in the picture appeared bent over as if he couldn't get up. Andi remembered something Lux had told her about Donalys.

"Lux said that he," she cocked her hand at Donalys, "was old. Something like millions of years. But that his mind and body were those of a ten-year-old."

"Anyway," Andi continued, "Lux didn't say years. I don't think he measures time like that. Just that Donalys is, well, *old.*"

"So," Jubal continued excitedly, "that could mean that they were stuck in that place for a long time. An immeasurable amount of time. Stuck. No time passed at all in that place. Maybe to them, they were there for one second, but to us it was millions of years." He smacked the drawing with the back of his hand, an action that made Andi giggle and Donalys frown. "This was probably a pocket universe."

"A *what?*" Andi spluttered. "Just what is a pocket universe?"

Artie had leaned forward, still seated in Indian position, his face focused, interested. Jubal continued.

"A pocket universe is, well, just a theory. But ..." His voice rose in excitement. "If Donalys is telling the truth, then yes, this could be a pocket universe."

"Jubal," Andi replied with an edge in her voice, "just what is a pocket universe?"

Jubal stared at her and began to stammer, becoming aware that his excitement had run away with him. "It's ..." He grasped at words for an explanation. "It's a universe within a universe. A universe that is um, *deflated,* smaller than this one. With its own rules. About space and time."

"And just how many universes are there? Do you know?" Andi asked, a tired note in her voice.

This time it was Artie who spoke. "It could be one, or it could be many." His voice was eager. Andi turned around and looked at him. He never spoke like that. Artie always spoke in a more level voice.

Jubal raised a hand as if pointing to an invisible object. "These universes could be part of our universe but separate. They're like—they're like bubbles. Different sizes and shapes. And different rules that come with them."

"*Maybe,*" Artie interjected.

"But, but ..." Andi could not finish, lost as she was. She swallowed. "So these bubbles have their own rules. Do ... they ... ever become part of ours? Then our rules become like their own rules? Or vice-versa?"

Jubal sighed. "I don't know." Artie nodded.

Andi did not understand, but a small idea was growing in the back of her mind. Before she could begin to verbalize it, she needed to find out something. She adopted her best motherly posture and put her hands on her hips. *Well, it worked with Donalys taking a bath anyway.*

"So," she started, smiling sweetly at both Jubal and Artie, both of whom looked taken aback by her change in mood. "Just how did the two of you discover the idea of pocket universes?" She spread her arms apart. "I need to figure this out, so could you help me?"

Both boys looked abashed to Andi's immense, secret satisfaction. Jubal and Artie looked at each other guiltily before Jubal finally answered her.

"Comic books," Jubal said.

Andi snorted so loudly that she startled all three boys, including herself. She looked at them, and they back at her. Then they all broke out into peals of laughter.

Fifteen

Hide and Seek

Andi found herself laughing much longer than the boys did. She wiped the tears from her eyes before letting out one last guffaw. All the stress, anger, and grief from losing Lux evaporated in her laughing fit. She was still worried about Lux, of course, but more hopeful that she would find him. She looked at Jubal and Artie and burst out laughing again.

"Comic books!" Andi roared.

The two boys smiled sheepishly but this time did not laugh. Donalys smiled, just happy to be able to join in somehow. Andi forced herself to be quiet. She studied Donalys' drawing again. A lot of what Jubal said had made sense. It also fit in with another idea that was starting to surface in her mind. She put the drawing down and pursed her lips.

To tell them what she was thinking would be equal to admitting that they just might be on to something with their idea. Pocket universes. She still couldn't get used to the idea.

"What?" Jubal said.

Maybe, just maybe.

"Okay," Andi said, "that cave where I first found Lux? Not Mom's cave where Lux's been staying, but the Underwater Grotto, the one where I had to dive and swim underwater?" She looked at Jubal. Artie nodded, understanding before Jubal did what she was thinking. Jubal looked at Artie, confused.

"Yeah ... what about it?" Jubal adopted an eager, listening face.

"What if ... what if ..." Andi struggled to complete the sentence. "What if the Underwater Grotto is ... what if that is one of your pocket universes? The way opens when the stars are in a certain position in the sky. That's what I was able to get from Lux's mother when she told me where she had hidden Lux." She also remembered how large the lake had been inside the underwater grotto; she had very serious doubts about it fitting under the cliff somewhere.

Jubal grinned broadly. Andi rolled her eyes. He was so happy that she was even entertaining the idea he and Artie had suggested. She continued.

"Lux's mother put him there to be safe." She looked around at the three of them even though she knew Donalys didn't understand. "Wouldn't it make sense for Lux to hide in that cave from the ship? Maybe he can get in and out easily because, well, he can teleport. *I* can't. Maybe I can only get in when those stars are just right, but it may be very easy for Lux. "

Again, Artie nodded while Jubal was silent. Then Jubal completed Andi's train of thought.

"That would also explain why you two haven't been able to communicate. It's so close but ..."

Andi picked up where he left off. "So close and yet so far away. If he's in another universe with its own rules and all that, then ... he may not be able to communicate." She frowned. "He may not understand why he's not able to communicate. He's scared, wondering why I haven't come to get him yet." Her eyes began to sting.

Jubal finally nodded. "It would make sense if it's true. But if that deep cavern ... where you had to swim underwater for such a long time ..." He trailed off, shuddering. He shook himself and came to. "The fact is there's an opening to it. It's not closed off from this ... universe."

Andi continued. "My question is this. How did that ship get from there to here?" She pointed to Donalys' drawing of the ship floating in the purple world.

It was Artie who replied, surprising them all because of how silent he normally was. "Lux and his mother." Jubal looked at Artie, expecting more. But Artie remained silent. This was the one thing about Artie: he didn't waste his words.

Andi picked up on what her twin was trying to say. "You're saying Lux and his mother can make these universes ... connect to ours?"

Artie nodded, now looking directly at Andi. "The earthquakes?" At first Andi did not understand, but then she made the connection. She gasped. Jubal looked at her.

"The earthquakes," she said. "The ship appeared during an earthquake. It disappeared. But then it came back and stayed this time. Lux using his powers is causing these earthquakes. Because we were in the purple world with them, Lux using his powers must have somehow freed the ship, allowing it to come here." Andi's heart was racing as she said this. It all made so much sense now. "We freed it in the purple world, but then ... it followed us. It was Lux using his powers. A kind of door opened for them."

Jubal's usual cheery expression gave way to a more sober one. "And the ship has figured that out. That's why they're after Lux. They want him to help them."

"But what if he doesn't want to help them?" Andi's face was scarlet with indignation.

"If the crew was stuck there for millions of years ...millions. If I were one of them, one of the people on the ship, I'd want his help." He paused. "I'd probably do anything I could to get his help."

"You said it only was like a second to them," Andi began to argue.

"It may have been a second," Jubal replied. "It may have been much more. All I'm saying is that their concept of time as compared to ours is, well, *different*. They're figuring out time here in this world, this universe. And Lux is the key to that," he ended soberly.

Andi shuddered to think of what that could mean. They needed to find her dolphin soon. "Is there any way the crew could know about the cave? The one where I found Lux?"

Instead of answering, Artie came over and hugged her tightly. It weakened her resolve to understand and argue. She heard Jubal answer her question even as Artie continued to hold her.

"Andi, I guess we don't know. We don't know these people. All these ideas we're having ... they could be wrong. These ideas ... all they do is connect everything together. That's all they do. There could be a totally different explanation. Something that connects all this better. Something we haven't hit upon yet." Jubal paused. "We're just twelve- and thirteen-year-olds, Andi." There was a helpless tone in his voice that made Andi feel guilty. She'd dragged them into this, even Donalys.

Although Donalys might be better off now than he was before. He wasn't freezing in a cave. Jubal and Artie ... they hadn't asked for this. Grandma hadn't either.

Grandma. How many days did Grandma have left? At least Grandma Bea was going to die with her memories intact. Andi's heart constricted. She could see how Lux had been good in some ways. Many ways.

So she sat down on the basement floor and told them her plan. Artie was uneasy with it but agreed. Jubal did not like it, having experienced it once before, but agreed as well. Andi even went as far as drawing a picture showing Donalys what she planned to do, resulting only in a puzzled look. He shrugged and nodded, which Andi took for agreement. She was going to dive out from the cliff again into what she now called the Underwater Grotto. She had a hard time getting her head around the possibility that could really be a *pocket universe*.

Later as Andi prepared her plan, Grandma Bea walked into her room. "So you're camping out," she said. "So soon?"

Andi jerked up. Her grandmother remembered when she and Jubal had camped out in the backyard. Interesting. She hadn't recovered her memories yet at that time.

What would she do if she didn't come back? Would she ever talk with Grandma Bea about all the things she needed to talk about before she died? She'd nearly died before when she dove out from the cliff into the sea; would tonight be the one to finish her? Then it would be Artie who would be all alone, she realized. She would be gone, and Grandma Bea would be gone. Was she doing the right thing?

Fog floated over the island that evening, which made Andi nervous. She needed the night to be clear so that she could carry out her plan. The possibility that scared her the most was if Lux ended up not being in the cave after all. What would she do then? She had no other ideas of how to find him. And if Lux was not in the cave, how would she get out? Getting in had been hard enough the first time; getting out of the cave with Lux had been so much simpler.

He had to be there; that's all there was to it.

The four of them snuck out of the house at around two in the morning. After Andi closed the door behind them, they went around the house into the back, Artie still half-asleep. Jubal carried several blankets so that they would be comfortable. Donalys simply looked mystified but happy to be with them.

Andi saw her breath float right in front of her. She didn't want to think about how cold the water would be. It was still foggy, which worried her too. But she didn't want to wait another night. She might already be too late.

They had at least two hours left to wait. The Underwater Grotto was open only when the stars aligned in a certain way. But ... she shrugged off the thought. She didn't want to make a mistake, which is why they were so early.

Jubal spoke her unexpressed fear. "How are you going to find out when to jump into the water? The stars won't appear the same way they did before." Jubal paused. "I mean," he said, "they shouldn't be too different. Not as if it were late summer or something. But..."

He'd caught her. No one else had shared that fear. Well, Artie hadn't anyway. Donalys didn't know what was going on, so ...

"Jubal," Andi began slowly, "it's like ... it's like Lux's mother left a permanent map in my mind. If I don't think too hard about it, then I'm hoping that the map will sort of identify when I'm supposed to jump. The picture changes depending on the day I call it back up into my memory. It's not a static, still photo. It's still doing its job. Do you know what I mean? Anyway, talking about it sure isn't going to help."

"Will you be able to stay warm?" Jubal demanded. "It's freezing down there. You don't have the mother dolphin's power to protect you, and what if you don't find Lux?"

"I think ..." Andi faltered. She had so many thoughts. "I think that if I'm able to get into the passageway, I'll be able to have more warmth. But yeah, shooting down into the water is very, very, *very* cold." She shivered. "If it isn't open, I'll try to get to the beach as fast as I can!"Jubal was silent.

As they settled down on the grass, curling up in the blankets, Artie lay down next to her. In an incredibly warm gesture, he rolled over and put his arms around her. He was half-asleep. Andi realized how scared he was for her, something that touched her deeply. They had been through so much together. Was it fair for her to put him through this? Yet both she and he were now tied to Lux in ways they couldn't begin to comprehend. She knew that now. And she knew Artie realized this too. So they waited.

The fog swirled above them. At moments, the clouds would part, raising Andi's hopes, only to cover the sky again. Andi's nervousness grew. And for some reason, she could not help but feel that someone was watching them. She looked back at the house, which lay in darkness. She could see very little. She looked at her brother. Artie lay sleeping normally, his arms still wrapped around her.

Jubal looked up at her, and Andi wanted to whisper across to him that she felt someone was watching them. But she didn't want to wake up Artie. Andi pointed with one arm toward the house, shaking her head. Andi hoped that Jubal would understand. He frowned, turned around to stare in the darkness, and then nodded, agreeing that something was not quite right. He held his forefinger up in front of Donalys, telling him to wait, and jumped to his feet. He walked carefully toward the house, looking around the large backyard to see if there was anything afoot. There was nothing. Jubal returned to the group and shrugged his shoulders before jumping under the thick blankets.

Some of the fog was dissipating now. Andi's heart leaped. She could see the stars. Not quite in position yet but close. She nudged Artie, waking him up, and pointed up to the sky. Artie, brushing sleepers from his eyes, smiled tentatively, and nodded to Andi. He was still nervous, but he had accepted this was what Andi was going to do. Andi flashed him a grateful look before getting up, alerting both Jubal and Donalys. Andi looked up into the sky. She could still call up the image implanted in her mind by Lux's mother in perfect detail. It surprised her, but she realized that, knowing Lux, nothing should surprise her anymore.

Andi stepped toward the edge of the cliff, leaving her brother and friends several yards behind. She looked up. *Almost ... almost ... almost.* Then a yell rang out in the dark. Andi swung around. A tall, fat man with arms like tree trunks fell upon Jubal and the shocked-out-of-sleep Artie pinning them down to the ground. Andi froze in terror. Donalys jumped up and began to pound on the man's shoulders, screaming at him in his own language.

What could she do? Several other men dressed in clothes that glinted in the night tried to drag Donalys off the large man. When they succeeded, the large man turned and clasped Donalys in a firm embrace, even though Donalys kept pounding on him as he did so. Releasing Donalys from the embrace, the man faced Andi for the first time. Commands flew out of his mouth, commands that Andi could not understand. The men behind Donalys ran around Jubal and Artie toward her.

Jubal's voice screamed, "Go, Andi, go! Go!" He was fighting to free himself from the men holding him in their grasp. Artie remained paralyzed, his eyes wide in terror. Yet as scared as he was, Artie nodded to Andi quickly. Andi took one quick dazed look up at the stars above her, and while they looked like they were in position, she had no time to make sure. She turned around and dashed toward the edge of the cliff and jumped off, diving headlong into the sea before the men were able to grab her.

Sixteen

The Maimed Skull

The opening at the bottom of the ocean floor was open to her. Andi swam for it much faster than she had the first time. She was so upset she did not even think about losing breath. She swam into the narrow passage that led to the odd cave where she'd found Lux. Her back scratched against the top of the rock, and she remembered the trapped air just above the water line after swimming under the U. She pulled herself up and gasped to fill her lungs. She did not feel Lux. There was no trace of his consciousness touching upon hers. Andi struggled, hoping against hope. Maybe when she got to the actual cavern, their connection would restore itself.

Andi swam to the opening of the small underground lake. The tunnel continued beyond the opening, as it had before. She wondered if Lux had gone further in, *beyond* the cave. Her lungs exploding, she pushed herself off the bottom of the rocky passage into the small open-ing above where she first found Lux. Andi burst out of the water, her lungs burning as she gasped air in. She swam to the rocky edge and huddled on it, shivering.

There was no sign of Lux. Disappointment tore through her like a sword. She had been so sure that she'd find him here. And now what was she going to do? Jubal and Artie were likely gone to wherever those men had taken them. Donalys too. How would she find them? How would she rescue them without Lux? What was she going to tell her grandmother? That she'd lost Grandma Bea's other grandchild along with two of her friends? One of whom was thousands of years old and had been living inside her basement? It was more than Andi could bear. She broke into huge hiccupping sobs and stared down into the inky black water. How was she going to swim back out? Could Lux be waiting for her further in, past the opening to the cave? Andi had no idea how much further the rocky passage extended. She could die swimming through it, and no one would ever know what had happened to her. No one would ever be able to help Artie and Jubal. Remembering the look of terror in Artie's eyes just made her cry more.

Phosphoresce bounced eerily around the cavern. The stalactites hanging from the roof looked so precarious. Andi knew one small tremor would cause one to fall on her, killing her. Yet Andi was too tired, scared, and overwhelmed to go back into the water. She needed to regroup. She needed to figure out what to do next. She stood up on the rocky shore. The Underwater Grotto was very different from Mom's cave. The grotto phosphoresced, creating images of light bouncing off the stalactites. The stalactites were long and wide and hung threateningly above Andi. The shore here resembled a real beach, albeit a rocky one. The gray, rocky shore extended past that stone bier Andi had seen the first time she'd swum through the passage to find Lux.

It was the bier that held her attention. There were huge cracks running alongside its sides. Andi frowned. Those fissures in the rock hadn't been there before. She walked toward it and then moved around it, studying all sides. Four stalagmites rose from the ground, creating a rectangular formation. What Andi felt looked like a stone casket fit right into it. Andi looked at the top of the strange boxlike stone. Spidery fissures ran all over it. Suddenly Andi understood. The earthquakes must have caused the stone to crack. As she thought this, a chipped stone on the top of the coffin flew right at her, hitting her in the forehead as if to say *yes*.

"Ow!" Andi exclaimed. She stared at the box with some apprehension. How had that happened? There was a small indentation in the middle of the coffin's top where the flying stone had been. She put her forefinger in the small hollow. As soon as she did, the stone crumbled, spreading out from the center with a horrible splintering sound. Andi snatched away her finger, horrified. The top of the stone box collapsed. Andi stepped back quickly. She knew she did not want to see what lay inside. She turned around toward the water. She needed to start putting together a plan.

"Come here."

Andi stopped. It was *the voice*. Thin and raspy, with a commanding edge to it. Andi kept walking toward the water, trying to convince herself that she had imagined it.

"I said, come here," the voice repeated itself, a threat in its tone. Andi's heart began to thud. She put her foot in the water, determined to ignore it. Suddenly she found herself jerked back, flying all the way to the stone coffin, her back crashing against its side. Something wet and warm trickled down her back. She reached back, touching it, then looked at her hand. *Blood.*

"Turn around," the voice whispered. Sucking her breath in, Andi realized she had no choice.

As she stood. Andi looked down into the coffin and let out a scream. Inside was a very large skull with a huge crack on its right side. It had two large, curved horns rising from behind where its ears ought to be. There was no skeleton, just the skull—no, Skull. The Skull turned itself to the side so that its empty sockets stared straight at her.

The words hissed from the mouth of the Skull. "Lift me out," it said.

A strange lassitude formed inside Andi's mind, clearing out everything except for the Skull. She bent down obediently and closed her hands around the back of the Skull just under where the horns formed. It was surprisingly heavy, and she struggled in lifting it out of the coffin. It truly was a coffin; Andi knew that now. Repulsiveness ran through Andi as she held the Skull, but the compulsion to obey still held.

"Place me on the top," the Skull directed her.

Andi looked with new eyes at the four stalagmites rising from the floor. Andi slid the hole at the bottom of the Skull where the neck ought to have been on the top of the closest stalagmite. The Skull faced her. Relief at not holding it anymore coursed through her as she stepped back. She could not take her eyes off the grotesque sight, no matter how much she wanted to. She shuddered at the feeling that the Skull was examining her.

"You entered here," it said. "How?"

A part of Andi's mind began to remove itself from the compulsion to obey this … thing. It was as if one part of her looked on with horror while the other part quietly answered the Skull's question.

"I swam through the opening in the ocean floor," she replied.

Andi blinked. For a moment, something spectral seemed to form itself around the creature. But whatever she had seen, it was gone now. The other part of her mind screamed at her that this thing was evil— beyond evil—but still she could not shake the impulse to obey it.

"A golden creature?" the Skull asked. Andi stared. It had read her mind. She tried desperately to block Lux out.

As much as Andi was compelled to answer the question, the other Andi, the other part of her refused to let her reply. She struggled, feeling herself tremble with the desire to speak but still did not answer. Something trickled from her eye down her cheek. Thinking it was a tear, she found that it was blood.

The Skull remarked in a detached voice, "Ah." Then its tone softened. "You have freed me. Tell me what you most desire."

Andi tried to withdraw, to keep the creature from reading her mind.

"Take me with you," the voice said, "and I will heal her."

Andi stared at the creature for a long time. *Heal her.* Heal Grandma Bea. The weariness she felt made her want to answer *yes.* And yet, the part of her mind that screamed at her told her what to say.

"No," Andi heard herself say. The Skull was telling her what she wanted to hear. She was sure of it. Something deep inside her told her that if Lux could not prevent her grandmother from dying, then the Skull creature could not either.

Suddenly, she flew toward the wall, her forehead slamming against it. She then found herself suspended two feet in the air, pinned against the wall. Blood streamed down from her forehead, getting into her eyes.

"Look at me," the voice said. Still trapped in the air, Andi's body rotated from facing the wall so that she could see the Skull. She gasped. The creature now had wings outlining themselves spectrally from where its neck should be.

"You're in the shape of a butterfly," Andi said in revulsion. The wings surrounding the Skull were colorless and ghostly. Andi could see through them to the other side of the wall. They looked thin and sharp, as if touching one could cut her to pieces. Even though it was ghostly, not physical. Bile gathered in Andi's stomach. Butterflies were beautiful, and this was not. What was the word Grandma Bea used? *Profane.*

The Skull floated in front of her, level with her head. The grating, hollow voice echoed throughout the cavern. "I do not negotiate."

"Forget it." Andi spat the blood that had pooled in her mouth. "I'm not helping you."

"The more blood you shed, the more substantial I will become. Then I will be free."

Blood streamed from Andi's head. And yes, the creature's wings were becoming less ghostly by the minute, more solid. But there was a small part of her mind still speaking to her. Why did it ask her for help if all it needed to do was to hurt her, kill her? Then it would be solid enough to break out. There was something to all this that she didn't understand, hadn't grasped. It needed something from her. That was why she wasn't dead yet.

The Skull flew off the long-pointed piece of rock, flapping its ghostly wings. It came too closely to Andi's face. "Where is the golden creature?"

"I'll never tell you," Andi answered. "Never."

The Skull's voice changed to a more wheedling, coaxing one. "Tell me where the golden creature is, and I will let you live."

Andi closed her eyes. Her head was throbbing. She was starting to shiver. Blood was streaming down from her forehead. *Is this what going into shock feels like?* Her shoulders could not stop shaking, and her teeth were chattering. She tried to focus. Why did this thing want Lux? What did it have to do with him? Then she looked over at the cracked remains of the coffin.

"The earthquakes," she muttered to the Skull as it floated before her. Andi was just about to black out. "That's how ... that's how it started. The earthquakes cracked the coffin ... it wasn't me. It was the earthquakes." She remembered the first earthquake that hit just before she witnessed Lux and his mother swimming in the sea. It was that earthquake that had begun to crack the Skull's coffin open. It was that same night she'd first heard that thin, raspy voice pleading for help.

The Skull hovered in front of her, saying nothing. Yet Andi sensed an immense anger and even deeper hatred. Andi continued.

"No matter how ... solid you become ... you can't break out of here. You ... can't," Andi gasped. "Can you? You still need ... Lux. And I won't let you find out where he is." Andi's head fell forward, exhausted by the effort it had taken to get the words out. Then she heard a cruel laugh ring hollowly through the cavern.

"All I needed was the name," the Skull cackled. "The name allows me to summon him. He will not know until it is too late. For both him and you," the voice cackled.

The creature flew up close to the stalactites protruding from the roof and began to whistle. It was a whistle that started high and shrill before deepening to a sort of bellow. The cavern walls began to vibrate. She wasn't sure if it was her imagination or not, but because of the vibrations, Andi could begin to see through them. It was a strange sort of vibration that shook atoms and molecules apart. It allowed her to see through the wall to another cavern, a different kind of cavern.

Lux was there swimming in a lake. There he was! Andi swore, berating herself for not swimming further into the next opening. That way, this *thing* would not be torturing her now. As she looked at Lux through the wall, she realized he was very sad. There was no joy in his face or mischief in how he moved in the water. He swam around that place in a slow, haphazard pattern.

There was a small hole in the roof of the cavern, allowing golden sunlight to stream through. Unlike the cavern she was in now, the shore was sandy, and past the sand, a grassy slope stood covered with yellow and red flowers. Flowers that she had never seen before. Hazily, she smiled at its beauty, understanding why Lux was drawn to it. She found the grassy beach wonderful. Her head was still throbbing. She could barely hold the blackness back. She wished she were there with him right now.

Oh, Lux. Andi's heart ached. She'd put him through so much. Just then, Lux jerked his head up out of the water and looked around him. Andi swallowed. He'd heard her. She'd experienced their connection again, albeit faintly. Nothing compared to what it had been before. She wondered if their bond had weakened because of asking him to heal Artie. Had Lux been so disgusted with her? Or maybe it was what Jubal had said—he was in an inaccessible place.

Lux jerked his head up again. Andi looked up to the Skull and knew he had seen the dolphin. The malevolent face had turned toward the vibrating wall. Lux's erratic movements told Andi he was becoming confused. He heard the creature crooning to him and knew it was not Andi's voice.

I mustn't think of him. I mustn't reach out to him. Andi realized that he could hear her because of the wall vibrating so hard. It allowed them to resume their bond. Andi forced herself to think of other things but found it impossible. She kept looking from where she hung in the air toward the beautiful cavern Lux was in. It was a kind of paradise.

For a moment, Andi was sure that Lux could see her. She hoped this wasn't true. He looked at her from the other side as if unsure of what he was seeing. Andi forced herself not to reach out to him, not to think about him at all. She closed her eyes, shutting him out. It cut into her, and as wracked with pain as she was, closing Lux out cost her even more dearly.

Lux roared, a bloodcurdling sound. He roared again and flipped into the air before diving down to the bottom of the lake. Their bond was growing more and more with each moment. He was coming for her. His anger at what was happening to her grew more as he swam closer to them. He didn't understand why she was hanging in the air, bleeding. His devastation, grief, and anger at what had happened to her rose within her.

Lux, don't! It's a trap! Don't come. It wants to get to you. Don't come.

Andi? His voice was beautiful inside her mind.

Don't come, Lux. She paused. *Lux, I'm sorry. I'm sorry for what happened. I'm sorry.* Then she shut him out of her mind, pushing as hard as she could. Beads of sweat stood out on her forehead, mingling with the blood. She couldn't let anything happen to Lux because of her. She prayed desperately from where she hung suspended that he would not enter the cavern.

Her prayers did no good. Lux burst out of the lake into the cavern, flying straight at the Skull butterfly. He roared. He slammed into the spectral butterfly, the Skull falling to the ground. Lux let out a groaning sound as he floated in the sky. Could he fly? Lux turned to Andi before falling back into the water. He tried to rise out of the water toward her but could not.

"Look out!" Andi screamed.

A stalactite came whistling through the air straight at Lux's side. Lux dodged it. Andi heard Lux growl. Lux rose out of the lake toward the ground where the Skull lay to Andi's great astonishment. She had not dreamt he could fly. He had been able to levitate but....She wondered if Lux had to be angry to tap into the power. He'd tried to come to her but couldn't. Andi blinked, forcing herself to stay awake. She was going to pass out any minute. She couldn't. She *couldn't.*

Lux roared again. Then came one word, aimed toward the Skull. *Why?*

"She is important to you," the Skull answered, his voice flat and unemotional.

Leave her alone! Lux cried. *Alone!*

The Skull rose, its wings flapping, making no noise as they did so. It neared Lux. "I will leave her alone," it replied, "if you will let me out of here."

Lux fell into the water. She felt his anger begin to subside. Her heart sank. He was going to let the Skull out. Into the world. Her world. What unimaginable evil would that thing wreak on her world?

The Skull began to shrink, a circle of blackness appearing around it. Suddenly, Lux's skin started becoming less golden. Andi gasped. The blackness was draining Lux's light from his skin! The circle of black around the Skull contracted and expanded.

"You will provide me with a portal," the creature pronounced.

Lux was becoming gray, his eyes no longer sharp but wan. The light within his skin no longer blazed a fiery gold. *He could die,* Andi realized with a gasp. He began to look like his mother did when she died.

His mother.

His mother.

A memory rose to the surface unbidden. She gasped. Now she understood everything. She screamed both with her mind and voice.

"Lux! That thing is what killed your mother!"

The dolphin glanced at her in astonishment.

Even though she was about to pass out, Andi realized that Lux's mother *meant* to put him in the Underwater Grotto—in its second opening—the one where Lux just came from. Somehow she made a mistake and came here. That *thing* wanted her to break him out. Somehow it couldn't leave the grotto on its own. When she wouldn't, the Skull hurt her. The only thing she could do was seal the Skull up in that tomb, leaving Lux here, hoping that he would be safe. She was pretty sure that the monstrous creature had reached out from beyond the tomb and wrapped the mother in that darkness she had seen that night with Jubal in her mom's cave.

But then Lux had started using his powers, and the earthquakes had occurred in response...cracking the tomb.

The Skull's voice broke in. "It does not matter if you let me out of here. It will take me longer, but I will do this myself." Then it cackled with a note of triumph in its voice.

This made Andi turn her head toward Lux. The circle of blackness kept growing. There was something inside the circle; it looked like another world. It was like—it was like the creature was creating a path of some kind from Lux's powers. The portal wasn't complete yet, Andi realized. But it would be soon if Lux didn't get away from the Skull.

Lux looked at her, then at the Skull, then at her. Suddenly, he flew right at Andi where she hung in the air. She grabbed him and let him pull her out of her suspended position. They crashed into the water, her arms barely around his torso.

Lux swam quickly down to the underwater passage, pulling her through. Light began to return to his body. Rocks began to fall from the passage, pelting them from above. Andi turned around and gasped. The creature was swimming at great speed in the water toward them. Its spectral wings had become real, physical. Its wings crashed into the sides of the rocky passage as it swam in heavy pursuit of them. It was not going to let them escape.

Andi hung slackly at Lux's side, sensing that he was somehow keeping her from falling off. The light had returned to his body, bright gold shining through her fingers where she held on to Lux.

Andi sent him a mental image of the Skull zooming through the rocky passage behind them. Moments later, a great crash echoed through the tunnel. Stones had been teleported from the sea, blocking the passageway. The Skull was trapped. Andi felt it beat its wings against the collapsed passage looking for a way out. Then the world opened to them as they reached the end of the tunnel. Lux flew out of the water into the sky. Andi lay nearly comatose on his back, looking down at the ocean for a sign that the Skull had escaped. When it didn't emerge, Andi finally allowed herself to submit to the black dizziness rising within her.

Seventeen

Time, Space and Neither

Andi had no idea how long she slept. She had brief waking moments, but her vision was blurred, and she always fell back to sleep immediately. A few times she heard a lovely voice hum and murmur, soothing her. It was one of the most beautiful sounds Andi had ever heard. During one of those waking moments, her consciousness began dancing close to the surface. The beautiful voice helped Andi stir. It was talking with another voice, a gruffer and deeper voice.

"She has been through so much," the voice murmured. Water stroked her forehead, leaving behind a tingly feel. A good one. It made her feel like falling back asleep, but the other voice kept her near the surface. *Where was she?*

"Most of it her own fault," the deeper voice answered.

Andi almost opened her eyes in indignation. *Her own fault?*

"She protected our Donalys when no one else would. Seems to me that you owe her a debt for that," the higher voice said, with the slightest hint of reproach in it. Andi almost opened her eyes at the name Donalys but forced herself to pretend she was asleep. The big men she had seen pounce on Artie and Jubal had also dealt with Donalys, maybe in a gentler way but still. She wanted to see if Artie and Jubal's names came up in the conversation.

"Aye, perhaps you're right for all that," the gruff voice conceded. "Still, you can't help but see that trouble follows her. She attracts it." He paused. "Where did her wounds come from?"

"I'm not so sure," the other voice answered. "Whatever it was, it involved the golden creature."

The gentle voice continued. "She's the only one who can talk to the golden creature. We need her for that. And we still don't know the whole story. Those boys have helped fill a few gaps, but I think she is the one who can connect it all for us."

"Be that as it may," the gruff voice said, "this girl is bad luck. They all are." Andi heard heavy footsteps leave the room. She did not hear a second set of footsteps leave with him. Andi slowly opened her eyes. *Those boys.* Artie and Jubal along with Donalys ... they just might be all right.

There was no one in her room. And the room, it was *grand.* She was in what appeared to be a king-size bed covered with royal purple blankets. She stretched luxuriously, feeling the majesty of the bed even if she was a little sick. It was so comfortable. Andi sighed, resting back onto the thick pillows. But then she remembered. *The Skull.* Her stomach clenched. She lifted herself off the bed, realizing how lightheaded she was. Through a doorway, a sink stood in the adjacent room.

Figuring it was the bathroom, Andi walked toward it with one hand on the wall to support herself. She was dizzy. Once inside the room, she blinked. It was a bathroom that she had never seen the likes of before. The sink hung in the air, suspended over the floor. The toilet stood on a pedestal, and as she stood there, the toilet rose from a normal height to be level with her face. Taken aback, Andi leaned against the wall for a minute. Andi understood. She approached the tall toilet. The toilet bowl bent toward her, anticipating her need. Relieved, Andi vomited. The bowl waited until she was all done and then returned to its original position. Then the pedestal sank to the ground. To Andi's great surprise, the bowl was clean.

She limped out into the bedroom, still leaning on the wall. The bedroom before her stood paneled ornately with wood. The ceiling was a zigzag pattern of wood. It was hard for Andi to resist the temptation to stand on her bed and touch the ceiling, but she was still too light-headed. There was a chair with the same royal purple fabric found on her bed and two lanterns. She peered inside one. A small candle burned cheerily in it, but to her great puzzlement, the lantern gave off a lot lighter than the candle was making. *Should it work like that?* Andi wondered. She felt grumpy with herself. Her head didn't feel as if it were bothering her, but the room kept moving ever so slightly.

Yet the most intriguing thing about the room was the *cylinder*. A large glass tube filled with water stood in the corner of the room. Andi approached it cautiously. It was huge. Enough to fit one person. She put her hands on the glass, feeling its thickness and curve. Looking up, she noticed that the cylinder-like aquarium rose through the room like a chimney. Suddenly she understood. *The ship. She was on the ship.*

It was then that Andi moved toward the window—a small, round window in the center of the wall opposite her bed. Andi looked outside and gasped. They were on the water! She undid the window latch, opened the glass pane, and peered out. She should have realized a lot earlier that they were on a ship. That was why the room had been moving! She had been so lightheaded from the fight. Other than realizing she was safe, the only other things she'd thought about were Lux, Artie, Jubal, and Donalys.

A splashing sound from below startled her. Andi laughed. It was Lux! He was jumping up at her from the water, spinning and diving. The joy on his face at seeing her was clear. It was such a contrast to the grief and fury she'd seen in him when they were both trapped in the cavern. He jumped high enough the next time that she was able to put her hand on his head. Lux stayed there, suspended in the air. Andi gasped, before remembering the image she had of him flying in the cavern with her and the Skull. Then when they flew out of the water leaving the Skull behind ...

Lux, can you fly? Andi was not eager for others to hear her voice. She had no idea what to expect. She wondered if Artie and Jubal were on the ship.

Learning, can levitate, so trying to fly. Lux responded. Probing into his mind, Andi sensed he didn't want to talk about what happened or even about his flying. He was just so happy to see her.

She stroked his soft, rubbery, glowing skin. *Lux, I'm sorry. I'm so, so sorry.* She shuddered, remembering what she'd asked Lux to do for Artie. It had been so wrong. She had already apologized to him down in the cavern but felt she needed to do it again when it was peaceful without anything between them.

Forgotten, the dolphin answered her. Then he pressed his beak-like rostrum against her mouth in a kiss. His joy echoed itself in her. Then he fell back into the water making a gigantic splash. Andi laughed.

A voice floated down to her from somewhere above. "Lux is not in the front of the ship with us anymore. I heard a splash on the side. Andi must be awake!" *Donalys.* She could understand him! Then she heard Jubal's voice.

"Donalys! Slow down! If she's awake, great, but we do not want to wake her up, not with that gash on her forehead." She heard a second and third set of footsteps following the first. She guessed Donalys was on his way to see her. Artie and Jubal wouldn't be far behind. *Thank God.* They were all right. She didn't know what they all were doing on this boat—this ship, she reminded herself—but they were all okay. For now. *Donalys.* She could understand him. *Something on the ship was translating for all of them!*

Gash? Andi put her hand to her forehead. There was a sort of bandage. Andi slide a finger under it, and the cut went deep. Then she remembered the Skull and shivered. She remembered its howl as she and Lux had burst out of the rocky passage. Bile rose in her mouth. She did not want to be ill again. She lay back on the bed to calm her stomach, preparing to see the boys.

Donalys burst through the door and jumped up and down by the bed. Despite herself, Andi laughed at him. He beamed at her and kept jumping. Turning to the door, he shouted, "She's awake! She's a-wake!" He kept jumping up and down to the sound of the word "a-wake," laughing as he said it. *Where did he learn how to speak?* Andi rolled over to see Artie and Jubal at the door. Artie's expression was unreadable. *Why?* Andi wondered. She was always able to read her twin.

Jubal nudged Artie through the doorway. Artie stumbled, falling on the bed. And when he got a closer look at Andi, he burst into tears. Saying nothing, he got on the bed and put his arm around her. She put her arm around him, and he put his head next to hers. Andi held her hand in front of her forehead, warning him not to collide with it. "Careful," she said, grinning.

Then she turned to Jubal, who stood awkwardly at the foot of the bed, looming tall over her with his hands in his pockets. "So, hey," he said. He motioned over to Donalys, who was continuing to jump up and down throughout the room. "Just so you know, Donalys has learned what the word 'awake' means. I think we said it so many times while we were waiting for you to wake up that he figured out what it meant."

"Oh," Andi said. "How are we able to understand Donalys?"

"Well," Jubal said, "Calypso *is* translating. But at the same time, Donalys is learning. Tell you the truth, we're all pretty sick of hearing him say the word 'awake.' I think he's been waiting for you to wake up just so he could show off." He grinned.

Andi laughed. Then she remembered. "Jubal, Artie," she said, "how long have I been asleep?" *And who was Calypso?*

Artie drew in his breath and looked at Jubal, who winced. "Yeah, about that," Jubal started.

A booming voice interrupted Jubal's explanation. Andi's bed moved, as if at the sound of the words.

"Ah. So the girl has awakened!" A tall heavyset man entered the room, barely able to pass through the door. He stood beaming at Andi with his arms wide open in a welcoming gesture. Andi recognized his voice as the gruff one that had said she was too much trouble. She wasn't sure whether she could trust his welcome. She realized he was the same on who had pinned Jubal and Artie down.

The man's thick red mustache and beard were the same red as

Odalys's. The man clasped his large hand on Donalys' shoulder, and the boy winced. The man shook his head at Donalys, who shrugged back at him and said, "A-wake! Andi's a-wake!"

"Fiery hailstones!" The man turned to Jubal. "Did we not agree he would stop using that fool word?" Jubal smiled at the man with some discomfort.

"Well," Jubal began, "he knows that the word 'awake' means that Andi would be back with us, that she'd come out of her coma."

Coma? Andi wondered. She was about to say something when the man's voice shocked her into silence again. "Enough!" he bellowed. Donalys' face went as red as his hair. His expression froze into one of obedience. *And fear?* Andi wondered.

"Space and sea!" The man bellowed. He pointed at Donalys while talking to Andi. "This young man," he continued, inclining his head toward Jubal, "tells me that you do not put up with Donalys' nonsense. Good!" Andi's eyes were wide. No one had ever *bellowed* at her like that.

"I am the Captain of this ship," the man continued. "I am also the boy's uncle." Donalys stared up at the man as he said this. The stare held a great depth of feeling and emotion, both good and bad. The man bowed toward her as much as his paunch would allow him. "I am Captain Zare Grubb, and I remain at your service, milady. Thank you for taking care of my nephew."

Captain Grubb? Andi began to giggle, but Artie pinched her shoulder, and Jubal shook his head, a violent no. Andi maintained a straight face. She rose rather unsteadily from the bed. Artie had worry written on his face. She knew she would have to make an impression on this man as "nothing but trouble."

Slowly, Andi rose her head to meet the Captain's eyes. "Why did you throw Donalys overboard?"

Andi thought she saw a flicker of humanity behind the Captain's eyes.

"Because," he sighed, "we were disappearing back into the world we came from. We were being *pulled* back in. I didn't know if we would have another chance. We were trapped there," again he paused, "for a very, very long time. I had hoped by throwing Donalys overboard that he would have a chance." He fell silent. "A better chance than the rest of us," he added.

Andi could not be sure that she would not have done the same thing.

. Andi curtsied as deeply as her lightheadedness would allow her. *Well, I guess we're even.* Captain Grubb could not bow down all the way because of his weight, and neither could she, because of her lightheadedness. His booming voice was so strong that it knocked Andi backward.

"A proper little lady!" he roared, slapping Jubal on the back so hard Jubal grimaced. He bent over and slapped Artie on the knee. Artie smiled tightly but otherwise showed no discomfort. "A proper little lady!" He smiled at Andi, who, despite her misgivings, could not help but feel that his smile was genuine. "Anyway, Calypso has a theory." *Who was this Calypso?*

"The more your dolphin used his power, the more able we were to break free and *stay* free." He made a little flourish as he finished his thought. "Cook wants to know what you want for your dinner," he said kindly in a lower voice. His eyes sparkled with amusement. *Amusement at her,* Andi realized. She looked at Donalys again, who stood at the side of her bed, his eyes shining with a desperate need for approval. Andi wanted to stand up for the boy.

"Captain," she began. "Your nephew is wonderful. I'm sure he gets it from you." She turned to Donalys. "Why don't *you* decide what we all should have for dinner? Heaven knows you've eaten enough of *our* stuff."

Captain Grubb leaned backward and broke out in laughter. He could not breathe for a few minutes. Jubal stepped toward him out of concern, putting his arm on Captain Grubb's. Captain Grubb shrugged it off, still laughing. He winked at Andi, showing her that he knew what she was doing. Humoring his nephew.

The Captain bowed again to them. He swept out of the room

grandly, pulling Donalys out with him by the collar. Donalys looked back at Andi in dismay. He did not want to leave her. The door closed behind them.

Jubal, Artie, and Andi waited for the footfalls to fade. Then the three of them all looked at each other and collapsed in helpless laughter.

"Captain Grubb?" Jubal gasped. "Looks like he has *plenty* of grub!" They all howled again, even Artie.

Finally they calmed down enough to talk.

"So," Andi said. "You never told me. How long have I been asleep?"

Jubal scratched the back of his head. "Yeah, about that—"

"How long, Jubal?" Andi's voice was steel.

He sighed. "A day."

A day. She turned to Artie in dismay. "Artie, Grandma Bea has until only tomorrow! Or is it the day after? And she'll be so sick with worry about us!" *We should have told her. We just didn't want to shock her so much that she would die from a heart attack or even lost her memories again.* Andi kept shaking her head because of her own carelessness.

"Andi," Jubal said, "they rowed me to shore. I called your grandmother. She thinks you two are at my house. It will be fine. But yeah, you and Artie do need to get back to shore kind of soon so that you know, you can ..."

Who was Calypso? Why were they all on this ship? What did Captain Grubb want with them? They needed to get ashore as soon as they could because of Grandma Bea.

Artie's face was in his hands. Andi had a million questions, but first she pulled her twin into her arms. "Artie, Artie." She held him close. "I'm so sorry you had to go through all that you did, not knowing where I was and seeing me like that. All that on top of worrying about Grandma Bea."

"Too much," Artie said.

Andi looked back in his eyes sadly. "Too much," she echoed.

After a moment, she turned to Jubal. "Jubal, who is Calypso?"

"I am she," the same lovely musical voice Andi had heard in her sleep rang out. Andi looked around, startled. Perhaps the most beautiful woman Andi had ever seen floated in the water-filled glass tube. Her skin was a peculiar light blue, and her eyes were much darker. Her hair was the same color as her skin, only darker, and it fell in curls all around her. She looked only twenty years old, but Andi sensed she was much older than that. She wore a gossamer dress that reached to her feet. The dress floated in the water as the woman bounced up and down in the watery tube. A trace of the woman's feet showed through the dress, but they were oddly shaped.

"I'm so happy to encounter you, Andi." Calypso smiled at her through the glass. "You seem to have a special connection with everyone here." Andi realized Calypso was referring to Lux as well, who she could feel swimming close by.

Calypso continued. "It has been so long since I have been able to see or converse with another woman. The crew," she smiled, "they are all men. As much as I love them, their company sometimes leaves me a little lonely." She smiled kindly to Andi. "I do not think you realize the impact you have had on little Donalys."

Little Donalys? But Donalys was only two years younger than she—or was he? But then again ... "You're the loveliest creature I've ever seen," Andi said. "You're ... just so beautiful. Who—what—are you?"

The woman laughed in the water. But her laughter was infectious. Even Artie had a huge grin. "You, yourself, Andi, are quite lovely." The woman paused, thinking before she continued.

"I am what you would call a selkie. Your friend Jubal has some rudimentary knowledge of the word. It makes me wonder if there are others of my kind in this world. I live in the water. But I am human, just like you are. I am ... different." She gave a rueful smile.

Calypso continued, "Jubal thinks that we change into animals when we are in the water and become human when we are on land. We do live in the water, but we cannot live on the land. We would die if we did so. Some of us served as navigators of the great ships of our people. Our people created these ships to help our land-dwelling counterparts travel the seas and in other ways."

Andi had so many questions, and she could not think of which one to ask next.

"Is it true?" she asked. "Is it true you were stuck somewhere else for thousands of years?"

Calypso closed her eyes. "Our understanding of time may be different from each other's. But yes, we found ourselves trapped for an immeasurable amount of time."

Sorrow entered her voice. "I should explain. You should know where we come from and what our circumstances have been. Our world experienced a great cataclysm. The stars rained down on us, and the land sank beneath the sea." She looked at Andi. "Our world had a unique relationship with the falling stars. This much you need to know for now. Suffice it to say that the relationship went awry and resulted in the falling stars crashing upon and impacting the land. It poisoned the seas and killed most of our people."

"I'm sorry, I didn't mean ..." Andi began, but Calypso smiled.

"It is necessary. We desire a relationship with you because of the creature you call Lux.

Of this we will speak later. Based on our interactions with your friends and the creature, I have come to believe that you are worthy of our friendship. And of our trust. I hope you will come to feel the same way about us." She paused. "Not everyone agrees with me, but I am the ship's navigator, after all."

Andi wondered at her words. So much lay hidden in them.

"Our leaders had a plan," Calypso continued. "A plan to save our people. The great ships we had created would embark to a new world, an uninhabited world. We could not save everyone; that much was clear. We created a lottery where the some of the land-dwellers and selkies would be chosen from. These lucky few would sail forward from our dying world to a new world that awaited us." She paused. "I was selected. One other sister of mine was selected. My mother was not. The rest of my family was not. We boarded the great ships. I took charge of the *Kronos*. Yes," she said, smiling at Andi, "that is the name of the ship you are on now."

Andi looked around her. The *Kronos*. It was nothing short of magnificent. Her head swam with all that she had learned. So much death and grief but such a strong desire to survive. How were these people any different from her and Artie? She shivered.

"After the creation of the ships, only the Captains and navigators knew the results of the lottery. No one from the general population knew the results. It was the Captain's responsibility to disclose to those chosen where to rendezvous with the ship. We shared the news with those selected at the very end. How do you say it? The last minute?"

"Two terrible mistakes we made doomed us. At least, that is what some of us on the ship believe."

"Do *you* think it?" Andi asked curiously.

The selkie smiled at her. Then her face became serious. "One was a mistake of love. I

cannot condemn that. The other ... it doomed us." A faraway look appeared on her face, filled with such deep loneliness and longing that it pained Andi to the heart.

"Before the decision to create the great ships, we investigated several other options. None came to fruition." Her voice became hard. "Except one." She looked hard at them before continuing.

"A man named Portent created a terrible and evil thing. An abomination. He created life from nothing. It is a terrible wrong to create life from nothingness. The creature he made ... it was not alive. And yet it formed a consciousness of its own. And it had the power to destroy stars."

"It foretold destruction. Its purpose was to swallow the stars as they crashed upon the planet, thereby saving us from destruction."

Jubal interrupted. "But wasn't that the point? To avoid destruction? It seems that this thing Portent made might have been a good thing."

Calypso nodded sadly. "It did indeed seem like a good thing—at first. But the first star fell toward us early. We tested the creature on it."

Artie raised his hand as if he were in class asking a question. Calypso looked at him in fond amusement, and Jubal chuckled. Even Andi, in the middle of such a horrible story, had to grin at her twin. Artie looked around at them awkwardly before asking the question.

"Excuse me," he asked, "but these stars that crashed onto the planet, when you talk about them, do you mean comets?"

The selkie smiled at Artie. "From glancing through your mind, I think that yes, your word 'comet' describes what I mean."

"So when you say that this creature had the power to destroy stars, do you mean just comets or more than that?" Artie asked.

The selkie nodded in her glass tube. "Yes, more. This creature had the power to destroy suns." Her face was somber. Artie nodded, indicating that he understood and wanted her to continue. Artie hated interrupting others. Andi patted him on the shoulder.

"So, as the first *comet* fell," Calypso smiled at Artie, "we positioned the creature. It was ready to swallow the comet. And swallow it, it did. But he did more than swallow it. He didn't just destroy it. He erased it from existence."

"This threw our world in imbalance. We knew we did not have a lot of time left." She shook her head with sadness. "After that horrible tragedy," Calypso whispered, still lost in the horror of it, "our leaders asked Portent to destroy the creature. He said he would."

"But he didn't," Jubal guessed.

"Your guess is correct." Calypso's voice answered, laced with something close to hatred. "Portent was preselected to ride aboard the *Kronos*. There was no denying his intelligence. There was a lot that he offered our people. He was one of the few selected by our leaders to be one of the survivors. It was before the actual lottery began. But it seems that Portent snuck the Skull in among his belongings."

Andi froze. "What did you say?" Andi was dizzy.

Calypso put her hand on the glass, reaching for Andi. "Are you all right?" she asked.

"Tell me about the Skull," Andi said dully. Her forehead began to throb. Pain coursed through her eyes, causing Andi to blink rapidly.

"He created the creature from the remains of a Skull. Portent created a life from nothingness and imbued it into the Skull." Calypso hesitated. "The Skull took on ... different properties as a result. It became different from just a simple Skull."

Andi wanted to ask another question, but she was too afraid. She decided to let Calypso finish her story.

"So when Portent snuck the Skull onto the ship, he brought a deadly force aboard. Not only that, but it was also alive with no right of being so." Calypso looked at them. "The great ships were able to travel to a new world. To be clearer, we discovered a wormhole leading to this planet. Being a seafaring people, they and we were able to reconfigure the great ships into vessels that would survive travel through a wormhole—and in space. But our vessels were interdependent on each other. We all needed each other to make it to the new world."

"The Skull threw it into imbalance by just being aboard!" Jubal guessed. "You had no way of knowing, so that's how you ended up where you were," Jubal's excited voice rang in the room. He was proud of having put it all together. "You could carry only so many people aboard at a time, so without having the proper amount of energy ..." He snapped his fingers. "What happened to the other vessels? You said you were interdependent on each other."

Calypso looked sad. "We do not know, Jubal."

"What was the first mistake?" Andi asked. "You said it was for love."

Calypso sighed. "No matter what we have gone through or where we have been, I would not change it for anything," she answered firmly.

"What was it?" Andi was direct.

Calypso's face was sad. "Our leaders agreed that none of the Captains could bring family on board with them. The people who won the lottery who were able to come with us ... the Captains all had to feel the same grief and sorrow we all experienced at leaving our loved ones behind."

"Oh God," Andi said. She understood. Both boys looked at her curiously.

"Captain Grubb had one other brother. The brother and his mate conceived just before our people learned about the threat the comets posed to us. The Captain's parents were dead. His brother was older. So was his wife. They were not chosen in the lottery. So they asked the Captain to take Donalys. Captain Grubb agreed."

She sighed. "Captain Grubb told me just before the great ships departed. I told him that since Donalys was a baby that it would be fine. It would not need much change to calibrate the great ship for a baby." Calypso looked bitter.

"But with Portent ... and with the Skull aboard ... that much power ..." Jubal guessed, waiting.

"Yes, yes, it threw us off balance to the point that when we discovered Portent had the Skull on the ship, we ejected him—and the Skull—off the ship. But it was already too late." Calypso's eyes were sad. "We found ourselves alone in what you refer to as the purple world. Separated from the other great ships. We were paralyzed. We could not think, feel, nothing."

Jubal interjected. "If you were stuck in limbo for so long ... how did Donalys learn how to talk? Grow to be ten years old?" He looked puzzled. "Wouldn't he still be a baby?"

"I've told you all that you need to know for now. There will be other stories told later." She smiled gently. "All right?"

Artie nodded, satisfied. But Andi was not done.

"So," she began. "You threw Donalys overboard because ..."

Calypso answered. "We were being pulled back into the other world, other dimension—whatever it is—where we had been as unmoving statues. The Captain thought that the risk was great enough to give the youngest person on this ship a chance at life. But when we were pulled back into the other world, we weren't paralyzed. And so we kept looking for a door back here, and eventually we found one." She looked at Andi. "You do know that when your dolphin uses his powers, there is an equally great and opposite response to it."

"I know that now," Andi admitted. "I'm just glad he was able to break you out."

Calypso smiled. "So am I. Even if he did not know he was doing it at the time."

Jubal interrupted. "You weren't sure you could break out again. You broke out, then disappeared again, back into that—that," he grasped for words. "That prison. That limbo."

Calypso nodded. "We did not have much time to act. We wanted someone to survive. Donalys is the youngest of our crew. He deserved a chance to live. We knew a hole had opened, drawing us back into that strange world. We decided to throw Donalys overboard in the hopes of giving him some chance of survival. We knew we were putting him in great danger by throwing him overboard. It was the Captain's decision. He thought the danger of Donalys being drawn back into the other world was greater than if we threw him overboard. At least he had some chance." Calypso looked up at them. "Then we returned. And this time, there was no portal drawing us back into where we were paralyzed. We were free. Probably because of the increased activity of your golden creature's powers." She beamed at them.

Andi was quiet. The crew of the *Kronos* had gone through so much. Sacrificed so much.

"Then we began searching for Donalys." Calypso smiled. "That is how we came to find and meet you."

"I have one more question," Andi said, her voice shaking.

Calypso looked at her. "What is it?"

Andi's voice was flat and monotone. "The Skull. It had wings like a butterfly? Horns on its head?"

Calypso's face froze. She stretched her hand toward Andi, from inside her watery tube. But it was the answer Andi needed.

The Skull was still alive.

Eighteen

Navigation Lines

The Captain decided to steer the *Kronos* as closely as it could get to the shore near her home. Andi worried that Grandma Bea would see the ship coming from the sea toward her and have a heart attack. That was when Jubal stepped in.

"Andi," he reassured her, "we're hidden in the small curve of the bay. No one can see us unless they come directly down to the shore, and so far, no one has. It's your property and even you guys can't see it from your house!"

This made Andi feel a little nervous, but Jubal was right. He had it all figured out, didn't he? Not even they, from their cliffside home, could see directly below where the small curve of the bay was.

"What did happen to Portent?" Andi wondered. She was afraid that he, too, might have made it into this world, like the Skull had.

"We do not know, Andi," Calypso explained. "We ejected them both from the ship when we realized Portent had the Skull. But then it was too late for us. That is when we found ourselves in that other world. It is possible that Portent himself is in this world, but I do not think so. He and the Skull seem to have been separated. For all we know, Portent is dead."

Andi began hesitantly. "I think, I think it was Lux and I that freed you. From the paralysis you were in." She then told Calypso about her and Lux's jump from their planet to the purple and silvery world and how when Andi had touched the *Kronos*, it had come alive.

Calypso stared at her openmouthed. "So ... you are our savior. You are the one who brought us back."

"Please don't say that," Andi answered, blushing. "I really didn't know what I was doing. But you *knew* what you were doing, having me brought aboard. Please tell me how to help you. After all you've done for me, I'll do anything." She wasn't sure about Captain Grubb, but she trusted Calypso infinitely. "What do you want Lux for?"

"Andi, the boys have told me about your circumstances, and I think we can help you. But I don't think we should talk about it right now."

Andi nodded enthusiastically, a little confused but for once not suspicious. Andi was unburdened and free. Lux was back. Grandma Bea was okay, and she would have time to say good-bye. She hoped Grandma Bea would not be mad at her for not telling the truth. They had been so afraid at what the news might do to her.

Calypso had told her privately that she would need to let Captain Grubb know that Portent's Skull was still alive and very close to them. It didn't matter if the Skull was trapped or not. She asked Andi if she could tell the Captain after dinner. "Because, well, the Captain likes his dinner," she explained with a twinkle in her eye. "I don't want to interrupt that for him."

Andi climbed up the stairs to the top deck. The Captain's table was in a stateroom with a glassed ceiling and many windows. The boys were already there, and so was Donalys. His eyes were puffy and red-rimmed. He avoided meeting her gaze as she walked by him. Seized by a sudden urge, she asked Artie, "Do you mind?" Her twin understood her perfectly. Andi placed her hand in Donalys', and he looked up at her in surprise and mute adoration. She pulled him out of his chair and seated him next to where she sat, at the head of the table, directly opposite Captain Grubb.

Andi leaned over to Donalys and whispered a word to him mischievously. "A-wake!" The Captain looked up at her, startled. He smiled uncertainly at her. Andi smiled sweetly at him. Donalys clasped his hand to his mouth to cover up his laughing. Calypso rose into the tube directly behind the Captain's chair.

Andi heard laughter enter her mind. She gasped. She saw through the window that Lux was floating over the water near them. She got up, went outside, and hugged him hard. Suddenly, she investigated his mind, seeing blood stream down her forehead, suspended in the air, begging him not to risk himself.

All right? Lux asked.

"Perfect," Andi said.

The dolphin did not lower himself back into the sea but floated just above her, staying near her window the entire dinner. Andi realized this made the Captain very nervous. He gulped a drink down and examined her more closely. He pointed to Lux with a strange utensil that he had just been eating with.

"You can talk with him?" Andi saw this made the Captain nervous.

"We're very close," she said. "We can read each other's thoughts. Talk with our minds." What was she doing? She was egging the Captain on, playing on his fears. Andi knew she shouldn't be doing that. If only he hadn't yelled at Donalys.... He *must* be nice, right? He hadn't wanted his nephew to die...

"Can you talk to him for us?" Captain Grubb asked the question awkwardly, as if he did not want to depend on a twelve-year-old girl.

So. They needed her to talk to Lux. But why? Andi realized she was feeling suspicious again.

"Is that why we're all here? So that I can talk to him for you?" she asked.

There was a long silence at the table before Captain Grubb said, "He will not speak with us, which is why we need you."

Andi continued eating, selecting food from her plate. She said in a much smaller, more dignified voice, "I see. That explains a lot."

Jubal kicked her under the table. But she didn't care. The Captain had gotten on her nerves with how he treated Donalys. *Even though he had been trying to save his life,* she admitted to herself grudgingly.

"Will you help us?" Captain Grubb's voice betrayed a hint of desperation.

"Even though I attract trouble wherever I go?" Andi asked sweetly, making eye contact with the Captain. "Make up your mind, Captain. Am I helping you or am I making trouble for you?"

"Girl, you are going too far!" he bellowed, slamming his fist on the table. Artie looked shocked. Jubal was making the slitting-your-throat-with-a-knife gesture at her. But Andi stared the Captain in the face.

"I find it disgraceful, Captain, how you treat your nephew. I find it horrifying that you would refer to a person whose help you need as someone who attracts trouble wherever she goes."

Artie was rocking in his chair, back and forth and back and forth. Andi hung her head. *Oh no.* She *had* gone too far.

But then the Captain did something completely unexpected. He sat back in his chair and roared with laughter. "By the universe! You are a grand girl." He stood up and turned to Calypso. "When was the last time you heard someone speak to me that way?"

"Never." Calypso's answer was unequivocal. She smiled at Andi.

The Captain slapped his knees in agreement.

He came around the table and put his hands in Andi's. "Girl, you can sail with me anywhere as far as I am concerned."

Andi froze. *Sail with him?* She looked over at Artie. His hands were over his ears, and he continued to rock back and forth, his eyes closed. Jubal looked as if he had swallowed something enormous and wasn't sure if it was going to go down or not.

"Sir," Andi began, getting up to her feet, bending over Artie. "I'm sorry I was rude. I'll try not to do that again." She murmured what she hoped were soothing words in Artie's ears. He slowed down his rocking but didn't stop.

"By God, I hope you do, girl. I need it." The Captain wasn't laughing anymore. Indeed, he appeared quite sober. He motioned rather rudely to Artie as if to ask, *What?*

"I think I need to take him downstairs and be alone with him, to calm him down a bit. Is that okay?" she asked the Captain. He nodded, still confused at what was wrong with Artie. She murmured again into Artie's ear, and he nodded slowly. Andi tugged at his shoulder. He put his arm around her, and she put hers around him.

Andi and Artie descended the stairs. Andi looked around. They were on a deck. It was too public. Slowly she motioned to her twin to follow her to the bedroom.

Andi tripped in the hallway as she opened what looked to be a door into her bedroom. It wasn't. It opened into a larger room, completely dark. Her arm bumped against something that fell with several loud thuds onto the floor. Andi let go of Artie. Kneeling, she rummaged around on the floor in the dark. Her hand finally felt cold metal. Slowly, she and Artie went back out into the hall. She had several bars of gold in her hands. Not the kind of bars of gold that were shaped into shapes of brick. These bars weren't heavy. No, these bars of gold were oval. Quickly, she unloaded some of them into Artie's arms.

Silently, Andi went back into the dark room and came out with as many gold bars as she could carry. Andi could tell that Artie understood what she was doing and why she was doing it. Andi finally found her bedroom and motioned her twin to follow her inside.

Artie collapsed in her arms right after depositing the bars onto her bed. He slapped her on her shoulder. He was really upset, Andi realized.

"Why?" Artie screamed. "Why?"

Andi grabbed him by the arms and made her look at him. "Artie, I did it because it's disgusting how the Captain treats Donalys. *It is disgusting,* and someone had to protect him. I'm sorry." She hesitated. Finally she said, "His mood changed awfully fast. Don't you think?" She hoped this would calm him down.

Artie answered. "Captain of a ship. Hard decisions."

"I don't think I'm overreacting, Artie." Andi was mad. "He needs to treat Donalys with consideration."

"He does," Artie said. "He didn't try to save himself. He didn't jump overboard to save his own life. He wanted to save Donalys'." Andi was alarmed. This was a lot for Artie to say all at once. And he was right. She had misjudged the Captain.

Finally Andi spoke. "You're right, Artie. You are right." Andi sighed. "I'm putting off going home, you know? Grandma Bea will come right to us as we come through the door. And then, and then—I don't want to think about that." Andi didn't cry. She was out of tears for now.

Artie nodded. He paused. "How?"

Andi frowned. "How what?"

"Grandma?"

"How will she die? I don't know, Artie." Andi took in a deep breath. "I don't know, but one thing I do know. We do it together. We say good-bye to her together." She held her hand out to him. He took it.

"Okay." He smiled at her, finally.

They slowly walked the stairs. They emerged back up on to the main deck. She could see their house from this point right on top of their cliff. *It was coming,* Andi realized.

Soft footsteps approached them. Andi turned. It was Jubal. She went to him, an apology on her lips, but Jubal waved it off. He smiled, amused. "That Captain is very taken with you."

Andi shrugged. "Because I tell him the truth? He hasn't heard the truth for maybe thousands—no, millions of years." She smiled up at Jubal before finishing. "Must be a refreshing change for him. I don't know." She was very tired, and as much as she dreaded doing so, she was ready to go home.

Jubal looked at her. "You're ready to go home?"

"Yes," Andi said. "I'm going to ask them a few questions before we leave though." She paused. "Jubal," she said slowly, "can I use your backpack?" He'd brought the backpack with him when he was camping outside on top of the Cliff. When they'd captured them, Andi guessed they'd brought his backpack on board.

"Huh? Oh I see. Sure. Here you go." Jubal handed his almost-empty backpack to her. She dumped the armload of gold bars she had in them. She marveled at how *light* they were.

Jubal pointed backwards with his thumb. "Calypso just told the Captain about the Skull and what really happened to you." His voice was somber. "He doesn't believe it. I think you better go help her explain everything, Andi."

Andi sighed and began to walk toward the staircase up to the Captain's table. As she did, Lux rose in front of her from the sea. She stopped, allowing Artie and Jubal to continue ahead without her.

Proud of you, her little dolphin told her. Andi realized he'd grown over the last two weeks. He wasn't so little anymore.

"Why?" she said aloud.

Artie. Lux cocked his head toward Artie's departing figure. *He feels your love.*

Andi sighed. "I hope he always does."

You teach me how to keep my heart strong. With that, Lux lowered himself back into the sea. Andi's eyes watered.

When she reached the deck, she came across Calypso tall in her glass tube, her arms folded, staring at Captain Grubb with a stern look.

"I cannot accept this," Captain Grubb said, sinking heavily into a chair. He pointed his finger at Calypso. The larger tube that Calypso floated in was the tower Andi had seen from so far away that other night. A solid gold steering wheel was attached to the outside of the cylindrical tower for Captain Grubb, presumably to steer. And Calypso floated in the tube right behind it, to navigate. They made quite a team, Andi thought admiringly.

Calypso sighed, her arms folded across her chest as she looked at Captain Grubb. Andi realized that Calypso was used to the Captain's outbursts and had probably learned how to navigate her way around them. *Navigate.* Andi smiled, thinking about how the word had a double meaning when it came to Calypso. What lay ahead of them still haunted and nagged at her but being on the *Kronos* was wonderful. It felt strangely like *home*. People here cared about them.

Andi realized that ever since she'd found out about Grandma Bea that the house standing on the cliff way above the ship looking down on her no longer felt like home. She wondered if Artie felt the same way.

"Zare, I know you feel that it is impossible, but examine the evidence for a minute," Calypso responded soothingly, pressing her hand on the glass, reaching out to the Captain.

"We ejected them from the ship. We had no idea where they went. After we escaped that, that limbo we were stuck in, we found ourselves here. Wouldn't it stand to reason that we might find the Skull here too?" She nodded toward Andi. "The Skull is here. They trapped the creature in an underwater passage. Yet how long can it stay there, Zare? Answer me. How long?"

Captain Grubb's cheeks were a fierce red by now, matching his hair and whiskers perfectly. Instead of answering in his customary bellow, he whispered, "I can't believe it's come to this. All this time trapped ... only to be free then ... we find it here." He stared at Calypso.

"Zare," Calypso said quietly yet firmly. "We have found the golden creature. We can go home."

Home? Andi wondered what Calypso meant by this.

"That's only if she agrees," the Captain said with a scowl. He turned in his chair to Andi. "This one's a firebrand, aye, she is at that, spark all over."

"And all heart inside," Calypso said, still firm, but with a smile on her face.

Andi could not contain herself any longer.

"I'm sorry, you said something about Lux taking you home? Where? The home you came from or the home you were trying to get to in the first place?" Her voice was level, yet behind it was a note of steel. She'd fought that evil creature in a deep cavern that, for all anyone knew, wasn't even really part of this world at all. She still had a hard time wrapping her head around Artie and Jubal's idea of a pocket universe.

"Your creature," the Captain began gravely, "can it move from one point to another," he spread his hands apart while doing it, "without traveling the intervening distance?"

Andi frowned. The way Captain Grubb described it, it made sense.

Andi answered hesitantly. "I think he can. We call it teleporting. I'm not sure if he's mastered it yet. Sometimes we just, you know, disappear, and then we find ourselves in another place." Andi's head hurt as she said this.

"So he can create tunnels?" Calypso asked intently.

"I—I'm not quite sure what you mean," Andi stammered. She was growing tired of this. She was ready to go back to shore, to see Grandma Bea and to say good-bye.

"I'm sorry, Andi," Calypso said, studying Andi. "We have been lost and stranded for so long that we are eager to find our people again, to create a real home of our own."

Andi knew the uncertainty Calypso was referring to. For so long, she had lived in fear of her grandmother's memory loss being found out and both she and Artie being taken away from their home. She understood the need to find and call a place home. She looked up to the house atop the cliff. It was the only home she had ever known, and very soon it would be home no longer.

"I can understand that," Andi replied finally.

"Andi," Calypso replied, her face grave, "Artie and Jubal told us that your grandmother is dying and that you have no other place to go. We need him—we need your Lux to take us home." She stared at Andi intently as she said this. "You would have a home with us. We would be very happy have you." She looked at the Captain. "The Captain is ... well, the Captain—but you have already gotten under his skin." Andi looked at the Captain, but he was looking at his shoes, refusing to meet either Calypso or Andi in the eyes.

"Here?" Andi was stunned. She turned to Jubal accusingly. "Did you know about this?"

He met her eyes guiltily. "They need you, Andi. Well, they need Lux, which means that they need you too, since you're the only one who can talk with him. Because you're bonded or something like that? I think Lux understands the rest of us just fine, but because your minds are tied together, you're the only one he'll talk to. The only one he *can* talk to," she amended.

"Andi," Calypso said, "I cannot read Lux. But I can read his body language, his movements. He is devoted to you. And I can read you. You feel the same way. Because of your bond, he cannot leave here without you. And he would never do so anyway because of your mutual devotion to one another." She smiled.

"H-how?" Andi stammered. "How would Lux do this?"

Calypso smiled gently at her. "He would take us into space. Where we would search for our people."

Space? Andi was openmouthed at the idea.

Jubal said jokingly but with a serious undertone, "It would be like the reindeer pulling Santa's sleigh." But Andi understood what he meant. So. Lux would be pulling the *Kronos* out into space.

The Captain broke into her reverie. "Young lady, you say I do not love my nephew. 'Tis true enough I do not know how to bring up a boy. Yet I set out on this journey intending for our Donalys to have a home. To have some knowledge of his heritage. I would like to give him that at least, after everything ..." He faltered.

Andi turned to Artie. "Is this what you want?" she asked quietly. "To live here? On this ship? To travel with them?" *Space?* She wondered again.

Artie nodded, his eyes shining. Andi understood. So many of the islanders regarded Artie as someone who was damaged, who was something less than. *Someone less than.* On this ship, he could maybe be seen as unique, as someone who had something to offer. She hoped so. If Artie understood pocket universes, then he could be a real asset to the *Kronos*.

"This gold," Andi said abruptly, changing the subject. She unzipped Jubal's backpack and showed it to them. "May we have it?" Her stomach churned. She was being presumptuous, and she knew it.

The Captain sized her up carefully while Calypso had a sad smile on her face.

"As currency?" The Captain asked.

Andi nodded.

"You may have it," he said magnanimously. "But I hope you come back," he ended, a shadow on his face. Andi knew that the Captain knew she and Artie could use this gold to run off. It was a sign of his trust in her, she realized. That nearly made up her mind. But first ...

"I'm going to have to say good-bye to my grandmother before I can think of anything else," she answered quietly. "Do you think, do you think ..." Andi was shocked at how tired and strained her voice sounded suddenly. "Do you think we could go to shore now?"

Captain Grubb nodded as he got to his feet and started ordering the crew to prepare a boat to take them to shore. She stared up to the house on top of the cliff. *This is it.* Andi braced herself. *One way or another, this was it.*

Nineteen

Crossing Over

Before they climbed down to the lower decks, Calypso beckoned to Andi and then pressed her hand against the side of the tube. Andi understood she was to touch the same spot so that their hands would meet, separated only by glass. When she did, she had a sudden vision of something old, beautiful, ancient, and lost. A people with Calypso's color skin swam in the sea. She heard songs sung in the water. Andi marveled at Calypso's comfort in the memories, comfort followed by a shockingly cold tide of loss. Yet Andi felt the truth: Calypso was upheld by the memories she had, by the love she felt within.

"I didn't know you could do that!" Andi exclaimed.

Calypso grinned at her through the glass. "How else do you think I've been able to translate? I've had to look in all your minds for words and their meanings. I haven't violated any memories of yours, of course," the selkie added hastily.

"I trust you." Andi grinned. Her mind returned to what Calypso had shown her.

Calypso answered her unspoken questions. "The love is still there." She examined Andi closely. "It hasn't disappeared. Do you understand?"

Andi nodded. It was too much to bear. She understood the opposite was true: while it might be too much to bear, Calypso could never bear to lose her memories. *A paradox*, Andi realized, remembering Jubal's definition of what a paradox was. Two opposite things being equally true, or two things existing that should not exist in the same place at the same time. Yet Jubal never used the word paradox in matters of the heart. It was always used in science or math or something else.

Andi realized that she didn't remember her mother or father in the same way Calypso remembered hers. Her father had left when she was so young and didn't have time to know him. There had been no explanation for her mother's presumed death. She'd had no closure. But she knew that she would remember Grandma Bea in the same way Calypso did her people. She would remember her with longing and laughter. With comfort and sorrow and loss and grief and thankfulness for having had her at all. The enormity of it was enough to knock her backward onto the chair the Captain had been sitting on.

"Andi!" Calypso cried, alarmed. "You're in the Captain's chair! Don't—" But it was too late. The Captain entered exactly when Andi was reclining in his chair. But instead of losing his temper as Calypso believed he would, he just laughed.

"The lady!" he muttered under his breath. "The lady!" He chuckled as crewmen cleaned the Captain's table. Calypso gave Andi a quizzical look. Gulping, she jumped up.

The Captain had arranged for a boat to take Andi, Artie, and Jubal to shore. A crew member asked the three of them to follow him to the small boat. The boat slid down to the sea. The sun was just starting to set, shining through the fog. A crewman rowed them to shore while Lux swam alongside. Tired and overwhelmed, Andi let her hand glide on the water. Lux enjoyed coming up from below so that her hand rested on his head. It was a game Andi was happy to play. It kept her mind off what was to come.

Andi fixed her eyes on the ship as they rowed toward shore. Andi stared at the ship. The *Kronos* consisted of thick wood. She noted that the wood was whole; she could not tell where one part ended, and another began. Andi finally concluded that the trees or wood where the people of the *Kronos* came from must be incredibly huge. It looked as if the *Kronos* had been carved out of a single piece of wood. Then the *Kronos* began to fade out of sight in the gathering fog.

They disembarked the boat near her mother's cave. Andi made sure Lux was situated there before she headed up the ridge path with the boys. Jubal bade them farewell. Andi had not realized that Jubal would part from them here.

Upon arriving at the top of the cliff, Jubal put his hand on her shoulder. "Listen, Andi." His voice was serious. "I need to talk to my mother about ... a few things. About a lot of things. Then I'll meet up with you soon, okay? To say good-bye." He smiled a sad and sweet smile before walking down Edge Street toward the village below. For a moment, Andi watched his departing figure, feeling lonely. She'd been with so many people on the ship, and now it was just her and Artie.

What did Jubal mean he needed to talk to his mother? About what? Surely he wasn't going to tell her about everything that'd happened. His mother would think Jubal was a lunatic.

Andi turned and put her arm around Artie. "Let's do this," she said. Together, they trudged up the way to the house that lay atop the cliff. They both knew that soon the house would no longer be theirs.

They entered quietly. It was so cold Andi could see her breath. Grandma Bea had turned down the heat, trusting that blankets would be enough to keep everyone warm. As soon as they opened the door into the house, they heard their grandmother moving around in her bedroom.

Artie turned to her. "Now what?" he asked.

"Tell her the truth," she replied with finality.

They sat on the couch holding hands. They heard their grandmother descend the stairs. Grandma Bea turned from the stairway into the living room and shouted.

"Andi! Artie! The two of you gave me such a scare!" Andi could not read Grandma Bea's face. She hoped Grandma Bea could not read hers. Dread and sorrow were welling up in her. She could feel the tension in Artie's hand as his grip grew stronger.

Grandma Bea finally spoke. "I get the feeling that you two haven't been at Jubal's house. Am I wrong or am I going crazy?"

This was what Andi had been waiting for. "Grandma," she began, her voice clear and strong, "it is time for us to tell you everything. But first, let me tell you that you're not crazy. I think I might be crazy." She laughed. "But you're not. So much has happened over the last week and half. Right, Artie?" She looked at her twin.

Artie's face was white. His eyes glittered with tears in a face so white it made Grandma Bea ask, "Are you sick, Artie? Maybe what you need is—"

"I think," Andi said, cutting her off, "that we just need to explain." Grandma Bea sat back, her eyes open and curious.

Andi told her about the walk up the cliff when she'd heard that unforgettable song. She explained about finding Lux's mother, of her directive to find Lux. She described Lux and their incredible bond. She shared about the trip she'd taken with Lux to another world, her injury, and the place Lux sent her to heal. She showed her grandmother the scar. And about waking up in her bed and finding out there'd been an earthquake. She explained that she'd asked Lux to restore Grandma's memory.

Andi chose not to tell her grandmother what Lux had said about her dying. Not yet. Grandma Bea licked her lips as if letting everything sink in and did not contradict her granddaughter.

Andi continued by explaining about Donalys and the trip to see their father. She even gave Grandma Bea the exact address of his home. She described the *Kronos* popping in and out of reality. She explained how Jubal theorized they had been stuck for a long time in some other place with maybe no sense of time. She told her about Donalys, the Skull and Captain Grubb and Calypso.

Finally, Andi swallowed hard, finishing her story. She looked at the clock, filled with dread. Time was passing inexorably.

Grandma Bea sat in her chair looking at Andi and Artie with a bemused expression. She sat there forever, not saying anything. Andi glanced over at Artie. His face was white, and she guessed hers was too. Grandma Bea got to her feet and went up the stairs. The twins stared at each other. Was she angry? So upset she wouldn't speak to them? Then they heard her feet on the stairs again, coming downstairs. She was wearing jeans, a rain slicker, and boots.

"Show me," she said simply.

The twins looked at each other and then leapt to their feet. Andi began to push out her mind toward Lux, although she was sure he would just feel the fact that she was coming to Mom's cave and needed him. They walked out the door with flashlights. They walked down single file down the ridge path. Her grandmother walked slowly, navigating its little footfalls. Finally they reached the thin strip of rocky beach that lay under the small jut of the hill of the haunt's cliff face. They could feel the wetness of the rock through their shoes as they kept moving toward the mouth of the inlet cave. Every now and then, her grandmother looked out to sea toward where the *Kronos* was hidden, wrapped by fog and night, trying to make it out. Andi knew if she couldn't see it, neither could Grandma Bea.

As they approached, a faint light glowed from the mouth of her mother's cave. Her little dolphin was there waiting for them, and finally Grandma would know that she was going to die. They entered the cavern.

The light became brighter. Then Lux showed himself. He stood tall on the water before them, balancing himself again on his fins. Lux always looked like he was smiling (and indeed Andi knew that he was always smiling inside), but today he was not. He stood before the three of them solemnly as he continued to balance himself on the water. He danced on his fluke on top of the water, much brighter than he usually was. He drew near them.

Grandma Bea's arms stretched toward him, and then she hesitated. Andi prompted her.

"Go ahead, Grandma. He wants you to."

Grandma Bea looked at Andi, nodded, and then stepped forward toward Lux. He came to her, as tall as she was. Grandma Bea put her hands on Lux's sides. A sense of profound pleasure emanated from Lux at the fact that she had finally brought her grandmother. His golden sheen shone through the space between Grandma Bea's fingers.

"He's just lovely," Grandma Bea declared. She looked back at Andi and Artie. "He—he's a miracle."

Feeling her grandmother's joy, Andi spoke silently to Lux. *You can't do anything for her? It's impossible?*

Cannot do it. Want to, she heard him say sadly. *Want anything? Try give.*

Andi voiced aloud, "Lux wants to know if he can do anything for you. He feels honored by your visit." She was close to tears.

"Can I speak to him?" Grandma Bea asked.

"Yes, yes, you can," Andi said. "He understands you just fine."

Grandma Bea let go of the dolphin and stepped back so she could see his face as she spoke to him.

"Hi, Lux. I'm Bea. I'm their Grandma Bea." She cocked her head at Andi and Artie who stood just behind her. Wild, joyful, unearthly music filled the cavern. Grandma Bea looked around her in wonderment.

"I'm dying," she said to Lux, shocking both Andi and Artie. "I'm sure that you, being whatever—whoever—you are, already know that. I—I found out from a doctor."

The music changed to a more sorrowful tone. Andi looked at Artie. His face looked pained, but there was a sort of peace within it, an acceptance. She understood, feeling the same way. Lux's dorsal fin touched Grandma Bea's face, brushing against her cheek. After Lux glided backwards to the center of the pool, Grandma put her hand on where Lux had touched her, as if treasuring the touch.

"My question is," she continued, "what's going to happen to them? Andi and Artie? I love them both more than anything in this world. They are my heroes. They've gone through so much more than they should have at such a young age." Grandma Bea looked up at the roof of the cavern.

"Andi is a nurturer. She doesn't know it, but she is. She loves so deeply and so fully that she becomes depleted. And yet she goes on loving. It's as if she can't help it. Her just being there has been—"

Grandma Bea's voice broke off into a sob. "She keeps me afloat. A child shouldn't do that for an adult. Really, they shouldn't. Yet she has. She's so smart. In fact, she's brilliant. But there is no division between her mind and heart. Because of that, she takes everything in. She has no filter. She knows and understands so much, too much sometimes. I'm afraid for her. So many people will try to use that for their own selfish needs and purposes." Grandma Bea stopped talking as if the effort was too much. She took in a deep breath and started again.

"Artie's mind is like a labyrinth. And only he knows all the turns and crooks of that labyrinth. Even if you follow him, you don't always get to the end of the labyrinth with him. Sometimes you do, sometimes you don't. But whenever you do come to the end of the labyrinth, it's such a different way of seeing the world and how it works. I need that viewpoint. It's so hard to get to that place, but whenever I do, I find that everything I know to be true, and right is only part of the picture. There's so much more, so much more."

"But see here, Lux the dolphin, this is the thing. Andi loves Artie so much, and he loves her back equally. They make each other who they are. I don't think Andi could love so much if it weren't for Artie. And I don't think Artie would ever be able to come to the end of the labyrinth himself if Andi weren't there."

Andi's eyes were wet, and she could see Artie's eyes were, too. The reality of death floated all around them. In front of Andi, Grandma Bea's solitary figure trembled. She was a silhouette against Lux's deep golden glow.

"My question is," Grandma Bea continued, addressing Lux, "what's going to happen to them? Are you strong enough to protect them? To keep them from parting, separating from one another? I see them going to separate homes, because one suits Andi better while Artie's needs are met by going somewhere else. I don't see any other way around it." Her voice was pleading.

The twins looked at each other again. Andi grimaced. *So all her suspicions were correct. No one would take them, not even her father. Her stomach* turned as she remembered the image of her father and little half-brother she'd seen through the window.

Andi, Lux's voice rang through her head. *Will speak.*

Can you? Andi asked.

The bond is very close. Between you and the grandma. I can do it. There was silence for a moment before Lux acknowledged his struggle with two words: *Very hard.*

Andi understood. Lux could not speak into minds with ease except for hers because they were ... bonded? Because of her bond with her grandmother, Lux was going to be able to speak into her grandmother's mind.

Go ahead, Andi thought.

Bea. Grandma Bea whirled around, startled, hearing his voice in her mind. Artie blinked, hearing it too. Because of how hard it was for Lux to communicate with anyone except for her, this might be the first and last time Artie would hear Lux. Andi stared at Lux. This must be very hard for him, to do both at the same time. Grandma Bea looked hard at Lux. Lux made a small nodding gesture. Grandma Bea's eyes were pleading and open.

Andi and Artie will stay with me, the voice in their minds spoke. *Together.*

The voice continued. *Cannot promise we will be safe always. But together, yes. Love and serve them, yes. Protect them, yes. Always okay? Do not know. Succeed? Sometimes and sometimes not. I will try hard.*

Grandma Bea's eyes were moist. She shrugged and nodded as she answered Lux. "What more can I ask for?" She wiped her tears away with the backs of her hands.

Andi, Lux voiced only in her head, *offer the grandma something. Is it okay?*

"It's okay," Andi said aloud, surprising Grandma Bea and Artie before both realized she was responding to Lux.

Bea, the voice rang in their heads again. *Today will die.*

"Today?" Grandma Bea's voice was incredulous.

You will become ill suddenly. For you I do not want that.

"Well, I guess I can understand that," Grandma Bea answered, her voice wavering. Andi sensed her grandmother's shock at Lux's statement. She found herself half-wishing she hadn't agreed to let Lux talk to Grandma Bea. But she changed her mind after the next statement.

I can open door to other side. Do you want this?

Grandma Bea's head shot up at this. She stared at Lux to make sure she had understood. Even Artie looked hard at the dolphin.

Show can. The voice stopped for the moment. Andi turned and gasped.

Fog had begun pouring into the cavern. Thick and heavy, it flooded the entire area. None of them could see each other except for Lux whose light shone through the darkness. Lightning crackled, and Andi jumped backward.

The voice began to speak again. *Bye to Andi and Artie,* the voice insisted. *Now.*

Grandma Bea stumbled in the darkness, her hands groping for Andi and Artie. Andi's heart was breaking. She wasn't sure what was happening, but she had a sudden and frightening feeling that it was going to be quite final. She shot a question of hers toward Lux. His answer came back at her. *Do not worry.*

They found Grandma Bea. She sank to her knees onto the rocky ridge floor, pulling them down with her. "I wish I had more time," she said. "I wish—I love you both. So much." She kissed them on their foreheads, stroking their cheeks.

"My life, it ended well. It ended well because of you two." Grandma Bea's voice was breaking also. "Most people don't ever have that; it was a gift. You two. My gifts. You made my life so wonderful at the end."

Artie's voice came through the darkness. "It was always wonderful with you, Grandma. Always."

Andi's grandmother finally became clearer in the mist. The love and kindness etched upon her face made Andi sob. Calypso was right. The memories were better than the loss but just barely. *Just barely.*

Andi began. "Grandma, I ... you," she faltered. "You saved us. After Mom. You saved us. I don't know what we would've—"

"You saved *me*," Grandma Bea cut in. "You shine. You shine just as bright as your dolphin over there. It's so real and true. There's nothing truer." She paused. "That's why he chose you."

The fog covered her grandmother's face, and her touch left their cheeks.

Ready? Lux's voice rang in their minds.

"Ready as I'll ever be," Grandma Bea said in a brave voice.

Two bolts of lightning struck out from the fog. The bolts hung suspended from roof to floor of the cavern. They were blinding, frozen in place. And blinked. The two blazing bolts came closer and closer to each other until they finally met. The lightning bolts separated from their intersection. A thin slit appeared between them, growing larger by the second. At first it was just blackness, but then lights appeared inside the portal, whirling. The lights became constellations and planets all spinning together. Andi realized what she was seeing. It was the image of the sea brilliantly lit from the inside with the beautiful night sky standing above it.

Andi felt the ground beneath them shake. Andi breathed slowly. She had forgotten how Lux's use of his powers caused earthquakes. The earthquakes had freed the *Kronos*. She looked at Lux in alarm. What could it do this time? The tremors passed, and Andi looked up from the ground toward the now-large slit opening into another world. Not another world—another *place*.

The outline of a man formed in the middle of the vista. It was her grandfather. He looked the same as when she had seen him several days before. His hair was still white, but it was thicker, and he looked neither old nor young, his wrinkles having disappeared.

"Tomas," Grandma Bea whispered in a broken voice.

The man looked toward Grandma Bea. Their eyes met. He started to walk toward her. He stepped out of the strange, starry world onto the thin ridge encircling the inlet pool. He continued to walk toward

Grandma Bea, his focus intent and unwavering. He reached her, took her into his arms, and enfolded her in his embrace.

"It's been so long, Tom," Grandma Bea said. "Too long."

Andi's grandfather said nothing, but he didn't have to. The look in his eyes said it all. He nodded toward Andi and Artie, raising his hand in salutation. Andi and Artie simply nodded back, their mouths open in amazement. Then Grandpa Tom took Grandma Bea by her hand. He stepped toward the large slit leading into the other world, pulling her in.

Grandma Bea stepped through the slit with Andi and Artie's grandfather, into the world that lay beyond. Once through, she turned back to wave one last farewell at her twins. She was younger, and her face appeared girlish. Yet here was an understanding and a serenity that surpassed a girl's youthfulness. Grandpa Tom nodded at the two of them, his arm around his wife. Then the slit closed, and they were gone.

Twenty

Loose Ends

Andi slowly picked herself up from the ground. She was very tired. One of her life's centers had disappeared. Thinking of Grandma Bea hurt her. Thinking of anything hurt her, because she knew that she would never be able to share anything on her mind or heart with Grandma Bea again. *Calypso.* Calypso had lost her entire family and would understand. Andi looked toward the mouth of the cavern. The tide was coming in. Lux did not remember much of his mother; he had not experienced the depth of loss of someone you have known your entire life. She wanted Calypso. Then she remembered: Artie.

It was not that she didn't want to be there for Artie. It was just that the pain was too much for her to bear without helping him carry his also. She walked over to him. She found him huddling against the stone wall. Bending down, she put her arm across his back, rubbing it the way he liked her to when he was upset or worried. But he did not budge. His hands remained clenched, his head pressed against the stone. Andi sighed, leaning back against the rock wall of the cavern. She smiled wistfully. Grandma Bea had looked so beautiful. She'd always been beautiful, but when she was across the threshold in that other place.

Andi shook her head, returning to reality. Lux had said that if Grandma Bea didn't cross that border into the other world, she would die suddenly. Because of illness. *Where was that place anyway? Heaven or ...*

Where was Lux anyway? She scanned the surface of the pool. Nothing. She looked deeper within the pool. Still nothing. Andi frowned, worried. She ran a frustrated hand through her hair. He'd moved Grandma Bea from here to there, spoken into all their minds. It was not an easy thing to do, she realized. Flying for Lux was much easier than speaking into more than one person's mind. Andi understood. Lux was recovering.

Andi lowered herself until she was flat on the ridge, her head an inch above the water. She peered inside. There was no light, no reflection, nothing. It was still foggy in the cavern. Her heart pounding, Andi wondered if he'd somehow managed to float up to the roof of the cavern from the pool. He did have a new flying ability after all.

Artie had risen from his kneeling position. Forcing herself to calm down, she took a deep breath and walked toward him, a sad smile on her lips. At first he did not seem to see her. Then he finally registered her. He shook his head, trying to shake himself out of his reverie. He finally met her eyes.

"I'm okay, Andi." That was all he said. Andi stepped forward to hug him, but he did not return the embrace. He stood limply while her arms went around him. Andi looked at him. His eyes dull, his mouth slack, he scared her. Andi realized with sudden terror that he was in some sort of shock. It had been too much for him. She waved her hand in front of his eyes, and his only reaction was to blink at her, his face and mouth remaining slack.

"Artie," Andi began, uncertainly. "We need to get out of here. It's dark."

They walked out into the open night. Andi noticed that Artie was breathing shallowly. Was she? Her insides were trembling. She held Artie's hand.

"Lux?" she said into the darkness, hoping for an answer.

Here. The golden dolphin surfaced in the ocean several yards out.

Andi called out, "Lux. Thank you. Thank you for what you did."

Sad. Did not want. The grief from the dolphin hit Andi hard in the stomach. Sharing a bond with him was wonderful, but it was also difficult, Andi realized. Especially at times like this. When they both carried so much grief and shared those feelings through their bond ... it was enough to knock her off her feet.

"Lux," Andi began, "Jubal said he'd be at his house. I think we should meet him there." It might help take their minds off things. Lux agreed with her— she felt his assent.

"Okay, okay," Andi said. "Let's just do this. Artie, let's get in the water."

Artie let Andi lead him into the water where Lux swam under their legs. They sat on his back. He had grown so much — while she did not think he had achieved full growth, his strength was formidable.

"Lux, is this okay?" Andi asked. He had carried her out of the cavern, away from the Skull, but she didn't know if he could support the two of them. Donalys and Artie had been holding on to Andi when they went to see her father. Artie sat behind Andi.

Growing stronger. More able. Andi realized Lux wanted to do this, because of what had just happened with Grandma Bea. Yet he hadn't done anything but help her.

The swim around the curve of the island was a short one. Andi was feeling tired but contemplative. Artie was behind her, his arms wrapped around her. She was so thankful for him. And Lux. Where would she be without him?

Andi allowed herself to feel all her emotions about her grandmother's death. She tried to focus them as if through a funnel toward Lux, so that he could see and feel them as she did. The joy of being able to say all that they wanted to say to Grandma Bea danced within Andi. She showed the astonishment of being able to see her grandfather and grandmother together one last time to Lux. Lux responded to the sudden, tearing grief Andi experienced when the slit in the air closed. Finally, she expressed her gratitude to Lux for intervening for Grandma's sake. For her own sake, Andi realized. He'd done it for her.

Lux responded in return by simply expressing his love for her.

As they rode upon Lux, Artie leaned his head against her back, maybe out of shock or exhaustion. It gave her a moment to think. What were they going to do now? Their only option was the *Kronos*. Why would the *Kronos* want to help her and Artie? It was because they wanted to use Lux for themselves. So that they could get home. And how did they expect him to get them to their home? Teleportation? Andi realized Lux's teleporting abilities were more complex than she originally thought.

Andi spoke silently into Lux's mind. She had changed her mind. *Gaby.* There was something she needed to do before going to Jubal's. She felt Lux acquiesce to her new plan. The dolphin moved quickly through the water toward Gaby's house. Andi hoped desperately that her plan would work out.

We are here. Andi looked up from where she sat on Lux's back, loosening Artie's hands from around her torso. Gaby's house stood there, as forlorn as it had been the other day. Andi slid off Lux, Artie not questioning her.

Andi walked to Gaby's door, hesitant. She slowly knocked on the door. The same heavyweight woman she had seen smoking while watching television several days before answered the door.

"Yeah?" she asked carelessly, squinting down at Andi through round, thick glasses in the dark.

Andi felt for the gold bars in Jubal's backpack. "I'd like to see Gaby, please."

Not inviting her in, the woman leaned back into the hallway yelling, "Gaby! There's a girl here for you." She nodded not unkindly to Andi before leaving the door.

Andi stayed just outside the door, dread building up in her stomach. She could feel Lux's encouragement coming from where he was waiting in the water. *But he's there while I'm here,* Andi thought glumly. *I'm the one who must face her.*

She heard Gaby's footsteps clicking on the hall even before she reached the door. Gaby examined her closely, a mixture of surprise and something else—Andi wasn't sure what. Gaby suddenly looked very afraid.

"You can't be here," she said. "My mom'll kill me if she knows what I said."

"What you said?" Andi answered stupidly, trying to remember.

Gaby's expression became even more confused. "That's why you're here, isn't it? To tell my parents about what I said—you know, about your brother." Her face flushed.

Andi ran her fingers through a lock that had come loose down on her forehead. "Oh that. Yeah, um, that's not why I'm here."

Gaby stared at Andi wordlessly.

Andi stammered, remembering the magazine clippings of all the flowers and gardens that Lux had allowed her to see inside Gaby's room. How was she going to do this? Then she squared her shoulders.

"I'm going away," she said, realizing that it *was* true the minute the words were out. "I wanted to give you something."

Andi slid the gold bars out of Jubal's backpack onto the ground in front of Gaby. Gaby looked down at the gold then back at Andi.

"What is this?" Gaby asked, her face a mixture of emotions.

"Real gold," Andi said. "I want you to have it."

Gaby's eyes narrowed, and suddenly Andi understood. *She was waiting for the other shoe to drop.* She didn't believe Andi. All she believed was that somehow Andi was here to exact her revenge for what she said the other day.

Andi wanted to shake Gaby, to try to make her understand. Andi suddenly sensed something in Lux's mind that shocked her. *She was just like Gaby!* When the crew of the *Kronos* had offered to help her and Artie, she'd been just as suspicious. Why would they want to help? That was why she was so eager to expose their motives for what they were. They wanted to use Lux for themselves. So that they could get home.

But instead they'd let her go. They'd let her and Artie go to say good-bye to Grandma Bea. They'd let her do that even though they knew she could very well run off with Artie and Lux somewhere with the gold where they could never be found. Andi had decided she meant to make their home on the *Kronos*.

"Use it," Andi said pleadingly. "Give it to your mom. The two of you —use it. Get out of here. Start a new life. Without your father." Andi finished this last part so quietly out of fear that the angry man she'd seen before might overhear.

Gaby's face turned deep red. To Andi's relief, she immediately bent down to pick it up, instead of leaving it there and rejecting Andi's offer. Gaby looked at Andi again, her face an odd mixture of fear, embarrassment, and something else.

"He's my stepfather. My father died a long time ago. How—how did you know?" Gaby faltered.

"I just do," Andi said firmly. "Look, if you don't believe me—you have clippings of flowers taped all over the walls of your bedroom. I'm not out to get you. Please know I'm not."

Gaby's stunned eyes moved from Andi toward the hallway. "He—he's not here," she said breathlessly. "I'll—I'll tell my mom. Ma-maybe ..."

Gaby looked at Andi, still disbelieving. "What's the catch?"

What's the catch? Why couldn't Gaby just believe Andi genuinely wished her well? That she wanted to help? Andi needed to show Gaby something—some proof that she meant her well, that she wanted to help. What would Lux say?

Andi stared at Gaby while these thoughts whirled through her mind. "My grandmother just died," she explained. "We won't be needing that where we're going. I just thought that ... maybe you could use it. You and your mom. For a better life."

Gaby looked down at the gold bars around her feet. "I'm sorry. About your grandmother," she said. Andi sighed. It was clear that Gaby had no idea what to say.

So, there. She'd done it. She'd given the gold bars to Gaby. Andi realized it wasn't her problem what Gaby did now. What she'd tried to do for Gaby—that was the important thing.

Andi thrust her hands into her pockets. "Good luck," she said, smiling at the girl's astonished face. "I really hope everything works out for you." She pointed to the gold. "I hope you can use it. For a new life."

Andi turned away from Gaby and started walking toward the shore.

"Wait!" Gaby called out to her.

Andi turned. Gaby still stood framed by the doorway.

"I *am* sorry," Gaby said. "What I said about your brother."

Andi was tempted to say *I'm sorry about the whirlwind* but what was the use? Gaby had a hard enough time believing that Andi was giving her the gold. Instead she just smiled and nodded.

The door to Gaby's house closed with a soft, silent *clink* followed by the sound of feet running to another room in the house—Lux must be letting her listen in, Andi realized—running as hard as they could. She got on Lux's back, ready to see Jubal.

Andi told Lux where to glide in closest to where Jubal lived. Motioning for Artie to follow her, the two of them jumped off Lux's back and walked up the stone beach up to Jubal's house. All the lights inside were dark except for one in the living room.

Andi paused in front of Jubal's house. She motioned to Artie to hide under the living room window—the one that was lit. Just until she figured out what to do.

They huddled together under the window. Suddenly she and Artie heard voices coming out of the window. Jubal's and his mother's. And someone else's. Andi's eyes widened. *It was Ms. Dugger!*

"My father Greg Fielding was not responsible for your husband's death," she heard Ms. Dugger's voice say. Her voice sounded firm yet entreating. "Both of us are entitled to the *treasure*."

Andi gasped. The man who had drowned—the drownings everyone initially blamed Andi's grandfather for—one of them had been Jubal's father! Why hadn't he told her?

"What is she talking about, Mom?" Jubal sounded confused.

So he didn't know! Andi took a deep breath.

"Do not listen to this woman," Mrs. Smith's voice said angrily to Jubal.

Andi heard Ms. Dugger say to Jubal in a sneering tone. "Don't you know? Your friend—her grandfather is responsible for your father's death."

"That's not true, Jubal," Mrs. Smith said. "Actually, it was this woman's father who was responsible." There was a pause. "I'm sorry," Andi heard Mrs. Smith say. "Just how did you get a teaching job on *this* island? This island of *all places?*"

Andi smiled inwardly. *Good for Mrs. Smith!* Andi might not always like her because of her anger issues and how she took them out on Jubal, but Mrs. Smith had sure scored today.

"Andi's grandfather would never have made a mistake like that!" Jubal's angry voice rang out.

"Be quiet, Jubal." Mrs. Smith's voice was surprisingly calm, controlled. In response to Ms. Dugger's question, she said, "You should be happy that I'm not escorting you out by force."

"You wouldn't." Ms. Dugger's voice had a sneer in it, but there was fear too.

"Oh, I *could*," Mrs. Smith said. "Get out. Now."

"Trust me, lady," Andi heard Jubal say to Ms. Dugger. "My mother *can.*"

"But the treasure—" Ms. Dugger was stammering now. Clearly she had not expected Mrs. Smith to reject her so out of hand.

"There is *no* treasure. Your father was responsible for my husband's death. You have everything all mixed up." There was a note of pity in her ironclad voice.

This did it for Ms. Dugger. "I don't need your help—or anyone else's," she said, stamping her foot. Before Andi knew it, Ms. Dugger stepped out of the front door, slamming it behind her.

Artie gasped. Andi tried to shush him, but it was too late. Ms. Dugger had seen them. But she wasn't looking at them. She was looking beyond Andi and Artie. Andi spun around. Lux had flown out of the water the moment he realized Ms. Dugger was there. Andi sensed his anger.

Andi turned back to Ms. Dugger. Her eyes had changed. They didn't seem—they didn't seem *rational*, Andi realized. Had she ever been? Her former teacher rushed toward them.

Before Andi knew it, Ms. Dugger was on top of her. Andi tried to wrestle her way from under, but she could not.

Ms. Dugger's voice shocked her, filled with so much hate. "You— you—" The words came through clenched teeth.

Suddenly Ms. Dugger was pulled off. Jubal pushed Ms. Dugger to the ground. His mother stood behind Jubal, alarmed. Then Mrs. Smith opened her mouth, but no sound came out. She crumpled to the ground, drool coming out the side of her mouth. Andi knew it was the shock of seeing Lux. Andi could still feel his anger as he approached Ms. Dugger. Andi realized Lux had helped Jubal push—not pull —Ms. Dugger off.

Ms. Dugger's face filled with terror as Lux approached her. Without warning, she jumped up and ran toward Andi again. There was no sense of the woman who used to be her teacher in the wild eyes running toward her. Even though Ms. Dugger was afraid of Lux, her fear had pusher over the edge. Andi pulled Artie up and began running from Jubal's house to the cliff, dragging Artie by the hand.

Artie kept stumbling behind her, almost falling. Andi refused to let go of his hand. She heard more than Artie's footsteps behind her. She looked behind her. Lux kept slamming into Ms. Dugger, making her stumble, but she kept getting up and running toward Andi and Artie. Her eyes were wide and *obsessed*.

Jubal was running behind them, trying to help Lux keep Ms. Dugger down. The darkness of night was starting to fade. Andi looked in the opposite direction. The horizon was beginning to light up but no sign of the sun yet. They'd been up all night. That was why Ms. Dugger was able to still hound them. They were all so tired and couldn't outrun her. Andi's heart was pounding. She wondered why Lux wasn't better able to stop Ms. Dugger. Even as she ran, she touched his mind. He was trying to follow her instructions—not to hurt anyone badly, especially after last time when Ms. Dugger hit her head. She understood.

He didn't want her to end up in the hospital. But she felt Lux's anger growing rapidly.

The ground beneath them shook. They stumbled together, trying to keep each other up even as they ran. It didn't work. Artie fell, dragging Andi down with him. Andi gasped. Ms. Dugger was nearly upon them. Andi sensed Lux's anger flare as he crashed into Ms. Dugger harder than before. Ms. Dugger rolled down from the sloped path out of control. Her former teacher screamed as she continued to fall. Jubal ran past the screaming woman toward them.

Another earthquake hit, toppling them against each other as they tried to rise from the ground but failed.

"What is *he* doing now?" Jubal gasped as he reached them. The earth kept shaking.

Andi, upset, said out loud, "Lux. What are you doing?"

But Lux was gone. He had disappeared. Andi turned around. Ms. Dugger was unconscious. Andi got up and began pulling Artie toward the cliff as Jubal followed right behind. Reaching the cliff, they began half-walking half-running down the ridge path towards the *Kronos*. Dawn was still faint, making it difficult to see.

A third earthquake struck. Knowing this might happen, Andi had balanced her weight on the ridge path so that she hit the rocky wall instead of falling over. She grabbed the back of Artie's shirt when he began to fall forward. She didn't let go of his shirt again but held on to it as they slowly slid down the ridge path, keeping their backs against the wall.

Reaching the bottom, Andi squinted so that she could see. She fell backward.

"Artie," she gasped, groping for his hand.

A large dangerous tidal wave hung over them.

Twenty-One

A Tidal Battle

The wave was gigantic. It was frozen in place, not falling upon them. Andi had very little doubt that if it fell they would all be killed. It had been made through some sort of power, Andi realized. If it were a tsunami wave, it would be moving away from them because the earthquakes on the island would have pushed the wave *away from the origin point*, not bring the wave *to* it. This was something entirely different. And what was that sound?

The immense wave hung frozen in the air. If loosed, the wave would hit the cliff as well as its rocky strip of beach. The wave towered nearly as high as the cliff. Andi pushed out desperately with her mind, *Lux, where are you?* She sensed that he'd heard her. He did not respond. Andi licked her lips.

The water was *so* high. Where was the *Kronos?* What would something like this have done to the ship?

A plume of water hit them as if aimed right at them. It was enough to slam Andi and Artie down onto the ridge path. Andi sat up on the rocky shore gasping and coughing. Artie lay next to her, his head on the rock, looking up at her, confused. Jubal lay behind them coughing. It had hit him too. Andi scrambled up to her feet.

Andi stared, disbelieving. How had the water hit them so precisely?

Andi thought that maybe she understood. Someone was trying to make the wave crash down on them, killing them. Someone else was keeping the wave from crashing. *The Skull had clawed its way out of its prison. It was responsible for this. Lux was the one holding the wave back.* The earthquakes of the previous night must have freed it.

As the sun dawned upon them, Andi realized that the wave was a massive wall of water. The Skull had taken no chances. It wanted them dead. As tall as the cliff, the wave was frozen, refusing to fall, a tidal wave lining the entire shoreline of the bay surrounding the cliff. Andi stumbled backward at the sheer sight of it.

The huge wave was almost even with the top of the cliff. Andi started backing up slowly then began running up the ridge path. Artie and Jubal were behind her. As they climbed the path, the huge wall of water started to push against whatever was keeping it frozen. Andi looked up at the wall, terrified. If it hit her with as much force and weight as it looked like it would, they would be dead.

The wave kept pushing, stopping just short of hitting her and Artie, freezing again in motion just inches away from impact. Andi fell onto the ridge path, pulling Artie down, with her rolling over him, trying to shield him from the power and force of the waterfall. Jubal fell next to her. Yet the wave stayed frozen. After a long time, Andi looked up. The immense wall of water surrounding the shore was stuck. Andi knew this was thanks to Lux. He must be preventing the wave from collapsing on top of them. *But how? And what was that sound?*

Andi gasped. Someone lay on the cliff path above them. Ms. Dugger lay trembling on the path. The madness had gone out of her eyes, and all there was now fear.

Before they could help Ms. Dugger to her feet, an evil voice chuckled humorlessly from somewhere behind her.

"You have recovered from your wounds from our first encounter. How?" The voice murmured. Beginning again with a dry chuckle, it said, "I seem to recall a selkie woman ... with a gift for healing."

Andi kept turning around. It sounded like the voice was speaking from behind her, but no matter how many times she moved, it was never in front of her. The voice continued.

"So you know of the *Kronos*?"

"Yes," Andi replied angrily, feeling Artie's hand squeezing hers from below where he still lay on the ridge path.

"They know of the golden creature?" Why did it want to know?

"Creature?" Andi replied stupidly, playing for time. She eyed the rest of the ridge path, which stood several feet away. Judging by its distance from the giant wave, which stood only inches from her face, could she grab Artie in time to run up the path? Could Jubal follow? Probably not. The Skull was going to win. She looked down at Artie. His face was like death, his eyes closed. Jubal lay on the path, still paralyzed.

"You know of whom I speak."

"The creature that's holding the wave up? This wave that you've made?" Andi was cautious, trying to buy time. If the wave collapsed, it would fall on them, killing them and pulling their bodies out to sea. Andi could not see a way out of this. She could not say Lux's name. Or the Skull would find him.

"Do you mean my friend?" she screamed.

"Yes," the creature responded, irritated.

"My friend who saved me?" Andi screamed even louder. The Skull wasn't stupid. It wouldn't take it long to figure out she was stalling for time.

"What are you doing?" The Skull was suspicious.

"You're not the one stopping this wave from falling straight down on me, are you?" Andi asked. "It's my friend who's stopping it." *That was why the earthquakes had happened in rapid succession.* Lux was preventing the gigantic wave from collapsing on top of them. But how? He didn't have powers like that ... did he? Looking at the wave, she saw that while it stayed in place, it was not as frozen as she realized. *Air,* she realized. The sound she was hearing...Lux was teleporting immense amounts of air to hold the wave up. She looked up into the night sky, even though she couldn't see the Skull. *The amount of air required to hold the wave back...*

"You're the Skull that the *Kronos* told us about, aren't you?" she asked.

The voice adopted a sneering tone. "I am."

Still stalling, Andi asked, "What's your name?"

The Skull did not answer.

"You don't have a name, do you? You're just ... a Skull. Nothing more. No wonder your master abandoned you."

"I and my master are one." The Skull's voice was stiff.

"Really?" Andi asked, still playing for time. "So ... where is he? Where's your master?"

"Enough of your games. Answer my question. The crew of the *Kronos* met your golden friend, did they not?"

"Why is it so important for you to know?" Andi asked.

Artie's hand grasped her leg from below. She knew that he did not understand what she was doing. She tried to nod to him as if to say *trust me*. She wasn't sure if he could trust her though.

"You know what?" Andi said to the darkness, toward the Skull. "I'm not going to answer any of your questions. You can go ahead and kill me and my brother now. Stop wasting my time." It was a gamble, but she did it. "I'm not going to tell you anything about my *friend*." She hoped that the emphasis on the word friend would be like a megaphone.

It did the trick. Andi heard a powerful collision in the air somewhere above her. The wall of water trembled, starting to collapse, but then firmed up again.

"Come on, Artie, Jubal. Let's *go*," Andi gasped. The Skull howled in rage, but they kept running. Andi heard a deep and furious growl, and this time it was not the Skull's. It was Lux. Sounds of fighting came from above her. She didn't dare look, just kept running up the pathway with Artie and Jubal.

In their hurry, all three tripped more than once, pulling or pushing each other down. Sometimes Artie ran ahead of her, sometimes Andi did. Jubal always stayed behind. Their knees and elbows bled, but neither of them noticed. They kept scrambling up the pathway to their house.

Ms. Dugger stared at them when they reached her, gasping as they did. Even though anger rose within her, Andi helped pull her up to her feet. The teacher was trembling as she held Andi's hand.

They finally reached the top. Andi whirled around to see what was happening. The sea wall remained high and thick. She saw Lux's shining figure as he slammed against something in the air. Ghostly white spectral wings retaliated, flying into Lux. Lux looked stunned, and Andi gasped as blood dripped down his golden side. Lux had become less golden. The Skull was sucking power out of Lux like a leech. That was why she could see the Skull so much more now than when it was in its prison, Andi realized. The more Lux bled, the more the Skull gained mass. It wasn't just because of the rising sun. The bleached white of the Skull shone as it became more tangible, *realer*.

Andi ran past her home to the backyard. The others followed her. She could see Lux and the Skull fighting just off the cliff head. They were very close to the battle between the dolphin and Skull. Andi picked up a stone from the backyard. The horned Skull rammed its wings into Lux's side, drawing more blood. Lux fell straight to the ground, stopping just short of hitting the rock below, then doubled back to the fight. The dolphin was exhausted fighting the Skull and keeping the wave from crashing, Andi realized. She threw the stone at the Skull as it dove after Lux.

The Skull howled as the stone hit him, whirling around to face Andi, coming straight toward her. Andi picked up another rock and hurled it at the Skull's face. She heard the stone hit the Skull, cracking part of its bleached bone.

The Skull turned around from Lux and came at her, its wings flapping dangerously close. Andi saw that she had cracked a small part of the bone near the eye. "I can give you what you want," it said, floating in front of her. Andi turned around. Artie was on the grass, his eyes wide open, frozen in fear.

"Too late," Andi replied, sizing up the situation. "She's gone," she finished, trying not to think of her grandmother. She needed to figure out her next move.

"Not her," the creature said in a soft whisper. "Your mother." The statement floated down toward her.

"My mother's dead," Andi said quietly.

She heard the Skull laugh mirthlessly. "No," it replied. "She's alive. Only I know where she is. Help me with the golden creature, and I will take her to you."

Andi's mind exploded in grief and rage as she understood. *That* was why Lux hadn't been able to find her in the other place. Her mother wasn't dead. She was alive. *Had Artie heard?* She didn't think so. Her heart pounded heavily. She had one chance and took it.

Andi grabbed the Skull by its horns and tried to wrestle the Skull to the ground. It was futile. The Skull was much stronger than she was. It rose into the air, but Andi had locked her arms around both horns. Andi rose into the air with it. Both were flying. Andi looked down at the cliff and saw Artie and Jubal running toward her, waving their arms madly. She was flying. And it wasn't like riding Lux. *She was going to die.*

"Let go of me!" the Skull screamed.

"No," Andi answered in a blind rage. She had an idea. She began swinging herself back and forth with her arms wrapped around the Skull's horns. While she was not strong enough to hurt the Skull, both were sent reeling. The Skull tried to shake Andi off, but she would not let go. It would pay for what it had said. For what it had revealed. Andi knew the Skull wasn't lying. She also knew she couldn't hold on forever.

Andi opened her eyes and gasped. She was high in the sky, way above the cliffside, above the threatening sea wall the monster had created. Her brother and Jubal were screaming for her at the top of their lungs. Andi saw through a haze of furious heartbreak that she had to survive. Survive for her brother, for Jubal. For Lux. For herself. There would be time to figure things later. She was beginning to lose her grip.

The Skull changed its tactics, plunging straight down so fast that Andi fell off. Screaming, she fell in the air. She closed her eyes and found herself landing on something soft. She almost rolled off, but whatever was beneath her quickly counterbalanced its weight against hers so that she stayed steady.

Lux. He'd flown right under her, positioning himself so that she fell on him. His skin had become more golden. He'd recovered because of the time Andi bought him through her own fight with the Skull.

Grab! Hold! The dolphin's orders screamed throughout her head. Andi lowered her whole body, wrapping her arms around Lux's torso. She tucked her legs under him as well. He flew toward the Skull, slamming into him. To her great satisfaction, the Skull crashed against the cliff wall. She and Lux fell but caught themselves, a little too close for comfort to the rocky shore below for her liking.

The Skull slammed back into Lux's side, throwing them into the gigantic wave. Yet they fell *backwards into* it, instead of *in* it. It was so different from diving. It was like waiting to hit a wall then realizing that it was porous. She had been right. The water was not frozen in place. Lux was constantly teleporting unfathomable masses of air to hold the wave against crashing against the shore. *How was Lux doing this?* Andi fell off Lux. Dazed for a moment, she stayed in the water where she was. She swam near the edge of the wall of water. She felt panicky because she knew there was a chance of falling out of the tower of water down to the dry exposed shoreline. Instead of walking into the ocean and feeling it deepen, she was high up in the wall near its edge. If she swam out, she would fall out, hitting the shore below.

Lux called to her mind, indicating that she should swim underwater in the opposite direction and follow him. Nervously, she swam through raised wave toward where the sea opened before her into the familiar bay. Underwater was littered with all kinds of debris, seaweed, and sea life that had been caught up in the wave's fury. With a powerful kick of her legs, she finally launched herself out of the wave into the sea, swimming through all the debris, keeping a careful watch on Lux's golden figure. She finally came up gasping for breath. Lux swam around her, nuzzling her. Andi looked up. They were in front of the *Kronos*.

Lux, Andi relayed to him, *Artie, and Jubal. We need to get Artie and Jubal. She left, she left me ...* Lux responded in confusion to her jumbled thoughts. Even though she was above water now, Andi still couldn't breathe. The Skull's revelation had left her in shock.

Twenty-Two

The Slinky Solution

Captain Grubb and members of his crew were waiting at the front, the prow of the ship. She got on top of Lux they both floated up to board the *Kronos*. She began to revive as she got back onto the boat. *Help me not to think about it,* she whispered to Lux voicelessly. Lux nodded, gliding in the air alongside her as she walked wearily along the dock.

"Artie, Jubal," she cried, "they're still up there. We must get to them. Lux, can you take me there? We can't be here, not yet." In her desperation, the confusion over her mother began to fade, but Andi knew it was only temporary. There was a note of desperation in Andi's voice that registered with the Captain. The Captain approached Lux, who floated just above the ship.

"Bring them here?" His voice was steady and calm, which was what Andi needed. In response, Lux rose further up in the air and flew faster than Andi had seen him fly toward the cliff face. Andi could barely see through the heavy sea wall the Skull had conjured up.

"How did it—the Skull—do that?" Andi asked, inclining her head toward the towering mass of sea.

Captain Grubb grimaced. His red whiskers trembled with an emotion Andi could not quite understand. "Chaos," he replied quietly.

"That's its purpose." He turned to Andi. "It is very powerful. He can overturn whole cities if he wants to."

"Come with me," he continued. "We'll stay on the ship so that your golden creature can see us but come with me." There was a note of gentleness in his voice that Andi had never heard before.

Silently, she followed the Captain to where he steered his ship, just behind Calypso's large glass tube. Calypso's eyes were closed in concentration. She lifted her hand and pressed it against the glass without opening her eyes, as if in greeting to Andi. Andi pressed her hand against the opposite side of the glass. Andi felt Calypso share in her loss of Grandma Bea. As crazy as things were right now, Calypso still cared.

Captain Grubb motioned for Andi to sit down. Calypso opened her eyes and smiled at Andi. The Captain sat in another chair opposite Andi.

He sighed and hesitated.

Calypso asked, "Do you want me to talk to her instead?"

The Captain nodded.

Calypso turned to Andi and began. "There is something we need to talk about. There is information we do not yet have. You may be able to give it to us." Her eyes clouded as if she were seeing something else that Andi could not see. Then her eyes flickered and focused on Andi again. "What is your family's history with that mountain?"

"Mountain?" Andi asked, confused.

Calypso inclined her head toward the cliff face.

"Oh," Andi said, "that isn't a mountain. It's a cliff. It isn't tall enough to be—" She stopped. Lux was approaching her from behind. She jumped up and turned around. On Lux's back were both Artie and Jubal! She let out a cry of relief and joy, running toward the side of the ship where Jubal was helping Artie slide off Lux's back onto the deck.

"Andi," Artie gasped, "you're okay—" He stopped as if he couldn't bear to finish the sentence.

"Lux caught me, and it all turned out okay. Are you okay?" Andi stared hard at Artie.

The minute Artie had seen her, he had gone limp, looking exhausted beyond belief. Jubal grinned, looking pleased before becoming serious.

"Where is the Skull?" Andi asked. "Why didn't it follow you?"

"That—that thing—it attacked your teacher—" Jubal did not finish.

"Does she need help?" Andi demanded.

Jubal nodded soberly. "I think so."

Andi turned to Lux. "Will you—can you—"

I will if can. Andi understood. Only if Lux could outrun the Skull. Only if he had enough time to teleport Ms. Dugger to the hospital. *Only if, only if.* The list went on and on. She looked at Lux as he departed back toward the island.

"Can the Skull see us? Can he find us?"

Calypso replied, "Not yet. I am blocking the ship from the Skull's eyes, but it will not last forever. We have just a bit of time left."

"You can do that?" Andi was amazed.

Calypso smiled sadly at Andi. "My ability is very weak compared to others in my race. If only I were stronger."

Jubal interrupted. "Andi, the Skull—the thing—disappeared after attacking Ms. Dugger. The whole village is up in arms. They know about the wave. We heard screaming from down in the village. Also, the weirdest thing happened. A few minutes before Lux came to get us, Artie stood up from the ground and ran into the house. He came out with this." Jubal pointed at the toy Artie clutched in his hands—his favorite toy, the slinky.

"Oh, that's his favorite thing in the world," Andi replied. There was a look of indignation on Jubal's face, saying *the slinky isn't important right now!* She remembered and turned to Artie. "He needs it. Right, Artie?" All she cared about was that they were safe.

"Wrong," said a voice behind her. It was Captain Grubb, no longer seated in his chair.

He pointed at the slinky in Artie's hands. "How did you know?" He asked Artie.

Andi didn't understand what Captain Grubb was asking, but Artie did. He shrugged, a gleam of pleasure in his eyes. "Always known," he replied.

"About the golden creature?" The Captain's voice was intent.

Artie shook his head. "No. But what it can do." He stretched the coils of the slinky apart, allowing them to come back together again. Small ripples echoed down the length of the slinky, like music. *It was like a tunnel,* Andi thought. He threaded his fingers across the coils, allowing the ripple to move across it again. Then he made the coils came together. The tunnel of the slinky didn't look like a tunnel anymore. The slinky simply looked like coils bunched closely together. Something very important was happening, but she didn't understand what.

"This has always been Artie's favorite thing in the world," she said. "He studies it all the time. I never know just what he's thinking when he's playing with it. But if this means something to you ..." She paused, studying the slinky. "Then I bet you Artie knows what it means." Her eyes settled on Artie. "Right, Artie?"

Artie nodded, but he still did not speak.

The Captain said, "The great ships took routes toward our new world. To arrive at our new world within our lifetime, we used routes that traveled through space and time."

Andi frowned, not understanding. But she continued to listen.

Artie said one word. "Wormhole."

The Captain and Calypso's faces went blank, not understanding the meaning of the word. Andi was not even sure *she* understood the meaning of the word.

Jubal clapped his hands together excitedly.

"Of course! You created a path to where you were going. Like a shortcut. A short way of getting to where you're going. A wormhole is a tunnel in space and time. You were trying to travel a huge distance in a very short time."

He excitedly took the slinky from Artie. He stretched it wide apart, making it look like a tunnel again. Then he clasped the metal coils together. The distance had become much smaller. Andi gasped. She was starting to understand.

"It's still a tunnel," Jubal said. "Just much smaller."

Calypso smiled at him. "You begin to understand, Jubal."

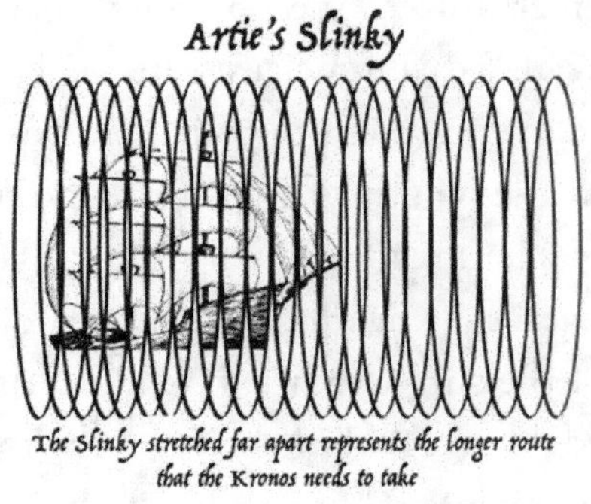

The Slinky stretched far apart represents the longer route
that the Kronos needs to take

Artie's Slinky

When coils are folded together,
the route shortens, which is what Captain Grubb
and Calypso hope of Lux's abilities.

Andi finally understood as well. She held her hand up as if to ask permission to speak. "But when Portent came onto your ship with the Skull ... and Donalys ... something went wrong. The tunnel was affected."

"The tunnel collapsed on the way, and you found yourselves in that... *limbo*. You got stuck." Jubal frowned, trying to complete his thoughts.

Calypso and the Captain stared at each other. Then Calypso answered, "Yes, the way you explain it is accurate."

"Do you know where Lux came from? How is it that he can do the things he does?" Andi interrupted.

"We do not know," the Captain answered.

"We wish we did," Calypso added sadly.

"So," Andi struggled to verbalize what she was thinking, "the Skull ... he kept asking if Lux had met you guys, the crew of the *Kronos*. It was very important for him to know."

The Captain and Calypso shared a quick glance, and Calypso nodded quickly to the Captain. He sighed and sat down again.

"Then if the Skull asked you that question, it means our suspicions are true."

"And that is?" Andi pushed for an answer.

The Captain replied. "You remember when you explained that your dolphin took you places where it would have been impossible for you to go otherwise?"

Artie and Jubal nodded, beating Andi to it. Andi hesitated. She liked the Captain, and she knew she adored Calypso. But she loved Lux most of all. She did not want him used.

"Yes," she admitted reluctantly.

The Captain let out a happy, satisfied grunt even though the tension remained in his eyes.

He looked at Calypso before they both looked back at Andi. Then Captain Grubb cocked his neck toward the cliffside. "The demon. It wants to reunite with its master. The golden creature is the only way how."

"Portent's *alive*? The man?" Andi asked.

"We do not know," Calypso answered sadly. "We never expected to find that evil creature here in this world. We ejected Portent and the Skull off the ship when we realized that the wormhole taking us to our new world was collapsing. We had hoped that by ejecting them, we would be able to stabilize the tunnel, but we were not able to. As for what happened to Portent and the Skull, that is a mystery. What is clear is that the Skull found itself here, without its master. I would guess that," Calypso looked at Captain Grubb, "Portent is not on this world. Otherwise the Skull would not be in such pursuit of your golden creature."

So that's why it wants Lux, Andi thought.

Jubal asked the Captain, "So? How does it help you that Lux can travel to other places just like that?"

Calypso answered for the Captain. "Because we think he creates tunnels," she broke off, nodding towards Artie slinky, "whenever he teleports."

"I don't understand," Andi replied. "It doesn't feel like a tunnel when he teleports."

Artie put his hand gently on Andi's shoulder. In front of her, the Captain, Calypso, and Jubal, he pushed all the coils of his slinky close together.

"Does that look like a tunnel?" Jubal asked. "No. But it is."

Andi looked at Calypso. Lux had gotten to her father's house in the wink of an eye. *That had been a tunnel.* She remembered the place with the statues. How they'd been there one moment, and the next, they hadn't. *Another tunnel. Wormhole,* if Artie and Jubal were right.

Jubal asked the next necessary question. "Can he take the whole ship?"

The Captain eyed Andi carefully. Calypso floated in her glass tube. Finally, it was Calypso who spoke.

"We do not possess the ability to create another tunnel. Our tunnel collapsed when we ejected Portent and the Skull overboard. We know that it will be a tremendous effort on Lux's part to expend that much energy, but we believe that ... if Andi is on the ship with us, then yes." Calypso trailed off. Andi understood. She and Captain Grubb wanted to find their people. Wherever they had ended up.

Andi's eyes moved to the woman in the watery tube. This was new.

"He has bonded with you. You two have a powerful link to one another. We believe ... that if you are on the ship with us, then Lux will be able to help us navigate through space. He would be pulling us at incredible speed, not always teleporting — I mean taking us through tunnels."

The expression in Calypso's eyes pleaded for Andi to understand their predicament. "He will not bond with anyone else," Calypso continued. "He can only read minds and teleport the person he has bonded with. If you are on the ship with us ..." Calypso trailed off.

"It's almost like Santa Claus having his sleigh pulled by reindeer!" Jubal laughed. Andi saw he was simply trying to digest the information. He wasn't joking, just framing it in his own terms.

"How do you know all of this?" Andi asked suspiciously.

Calypso bit her lip as she looked at the Captain. She began to explain. "Andi, where we come from, there are legends associated with the golden creature. We have never encountered them, but there was once a time when the golden creatures visited our world. The legends seem to be correct so far in how Lux is in his powers and how he is with you."

Andi looked up at Lux. "Do you know where they come from?" she asked Calypso.

"No," Calypso replied regretfully.

Andi felt Lux's disappointment ring like a gong struck inside her. He was listening in to the conversation through her. She sighed. She had already decided that they would have to go with the crew of the *Kronos*. And there was Artie. Of course Artie would want to go with them.

"So?" she asked her twin. "Will we go with them?"

Artie looked at her levelly. "Together."

"We would be together," Andi said, agreeing. So. This would be their new home. Somehow, she had won. She'd found a home where she and Artie could be together.

Andi had something to offer these people, and they had something to offer her: an opportunity to keep her and her brother together. A home. She somehow had a feeling it would be a long time before they found Captain Grubb and Calypso's people. Maybe they never would. She hoped she was wrong, but ... she looked all around her at the *Kronos*. This was her home now.

Andi smiled sadly at Jubal. If they survived, they'd leave him behind, never to see him again. Inwardly, she wondered if he would ever try to tell someone what he had seen and experienced. But Andi knew Jubal wouldn't. First, no one would believe him, and secondly, he was so loyal. She hoped he would work things out with his mother. She might be an alcoholic, but she had really stood up to Ms. Dugger.

Then Andi realized she'd forgotten one last thing. She had to ask Lux. This voyage in space would be his too. He'd be taking all of them with him toward a place they might never find.

What do you think? Andi asked her dolphin silently. They had never spoken over such a distance, but she was able to connect with him.

Yes, I can do this. Lux sounded excited.

When Andi asked him about his excitement, his answer was: *I want to stay with you. You. Me. Artie. Have a new home. Can carry them if Andi is on the ship.*

"But how?" Andi cried aloud, surprising the others with her outburst.

Our bond.

Won't you need water? Andi asked Lux. *Traveling in space...*she trailed off.

Do not need like other dolphins was Lux's answer.

Andi impulsively thanked her dolphin. She felt his smile reverberate inside her. She was overwhelmed at the powerful desire he had to stay with her. It was as powerful as hers, Andi realized.

Andi nodded to the others. "We will go with you." She hesitated. "I think I knew we were going to from the moment you explained to me, but I just wasn't ready." The Captain nodded at her kindly, and Calypso smiled, delighted. Artie squeezed her hand tightly. Andi looked at her brother softly. He had been as afraid of separating from her as she had been all along. She looked around the ship. *Home.* Then she stared sadly at the house atop the cliff. Grandma Bea was gone, and she and Artie were leaving. The Skull was hunting them.

"What do we do about the Skull?" Andi asked.

Calypso answered, "We protect you while Lux protects us. Hopefully we can leave now before it returns," Calypso ended, her eyes on Andi. "The Skull knows that if he can threaten your life, there is a chance Lux will help him leave this world and maybe find his master."

"That's why the Skull hasn't used its full power yet," the Captain said soberly.

Jubal understood. "He hasn't swallowed us like he did that comet."

"If that happened ..." Andi said. She was thinking hard. If they left, then the Skull would be free to do whatever he wanted in this world. She could not allow that to happen.

Calypso nodded from inside her tube. "Yes, any imbalance caused by the Skull would most likely consume us." She nodded toward the shoreline. "And your island as well."

"He hasn't tried to swallow us because ..." Andi could not bring herself to believe that the Skull was powerful enough to swallow Lux.

"He understands that if he destroys you, then Lux will never help him. He is being very careful. I imagine the Skull only fully understood the nature of your relationship with each other after he battled Lux above your....what did you call it? Cliff. It saw how determined Lux was to protect you."

Captain Grubb's eyes were penetrating as he answered Andi's question. "We have to do what we have to do, which is leave now." His tone was firm.

"But what about this world?" Andi asked.

"She's right, Zare," Calypso said soberly. Andi sighed inwardly, thankful to Calypso. Calypso understood why they had to fight and somehow trap the Skull again, so that this world would be safe. She suspected the Captain was more focused on getting his crew home. *He blamed himself,* Andi realized. A part of he understood this. She couldn't blame him. Still, she was thankful for Calypso.

The Captain drew in a deep breath and nodded, as if he had known all this time that this would be a condition of Andi and Artie going with the ship.

Lux returned, slowing down the nearer he got to her. Turning toward him, she was glad to see that the Skull was not behind him. But the Skull would soon be here. She grinned, feeling the same way. Andi stroked Lux's belly as he flew over them.

Will be all right, Lux spoke into Andi's mind.

Andi breathed slowly. Ms. Dugger would be all right.

"Andi," Calypso said, "can Lux seal tunnels on either end? Close both sides of the tunnel? When he teleports, I mean."

Lux, Andi asked mentally, *do you create tunnels when you teleport? Is that how it works?*

Yes. You cannot see. But I can.

Can you close the ends of the tunnel? Wormhole? Andi understood. They were going to try to trap the Skull.

Andi looked at Lux questioningly. The answer came. *I am not sure. Can try.*

Calypso breathed heavily. "We need him to seal the Underwater Grotto. The Skull was trapped there before Lux's mother opened a pathway between it and this world. We need Lux to seal the Underwater Grotto. We believe the Skull can be trapped if Lux closes both ends of the Underwater Grotto." Calypso smiled. " I believe the Underwater Grotto is what Jubal refers to as," the selkie's smile widened as she looked at Jubal, "a pocket universe."

Andi stared at Lux once more. She did not ask anything. She just waited for his answer.

Never closed before. I can try.

"He's going to try to do it, but he's not sure," she said.

Calypso looked serious. "I want to be clear that this is about closing both ends and not teleporting rocks to block the passageway."

Jubal asked eagerly, "So it is a pocket universe? The Underwater Grotto?"

Calypso replied slowly. "It is an area with rules different from ours—you may best describe it as a pocket universe. That if sealed," she added, "will trap the Skull."

"He's not sure he can do it and protect us from the water breaking loose." She pointed to the sea wall.

Captain Grubb grimaced. "That's my job, seems like. We are on the seaward side," he explained. "We might not be affected by whatever happens with the wave. But still ..." He grunted, stood up, and grasped the steering wheel. He grabbed a horn and started barking orders.

"Wait," Andi said. "Where is Donalys?"

"He's right here." The Captain pointed to the topmost mast of one of the sails. Two large crewmen were in it with Artie. Artie was learning from them! The boy grinned down at Andi as he waved down to her. He was one of the crewmen, Andi realized. She looked at the Captain with newfound respect. He was able to help his nephew feel included while at the same time protecting him. She turned to the floating dolphin right next to them.

"So ..." she began uncertainly. "What are you going to do?"

What they said.

"Does it make sense?" It did not make sense to Andi, but it did to Artie, the Captain, and Calypso.

Yes. The dolphin paused. *Afraid,* he said.

Andi understood that it would at least be hazardous. She asked, "Do you want me to come with you?" She added, "So that you're not alone." Andi thought some more. "Lux," she said slowly, "the Skull wants you. It also wants me. We could... distract it away from the ship."

Dangerous, Lux answered.

"I don't care," Andi declared.

The dolphin trembled slightly, sending ripples of gold through the air. Andi knew her own nerves were visible on her face, just as Lux's shimmered.

Calypso pressed her face against the glass as if preparing to beg Andi for something. She looked at Lux as she said it. "Seal the Skull up, Andi. Seal him. Contain him so that no one can ever escape from it again."

"Lux is going to try." Andi smiled sadly at Calypso. She hoped that whatever Lux could do would be enough.

"You have to help him with this, Andi."

"Me?" Andi voice rang out, astonished. "What do I know about that?"

Calypso's face was sad as she answered. "Only you two, my dear, can figure it out, if anyone can figure it out at all. Remember, you and Lux have bonded. He cannot bond with anyone else. If anyone can help him with this, it's you."

Twenty-Three

The Skull and the Dolphin

Suddenly, Andi heard a screeching above them and knew the Skull had found them. Captain Grubb yelled for his crew to man their positions. Calypso began swimming from interconnecting tube to tube, preparing the ship for what was to come. Andi walked over to Lux.

"The demon!" Captain Grubb bellowed to the crew. "It approaches!"

He pointed to the sky. The Skull's wings, no longer ghostly but a bright, scarily bleached white, were flying toward the ship. Andi knew that there was only one thing on the Skull's mind: *vengeance*.

Feeling Lux's body quiver below her, she leaned over and whispered to him. "Ready?"

Hold on with your arms. Tight. The voice was calm, as if Lux had resolved himself to what had to happen. The dolphin circled around from Calypso's tube toward the edge of the ship. Andi climbed to the edge, then climbed on her dolphin's back. Turning back, Andi took one long, perhaps final look at Artie. She tried to muster up all the love for him that she had in her heart so that he could see it in her eyes.

Artie met her gaze and nodded tightly. He came forward with the slinky. Artie stepped as close as he could to Lux without falling off the ship. He held the slinky up to Lux. The dolphin stared at Artie carefully. "Understand?" Artie asked the dolphin.

"Artie?" Andi asked. She was confused. *What was Artie trying to tell Lux?*

As if in response to Andi's thoughts, Artie explained. "It might help Lux. Just in case. Maybe if you have it with you ..." Artie trailed off. Andi smiled down at him.

The dolphin moved past Artie, past Jubal. Andi grabbed Jubal's hand and squeezed it. He squeezed it in return. They moved past him toward Captain Grubb. The Skull was upon them. He flew right in front of Andi and Lux and the Captain.

"You," it rasped at Captain Grubb.

Captain Grubb patted his belly as he met the Skull's eyes. "In all my glory," he spat right into the Skull's face.

"Where is my master?" the Skull asked.

A sly, taunting look appeared on the Captain's face. The Captain was baiting the Skull. "Wouldn't you like to know," he answered.

The Skull tried to attack the Captain, but before he could, Lux flew forward, slamming into the creature's face. Lux flew so quickly that Andi had to hold on as tightly as she could to keep from falling off. Driven back, the creature trembled with fury as it faced Lux. Lux slammed into it again. The creature's wings beat against Lux's sides, drawing blood. Lux's golden sheen began dimming again. In response, Andi kicked her feet against the wings as best as she could. She screamed in pain. The wing had sliced her thigh. *Not too badly,* she thought to herself.

"You will reunite me with my master," the Skull whispered, just loud enough for Andi to hear.

"No, we won't," Andi answered grimly. To Lux, she whispered, "Go!"

Lux zoomed off from the ship, the Skull in fast pursuit. Andi groaned in pain, but she did not let go. The wind whistled past them as they flew above the bay. Andi looked behind her. Despite how fast Lux was flying, the creature was keeping pace, even gaining on them. Its skeletal mouth was open in a snarl.

Hold on! Hearing the urgency in Lux's voice, Andi held on for all she was worth. Lux started speeding around the bay under the huge wave. *Lux was still teleporting air to hold it up!* She gently probed the inside of Lux's mind. She gasped. It was taking everything that he had to fly around the bay and hold the wave up! Andi screamed at Lux. *Let the wave go! Let the wave go!*

Wait! With the Skull right behind them, he flew under the teeming wave. Andi turned around. The Skull was following them under the wave! Suddenly the wave began to fall behind them. Lux was allowing the wave to fall on the Skull. He was still holding it up with air in front of them to allow them to escape! They flew under the rest of the wave as it collapsed behind them. Looking back, Andi saw that the Skull had been beaten down onto the shore by the giant wave it had created. It gave them a bigger lead, but Andi saw that the Skull was stirring to follow them again.

Andi screamed again as she turned to see where they were going. *Lux was flying straight into the cliff!* As they were about to hit it, they passed right through it. In a split second, they were inside Lux's cavern, the one Andi had seen him in from the Skull's cave. As they approached the other side of the immense cavern, Lux tried to seal it off by closing off the passage in the watery lake. It didn't work.

Lux entered the Skull's cavern where the raised bier had been. He sent out huge webs of energy spanning the entire cavern. The cavern shimmered as it began to contract and then expand in Lux's effort to trap the Skull. Refusing to slow down, Lux flew out of the cavern, flying toward the *Kronos*.

Blood from her leg dripped onto Lux's slender body and to the water below. They'd come out the other side of the mountain and were circling back to where the *Kronos* lay waiting. Only—the Skull was behind them! The trap had failed. They hadn't been able to seal the Skull in the cave!

The Skull had caught up and was now on top of them. She slapped the air behind her, trying to hit his face. Instead he flew closer, his mouth opening and then coming down hard on top of her hand. Andi screamed again. Indescribable pain shot through her hand. Yet she did not waver. With her other hand, she tried hitting the Skull.

It stared at her, its mouth open, ravenous. Suddenly, Andi felt herself rise off Lux's back, suspended in the air. The cut on her thigh opened itself up, cutting even deeper into her skin. She hung helplessly over the water, blood streaming down her leg into the sea. The Skull circled her, cackling eerily. Andi felt something slide between her legs at the same time it hit the Skull squarely in its face. It was Lux. He had doubled around to get her, and now he was returning to the *Kronos* them out of desperation. He was rushing at an even faster speed although Andi did not know how this was possible. He was trying to get her out of the Skull's range. Andi could tell that her dolphin did not know what to do. He did not know how to contain the Skull. They were fast approaching the *Kronos*. Andi began to fear that the Skull would attack the ship as a way of getting her to get Lux to do what it wanted.

It might have been better to leave the ship in the small universe it came from, she thought. She never should have touched the ship. No—what an awful thought. That would mean leaving Captain Grubb and Calypso behind. And Donalys.

Where the *Kronos* came *from*. Came *from*. An idea began to grow in her mind, yet it was as small as a seed because of all the pain the Skull had and was still inflicting on her. Her head throbbing, Andi shoved her idea into Lux's mind. Andi yelled internally into Lux's mind. *Go there! Go there! Can you go there?* She raised Artie's slinky above her head and tried to show it to Lux in her mind's eye. *Pull them!* She screamed into his mind. *Pull the ship!*

Andi sensed confusion from the dolphin and uncertainty. But he agreed with her very-good-yet-incomplete idea. Yet Andi was bleeding so much that she could not project any more to him than what she just had. Lux realized this and said *yes*, he would do it.

They were quite close to the *Kronos* now. They began to pass the *Kronos*. Andi turned around. The ship had suddenly begun following them at a very fast speed! How was Lux able to pull it? Andi realized. She wasn't on the ship! How was Lux pulling it? Then she understood.

Artie. Through her relationship with Artie. Her friendship with Jubal, even Calypso.

The ship trailed just right behind them and the Skull. Andi could see Artie and Jubal at the prow, their eyes wide open. Lux was pulling the *Kronos* behind them.

The Skull had caught up to them, flying beside and below them. He was going to try to grab her from Lux again and this time kill her. Andi was certain. She leaned over toward the Skull. She knew this was the last thing it expected her to do—and lassoed Artie's slinky so that its coils sank deep into its skeletal mouth. Pulling the slinky together like a noose, Andi tightened her grip. The coiled slinky stayed stuck in the evil creature's mouth. But the metal coils bit hard into Andi's hands. She was bleeding. If she kept holding on to the Skull, she would lose her hands or even die.

The Skull zoomed around frantically, trying to free himself from the slinky, distracted. *Now! Now!* Andi pleaded. She was in so much pain. Blood was streaming from her hands. Lux tapped into her emotions, letting her panic flood into his mind. That was what it was going to take, Andi realized, just now understanding. That was how they had gotten there and back before, in panic and desperation. Andi remembered what Calypso had said. *The two of them.* Only the two of them could figure it out.

Andi saw a something open in front of her. Through it was a purple sky with a silver sun. Lux flew through the circle. Breathing heavily, Andi sighed with relief. It had worked. *So far,* she reminded herself.

Let go! The dolphin's voice came at her. Andi was still holding on to the slinky. She turned around and stared at the ship, which was quickly following them in the silvery purple world. The Skull had come through also, lassoed by Artie's slinky. The circle had closed. There was no sign of Grey Cove. Andi finally obeyed Lux. She let go of the slinky, and the Skull fell crashing into the purplish sea. If she had held on to the slinky any longer, it would have cut through her hands.

Lux slowed down in the sea, throwing a suggestion toward Andi. She did not understand. She hurt all over and just wanted to rest. Still, she focused on the idea she and Lux shared. Andi smiled, seeing the *Kronos* behind them, matching their speed.

The Skull rose out of the water and began chasing the *Kronos*, trying to overtake them. Listening to Lux, Andi mentally nodded assent to her dolphin as the two mountains rose before them, with the tiny river from the sea running between the two.

Drawing in a deep breath, Andi's heart immediately connected with Lux's. For one moment, they were one person, their hearts beating in sync. Lux sped up to an unimaginable speed, and it was all Andi could do to hold on. Was the *Kronos* behind them? Andi asked Lux. She could not look back at this speed. *Yes* was his reply. Was the *Kronos* going as fast as she and Lux were? *Yes*, he replied.

The two statues were there. Lux sped into the small river between the mountains at a speed Andi had never experienced before. They passed the spot where the wooden and slate figurines had leapt up from their seats and fired their spears upon her and Lux. For a moment, Andi's scar radiated pain. All Andi could tell was that they had passed the midpoint of the river where they had been fired upon before.

She asked Lux, *Were we fired upon?* When his *no* answered her question, she asked the next. *Were they—was the ship—fired upon?* His response of *no* made her collapse with relief. When she asked the third question, her dolphin responded with *do not know.*

She and her dolphin turned around in the silvery purple water. The *Kronos* floated freely behind them, no longer being pulled by Lux. There was no sign of the Skull. Hope rose in Andi's chest, but she pushed it down, refusing to rest until she and Lux were sure. From where she rode upon Lux in the water, she smiled at her twin, just as Artie smiled at her.

Andi nervously told Lux to swim back slowly toward the river. As they turned the curve towards where both figurines were visible on their mountains, Andi gasped.

The Skull was struggling to free himself from two spears. One of them was like the spear that had grazed her shoulder, Andi realized. Both spears had crossed between his wings, paralyzing him in the middle of the small river. Andi could feel its rage. It was trapped, like Captain Grubb and the *Kronos* had been. She looked up to where the figurines were. Both were seated again, brand-new spears in each hand.

Andi knew they could not cross back towards the other side. The risk was too great. Andi turned back to the Skull and gasped. The two spears were dragging it down into the sea! Both she and Lux watched horrified as the Skull shrieked both in pain and rage as the two spears dragged its head beneath the sea. Andi felt as if she were about to throw up.

"Please rise up into the air," Andi voiced clearly to Lux. She had a question. Slowly the golden dolphin rose into the purple sky until it was level with the ship. They flew over to where Calypso floated, a look of relief on her face. The Captain's face looked happy.

"Did it work?" Andi asked Calypso.

"It would seem so," the selkie answered, her face full of relief.

Artie and Jubal had approached her and Lux from behind. They waited behind her. "Is the Skull dead?"

"I do not know," Calypso answered. "It should never have survived when we ejected it off our ship all those years ago. But it is trapped now and no longer on your world."

Both Artie and Jubal had broad grins. Andi got down from Lux. She beckoned for him to come down to her level. As he lowered down towards her level, Andi wrapped him in a large embrace. She didn't want to let go.

Finally, she turned back to Captain Grubb and Calypso. "So," she began, "we'll go back to Earth to drop Jubal off, and then Artie and I will go with you." She gasped. "Into space." She still couldn't wrap her head around it.

Captain Grubb stared at Lux soberly and then at Jubal and back at Andi.

"Lux closed the entry back to your world," he said to Andi gently, although he was looking at Jubal. "The tunnel he made—it is closed."

Told me to close on both ends, Lux spoke into Andi's mind. Shocked, she turned around, looking at Jubal. It was true. Lux had obeyed directions.

He had closed one end of the tunnel he made into this—*place*. Lux had closed the tunnel to Earth so that the Skull couldn't go back. She turned around to look at Jubal.

"Can't you just make another tunnel?" She asked Lux.

Cannot. Do not know why.

Jubal's mouth opened in realization. It looked as if he were trying to form words, but then his mouth closed again. He looked at them. Andi could not tell what he was thinking.

"He closed the passage, didn't he? In case your plan didn't work out. That makes sense." Jubal was covering up, trying to be kind. "He can't go back, can he? Right," he stammered. "I mean, right." He trembled.

Andi was frustrated suddenly. She said, "But it doesn't feel like a passage! We were there, and then we were here in the purple world!" She felt like crying.

Calypso looked sad. "Lux closed the tunnel as we passed through it—so that the Skull would not be able to return in case your plan to have those two Guardians capture him failed."

Guardians? Andi thought. She shook her head. It didn't matter. Not right now.

Andi turned to Lux. "Can we go back to Earth?"

Not now. The dolphin spoke into Andi's mind. *Maybe later. Do not know.*

Andi thought she understood. Maybe Lux could not teleport over such a great distance without a feeling of panic, rage, or something similar. He would have to learn how to teleport great distances on his own without those accompanying emotions. Or maybe there was another reason that they didn't understand just yet.

As Andi explained to everyone what Lux had told her, she could see how Jubal's pain pierced Artie, Captain Grubb, and Calypso. Even Lux.

Lux turned to Jubal. Instead of saying anything into Andi's mind, he floated close to Jubal's face. Jubal slowly raised his hands toward the dolphin and faced Lux.

"I know you did your best," he answered the dolphin.

The dolphin then turned to Captain Grubb. Lux whispered into Andi's brain. He was asking where to go.

"Where do we go?" Andi asked Captain Grubb.

The Captain was at a loss for words. He shook his head as he glanced at Calypso.

"Out of here might be a good first step, Captain." Calypso smiled at Andi before facing the Captain. The selkie floated before him, her hand on the glass.

"He can leave the other way? The end of this?" the Captain asked Andi.

"Of course," Andi answered him, listing to Lux's thoughts. Lux had closed the tunnel back to Earth. But he didn't need to make a tunnel to the other end. Captain Grubb would soon see. They would all soon see. She nodded to Lux. He knew what he had to do.

Andi found herself torn. She had won; she and Artie had a home, with Lux. Even though they could leave this place, Jubal was stuck with them. He hadn't spoken. He'd just gone to the prow of the ship, looking at the silvery purple world—or whatever it was. Right now, he didn't look devastated—he looked *awed*. Andi remembered the bruise on Jubal's face. *As much as he loved his mother* ... she stopped herself. She had enough to think about. Her own mother was alive, and she had left them.

Lux started to swim, pulling the *Kronos* behind him. The four— Andi, Artie, Donalys and Jubal—all stood in the front, at the prow of the ship. The read haired nephew of the Captain had joined them very determinedly in the front. The wind in their faces was gave them an incredible feeling. Lux swam faster and faster. Andi found that she could not look at Jubal. Artie slipped his hand into hers, transmitting to her the small sense of triumph that they were together. And that they would continue to be together. A tear trailed from Andi's eye.

Faster and faster. They were far out from the conical mountains now on the silvery ocean under the purplish sky. As they approached the horizon, the black space began to rise in front of them, full of stars. The purple horizon gave way to the starry universe. The black horizon with its many stars rose in front of them. Andi suddenly realized Lux was not swimming on water anymore! Andi saw the Captain pull a lever. A soft, giant bubble of oxygen began to envelop the ship.

The feeling of being on a skipping stone occurred again. They were out into the inky blackness—blacker than Andi could have ever imagined, a universe with glowing stars. The stars looked so real. They were not on a photograph. They were not viewed through the night sky. These stars were *alive*. Pulsating, moving, breathing.

Andi gasped, gripping Artie's hand as he gripped hers. They both looked out at Lux, their golden dolphin gliding out into the universe, pulling the ship behind him. Andi turned back from the prow to look at the *Kronos*, their home. They had made it. They were home. Then Andi saw Jubal's face. It was filled with grief.

Twenty-Four

Epilogue

WHAT'S IN A NAME?

They were home. They had won. No—she, Artie, and Lux had won. Home. The *Kronos* was her home now. She missed Grandma Bea horribly. Calypso was right though. The memories made up for the grief.

It was impossible to remember Grandma Bea without thinking of her mother. She had not shared the truth with Artie yet. She wondered if she would ever find out the truth about why her mother left. Left them. Left her. Was she alive? Had they left her behind on Earth? Andi had found out about her mother too late.

Lux floated in front of the ship, pulling the *Kronos* through space. The crew had created a false gravity on the ship so that they could walk just as if they were on Earth. The *Kronos* floated in space toward an unknown destination.

The two questions everyone had on their minds now were how to find Captain Grubb's people and how to help Jubal cope with the fact that he'd left his mother behind. She and Artie had pretty much cut all their ties when Grandma died. But Jubal hadn't. He seemed to alternate between grief and enjoyment of his new freedom. After all, Jubal loved the *Kronos* and was awed by its mission among the stars.

The boys were settling down on the front deck. Jubal had decided to teach Artie and Donalys how to play cards. He'd created his own. Artie had been able to learn, but Donalys had not. Donalys slammed his cards down in frustration. He left the game and skipped up to Andi.

"And-ee," he said plaintively, arms folded across his chest, brow furrowed.

"What is it?" Andi asked.

"Artie and Jubal say your name isn't Andi," Donalys said.

Andi laughed. She put her hands on her hips half-mockingly, making a face at Artie and Jubal, who looked all too innocent.

"And I suppose they told you my real name?" she asked.

"No."

"Well, good, then. They're not as stupid as I thought," Andi said, laughing.

Jubal and Artie grinned mischievously at her from behind their cards. Lux laughed inside her mind.

"What is your name?" Donalys persisted.

Andi smiled and began to speak, then stopped. She looked out at the stars.

"My name," she told Donalys, "is Andromeda."

First Chapter of Map of a Soundless Clock

MAP OF A SOUNDLESS CLOCK

THE PITFALLS OF GRAVITY

Captain Grubb slumped wearily and leaned against the steering wheel of the *Kronos*. His face was a mixture of disappointment and frustration. Andi wondered for a moment if he would fall. She imagined his immense heft ripping the steering wheel from where it stood on the upper deck—but it held. The captain's face turned as red as his hair and beard as he shouted down to her.

"He can't sense anything? Anything at all?" There was a note of pleading in his voice that Andi hated refuting.

"I don't think you understand," Andi began, her hand gliding over Lux's glowing skin. She liked seeing the golden light between her fingers.

"He and I have a mental bond," she continued. "That's it. He doesn't have a bond with anyone else. He can't sense things out there. That's not how it works," she repeated tiredly from where she sat astride the floating dolphin.

Andi and Lux floated several yards ahead of the bow. The captain's deck stood well above the main deck of the ship. Yet it was smaller in size, fitting only a group of twenty where the main deck easily fit more than a hundred. Captain Grubb looked down at them from behind the steering wheel. Crewmen stood on the main deck watching the exchange between Andi and their captain.

Andi refused to look out at the weightlessness of space all around them. Lux shone like a beacon in the very dark night of the universe. *The universe.* Andi swallowed heavily, turning back to face the beyond. *The beyond.* There was no other term for it. The immensity of the darkness of space, its endlessness choked the life out of her. The *Kronos*, an ancient sailing ship, was somehow floating in space, pulled out by Lux. Pulled out—out—well, towards *what?*

That's the problem, Andi acknowledged to herself grudgingly. She continued staring up at the captain. He was examining something on the top deck.

Yes, Lux answered her. *It is.*

Andi grinned despite herself. Most of the time, when she thought to herself, Lux chose not to comment. But when he did—rarely—it was always well timed. He knew her moods.

"And he's not going any faster," Captain Grubb continued, his mouth a grim line.

"Look," Andi shouted up to Captain Grubb, "I don't know how to make him go faster."

"But he was able to before—"

"I told you," Andi explained, reminding herself to be patient, "that he pulled us to that other place. He doesn't know how he did it."

Captain Grubb pulled off his golden cap, his long red hair cascading down his face. He rubbed his forehead. "He has showed us he can do it. We can't continue like this," he explained. "We don't have all the time in the world to look. We're done for now," Captain Grubb ended with finality. He disappeared. Andi knew he was going to check the ship's instruments to see if any signs of life had manifested themselves.

Andi turned from the ship, joining her gaze with Lux's towards the heavy blackness of space. She kept her eye fixed on the one star that was brighter, more solid than the others. That was the secret Calypso had shared with her. "Just fix your eye on one of them," the blue-skinned selkie had advised. "Let that star be your focal point. Don't let the blackness swallow you up."

So far, it had worked. It was not an experiment that Andi enjoyed. All she wanted was to be with her golden dolphin, to enjoy him and be together. And when Andi allowed herself to relax, there was more than one star—millions of stars stood decorating the black canvas of space, multicolored, varying in their hues. They did not twinkle—stars only twinkled when seen through an atmosphere. Instead, they were orbs of life, blazing out as if to say *look at me—see how alive I am!*

Behind her, Andi heard murmurs amongst the crewmen who stood on the below deck, as they monitored both her and Lux. Although she couldn't make out the words, they were clearly trying to figure out what she had said to Captain Grubb.

That was why Andi was so thankful for Calypso. Looking back at the captain's deck, the selkie floated in the glass tube nearby. The tube ran throughout the *Kronos*, allowing Calypso to move through it in her role as Navigator of the ship. She was also the ship's Interpreter. Her ability to read minds allowed her to understand the nuances of different languages, enabling her to translate. She hadn't translated Captain Grubb's conversation with Andi for the crewmen, choosing instead to respect their privacy. At other times, she translated for the entire ship. It always depended on what Calypso thought was right.

Calypso's human yet alien eyes met Andi's and there was in them a note of mute understanding. It was so hard dealing with Captain Grubb, and even harder to disappoint him. Sometimes Andi wanted to stop trying to help. It was so hard to keep disappointing everyone.

But as her twin brother Artie often reminded her, "They helped us. We need to help them."

Yep, Andi silently assented. Her best friend Jubal was more sarcastic about it than Artie was. Jubal had his own share of frustrations too, but even he agreed that they needed to return the favor.

"Lux," she said aloud to her dolphin, "take me back to the deck. I don't think we're going to find out anything today."

Turning around gently as not to upset her balance, Lux floated towards the main deck. Crewmen rushed towards her with their arms outstretched, ready to help. Not for the first time, Andi found herself wishing that they would let her slide off Lux's back by herself. She didn't need grooms helping her on and off like Lux was a horse! She knew they were doing it under Captain Grubb's orders, but it didn't make her feel any more comfortable.

Trying to be gracious, she murmured, "Thank you," as one crewman reached for her hand. She whispered another "thank you" when another crewman put his hands on her shoulders to help her slide off.

Captain Grubb was looking down on them from the railing of the top deck. "Did your instruments detect anything?" Andi made sure to insert a hopeful note in her voice.

Captain Grubb rubbed his red beard. "No, girlie. Nothing." His face looked bleak as he said it. A crowd of crewmen next to Andi looked up at him too, waiting for his answer. Andi heard a collective groan of disappointment. Calypso, knowing the conversation was about the entire ship, had chosen to translate for everyone.

Without saying anything more, the captain turned away. Andi knew that he had taken the stone elevator beneath the captain's seat leading to his quarters. She could no longer see Calypso. Andi guessed that the selkie had swum to where the tube passed through the captain's quarters.

It irritated Andi that everyone on the *Kronos* wanted her to do this or that with Lux. They never chose to include her in their discussions and plans. They simply told her what to do and when to do it.

But yes, Andi acknowledged to herself, *we have a home.* Where would they have gone if not for the *Kronos*? They had helped her, Artie, and even welcomed Jubal when he ended up on board by accident. Andi looked around her. All the crewmen were walking towards the large staircase where their quarters lay below deck. Andi still didn't know where they ate; she, Artie, and Jubal always sat at the captain's table on the top deck. Calypso always attended their meals but did not join them in eating. She merely floated in the glass tube nearby and made conversation with the group. They were also often joined by the captain and his young nephew, Donalys. Thinking of the boy, his red hair matching his uncle's, made Andi smile.

Looking around, there was only Lux, his golden figure floating half a foot above her. Lux was concerned for her. Andi smiled reassuringly, trying to quiet all the frenzied perspectives warring inside her mind. They were alive. They were together. And that was all that mattered.

Several crewmen remained on the main deck, absorbed in their responsibilities. Other than that, Andi found herself with Lux. Why did it feel like she was disappointing them? *Because I am,* Andi concluded miserably. If Lux continued pulling the *Kronos* out into space, there was hope. Yet that hope grew smaller and smaller the more they traveled. The longer they went without finding any clues about where to find their lost people.

How can we find them? Andi wondered. Wasn't it irrational to even try? Scanning the vastness of space around, above, and beneath them, the girl shivered. What was it Grandma Bea used to say? *Trying to find a needle in a haystack...* that was it.

Walking towards the front of the ship's bow, Andi climbed on the deck's railing and sat on its edge, her hands gripping the top of the railing. Her feet dangled over the bottom. Lux flew several yards out into space then reversed position so that he was facing her. Calypso had asked Andi in genuine bewilderment how the girl was able to do this. If flying through space scared Andi so much, why wouldn't she be afraid to sit on the railing? Andi had responded that when Lux was facing her instead of facing out towards space, she felt much safer.

Okay? Lux asked.

Great, Andi replied, beatific. Facing Lux, every worry and every concern slid off her back effortlessly. They were together. Taking in a deep breath, Andi scanned the universe around her, Lux squarely in the center of her vision. *He was a much better anchor than a faraway star ever could be,* she mused silently to herself.

Andi! Lux jumped, startled.

Someone slid their hands over Andi's eyes from behind. Letting out a startled scream, she slipped from her seated position. One minute she was falling and the next, Andi found herself floating, unable to breathe.

Scrambling madly, Andi grabbed at empty space, trying to gain a foothold. Spinning in the dark night of space, her lungs spasmed. Dots appeared in her eyes. *She could not breathe!* She was in space! There was a gravity bubble around the *Kronos* that kept air inside of it so that everyone could breathe freely. Losing consciousness, Andi blinked slowly in wonder as ice began to form on the tips of her fingers.

Lux slammed into Andi hard, bringing with him oxygen he stored within himself. She could breathe. Blinking, Andi mouthed to herself *I can breathe.* Lux stayed with her as Andi's hand reached for him. Her thoughts... becoming clearer by the second. She kept blinking at Lux who kept repeating one word at her through their shared bond.

Andi!

Andi!

Finally, a mental shout: *ANDI!*

Andi's mind focused on a single figure ahead of her: Donalys. The boy scrambled in space, freed from the gravity of the *Kronos*.

Go, Andi said firmly to Lux, sliding herself on his back. Weight. She had weight below her now. Lux shot forward, Andi holding on with all her might.

Donalys hugged himself tightly with his arms, still spinning. The *Kronos* was in the distance, crewmen running to the bow of the ship. Andi imagined hearing them shout even as she saw them point towards her, Lux and Donalys.

They were in range of Donalys now. *There... wait... there!* Andi grabbed the red-haired boy's hand, pulling him alongside her so he could breathe in from Lux's hidden reserves. As she dragged Donalys next to her and Lux, the boy's eyes shot up to hers in confusion and fear.

"Breathe," Andi said. "Breathe!"

Donalys nodded slowly, inhaling deeply. His eyes widened as he became more aware of his surroundings.

Okay? Lux asked frantically.

I've heard of people losing some of their brain function because they can't breathe! Andi relayed silently to him. She peered closely at Donalys. His eyes were clear, and he obviously knew Andi. Andi raised her eyebrows at him. Donalys raised his back at her in response. Andi calmed down. Donalys was okay.

Andi! Look! Lux shouted into her mind.

Several of the crewmen were jumping out from the ship towards them! *About six*, Andi realized with a sinking feeling. All had their arms linked and all jumped out from the bow of the ship towards them.

What are they doing? Andi asked Lux, stupefied.

Trying to help you! Her dolphin shouted back at her.

I can't grab all of them, Andi replied speechless. *I was barely able to get Donalys.* The crewmen were floating in space now, their arms still linked. Their legs were kicking hard, flailing as they desperately gasped for air.

Wait! Lux shouted into Andi's mind.

Approaching the *Kronos*, Lux started to pull it. The ship followed. Lux pulled the *Kronos* behind it as he flew towards the crewmen. Lux struggled to pick up speed.

What are you doing? Andi demanded.

Watch! Lux answered with a hint of desperation.

As Lux pulled the *Kronos*, the ship came closer to the crewmen. Lux dipped in his flight just so that the ship would pass below them.

"The gravity bubble!" Andi exclaimed.

Yes! Lux affirmed.

The top of the ship's mast flew below the crewmen. Then Lux pulled up sharply, the

Kronos rising behind him. It evened itself out into a straight angle. The crewmen crashed onto the top deck of the ship in a series of heavy and sickening thumps.

"You flew so close... the gravity bubble of the ship pulled them in," Andi voiced, amazed.

There was nothing but an echoing relief reverberating from Lux.

Andi heard groans rising from the deck. By the time she, Lux, and

Donalys finally rose above the top deck, they had begun to diminish in volume. There was instead a furious murmur. Artie and Jubal towards them, with a very angry Captain Grubb following right behind.

Lux floated down to the top deck. Andi slid off his back, pulling Donalys after her. The boy collapsed on the deck, huddled. He did not show his face, choosing instead to hide under the long mass of red hair he shared with his uncle. Andi sighed, looking down at the boy. Artie reached her first, clasping her on the shoulder wordlessly. Jubal grabbed her in a fierce hug. The large, rotund captain was spluttering with rage.

"What — what —" Captain Grubb spluttered. He stood looking at all three of them: her, Donalys, and Lux, hovering right next to her. Angry crewmen began gathering behind the captain, their faces murderous and glares fierce. One of them, a man with long black hair, looked as if he was about to speak. Captain Grubb's hands shot upward, signaling for silence.

"It's my fault, Uncle," Donalys whispered miserably, still huddled, not looking up.

"I'm not so sure about that—" Andi interjected before someone else jumped in.

"Make way! Make way!" Andi heard someone cry. "The Navigator approaches!"

Two men rolled out a glass tube on wheels. Calypso floated inside; her hands pressed against the glass. *A portable tube*, Andi realized. Something that allowed the ship's Navigator to reach where the ship's large glass tube would not permit her to go.

"What has happened here?" Calypso's voice was filled with concern, though none of the anger that Captain Grubb or the other crewmen displayed. Both she and the captain looked at Andi, waiting for an answer.

Feeling sheepish and unsure of herself, Andi spoke to Donalys. "Did you slide your hands around my eyes while I was talking to Lux?"

"Ye-es," the boy groaned. Captain Grubb looked even more scarlet, if that was possible. But Andi continued.

"And who taught you how to do that, Donalys?"

"What?" The red-haired boy finally looked up at her, confused.

Patiently, Andi asked again. "Sliding your hands around my eyes, Donalys. Who taught you that trick?"

"J-Jubal," Donalys stammered. "He did it to you the other day."

Jubal whistled, absorbing this new information. Looking at Andi, he answered. "So, he..." He ran his hands through his thick, black curly hair, his blue eyes offsetting his dark features.

"But there's one thing I still don't understand," Calypso spoke from inside the portable tube. "Why did the crewmen jump after you?" She turned to the men, still on the floor. Some had raised themselves to a seated position.

"The Golden Creature!" One crewman responded. "We have no hope without it."

"How would we ever find our lost people?" Another asked.

So, they were trying to save you, Andi thought silently to Lux.

The dolphin did not answer, his thoughts guarded from her.

"It is worth any risk," a third crewman said, rising to his feet. "Even at the cost of our own lives." He looked at Captain Grubb wearily. "If even just a few of us can find our home..." he trailed off.

The crewman with long black hair stepped forward, appearing ready to say something to the captain.

"Sir," he said to Captain Grubb, "the crew wishes to call a Forum."

"Must we?" Captain Grubb answered him, looking pained. "We have never called a Forum before."

The crewman brushed his hair to the side. "I think we must. There are some questions... that the crew requires answers to," he answered smoothly. Looking at Andi and Donalys, he continued. "The crew will not need atonement from them. We simply wish to... understand a few things." Frowning, the crewman added: "You have been keeping them to yourself. None of us know them or who they are."

"Fine, Calz," the captain answered wearily. "Proceed with the Forum."

In the time they had spoken, crewmen had erected a platform on the other end of the deck. It reminded Andi of a stage. Crewmen began to gather in front of it, seating themselves on the floor of the deck.

"Please follow me," Calz said deferentially, nodding to Andi and Donalys. "Oh, the two of you as well," he added, glancing at Jubal and Artie. "The creature too," he said finally, frowning. He looked as if he was trying to figure out how Lux would answer their questions. The four of them plus Lux walked towards the platform escorted by several members of the crew. Chairs waited for them on the raised stage. Andi understood. They—plus Lux—would face the crew and answer their questions.

As they seated themselves in the chairs, the crewmen formed rows. All sat on the floor across from them. Captain Grubb stood to the side, Calypso floating next to him. Calz stood at the front, speaking to the crewmen in a language she could not understand. She looked at Calypso.

"Yes," the selkie affirmed. "They asked me not to translate, although when they ask their questions, I will." Andi sensed an undercurrent of concern from Calypso; a feeling that perhaps she did not want Andi to pick up on.

Calz turned towards them, his face smooth. He looked as if he were in his twenties, Andi realized, as she remembered that the crew had found themselves trapped in some sort of stasis for millions of years. This made them very old. *But they sure don't look like it*, she mused to herself.

"A question," Calz began, with that same deferential attitude, "is why you were sitting on that railing at all. You fell, then were ejected into space where the Golden Creature helped you. Then the boy. Then our crewmen. The crewmen are injured. Because they were saving you." He paused. "Tried to save you," he amended.

"And I am very sorry for that," Andi tried to smile.

"As we understand it," Calz pursed his lips, ignoring Andi's apology. "Your dolphin is able to pull the *Kronos* out into space because you are on board." He spread his arms apart as he said this. "But when you fell off, he was still able to pull the *Kronos*. Are you—would he be—" he inclined his head towards Lux as he said it, "able to explain this?"

Andi blinked. That had never occurred to her. It was true. The only reason Lux was able to pull the *Kronos* was because she was on it. But—

You not on it when Skull chasing, Lux spoke into her mind, finishing what she was thinking.

That was true. "Then how were you able to do it?" Andi asked aloud. She realized too late that she had asked him with her voice and not with her mind. But maybe this was the best way to answer Calz and his friends, after all. That way, everything was out in the open. Another thing occurred to her. "But what about when I'm riding on top of you? I'm not on the ship then."

Bonded to you, Lux answered. *Bonded to no one else. But you are very close to Artie. Twin.*

"So, it's because of Artie? Because he's my brother?" Andi used her voice again.

Lux was silent as he digested her question. Finally, he answered.

It is one of them. Strongest reason. Only? I am not sure.

"So," Andi paused, searching for the right words, "Artie is the biggest reason but may not be the only reason."

You close to Jubal, Donalys. The captain is Donalys' uncle. Maybe those reasons.

"It may be… it may be that Artie being on board is one reason why Lux was able to pull the *Kronos*. But Jubal may be another reason. Even Donalys. We grew close when he was hiding in our basement. And then the fact that Donalys' uncle is the captain."

Andi looked at Calz as she said this. "It seems to be about how close I am to a person who is on the *Kronos*." Looking at Lux, she added, "If I'm close to someone on the ship then Lux's protection extends to them too. But only up to a point. Right, Lux?"

Yes, the dolphin affirmed. *Up to point only.* It sounded more like a warning.

The crew murmured as they heard Andi answer the questions. There was a newfound respect in many of their eyes. But not Calz's. He looked disappointed. The crewmen spoke to Calz and to each other at length.

Calz's face had remained neutral throughout the questioning, but now his expression changed. He smiled at the seated crew as the murmur rose, becoming more insistent, firm, as if demanding an answer.

Lux's anger hit Andi like a blow to the stomach. He had understood what they were asking. A powerful current of fury emanated from him. Andy remembered how angry Lux was when he found her bleeding in the Skull's cavern, hanging in the air. Was whatever Calz planned to ask *that* bad?

Calz spun around on his foot, facing the four of them again. He glanced askance at Lux. Andi understood. Calz was trying to communicate with Lux. It was as if he was pleading him not to act out on the cold fire of anger coursing through him.

Lux's anger only blazed as his golden light increased in intensity, less gold than fire. Andi squirmed in her chair. Something was very, very wrong. Artie looked at Andi in concern, followed by Jubal and Donalys. Then Lux did something very strange. He moved and placed himself directly above Andi's head. Lux stared out at the crewmen as if daring them to do whatever it was that had entered their minds.

Instead of his face becoming scarlet in anger, Captain Grubb's had gone pure white. He leaned over to Calypso's water tube and whispered something to her. Calypso nodded in response, her eyes never leaving Andi's. In them stood the same agitation and fury Lux carried.

Calz addressed Andi.

"In the event of your death, can someone else bond with Lux?"

THE PLAY'S THE THING

Jubal jumped up in his seat. "What the *hell* kind of question is that?" he shouted. Calz managed to look somewhat rebuffed but maintained his stance.

"We do need to know if the Golden Creature can bond with someone else in the event of her death," he answered soberly. "If he cannot,
then everything depends on the girl." He gave Andi a curt nod. "As
such, increased measures for her protection will be necessary." Turning
to Captain Grubb, he continued. "Isn't that so?"

Captain Grubb's face was still. His lack of response signaled that
this was not a new idea. Calypso, floating inside of her tube, looked at
the captain, as if incredulous. Calypso then glared at Calz.

"Put a stop to this, Zare," Calypso said to Captain Grubb, her tone
angry. "You can't let this happen—"

"He can, because he must," Calz interrupted. "When a crew calls a
Forum, the laws state that the concerns of the crew merit one or more
answers. The captain can do nothing." He shot a fierce glare at Captain
Grubb, as if daring him to try to do something.

The captain looked at him coolly. *He isn't falling for the bait,* Andi
realized.

"I say," a voice said from within the gathered crewmen, "wouldn't it
be better to discuss this without the girl? It's not worth angering the
Golden Creature." A very tiny man rose from within the audience. He
had a long white beard and a red pointed cap. Looking at him, Andi
irrationally wanted to giggle. Then she realized that she had understood
the tiny man. Calypso was still translating even though the little man
was talking to Calz, not her!

Shooting Calypso a grateful look, she found the gaze returned. It
said, *Of course I'm translating. This is about you!*

"Um," Andi began. Artie's hand was on her shoulder. She wondered
how long it had been there. Sitting up straight in her chair, she faced
Calz evenly. She prayed that she would not betray her upset stomach.
The blaze Lux gave off increased in heat. His golden sheen had disappeared; in its place was fire.

"I don't know," she shrugged, forcing herself to remain calm. "I don't
think Lux does either. Do you, Lux?"

No, the dolphin answered. Andi swore to herself. The heat coming
off him had gone up in seconds.

"And to be honest with you," Andi added sweetly, "I'm not going to try and find out." She enjoyed seeing Calz start in surprise at her statement.

The tiny man chuckled from within the throng. "She can bite back, Calz. Suggest you drop this line of questioning. After all, we *do* need her."

Need. There was that word again. They needed her. Of course. To talk to Lux. To help him do the things they wanted him to do.

"I did not want to ask the question, Ithak," Calz answered, his tone as cool as Andi's. "Our brethren insisted we do so."

"You tell our *brethren* to stop now, Calz," the man called Ithak answered. "They might decide not to help us find our people."

"But it's been months!" Another crewman stood up in the audience. "We are no closer to finding our people than when we first started!"

Captain Grubb stamped over to the tall man with the black hair. "That's on us, you fool. On us. This girl and her creature have nothing to do with it."

Yet another crewman stood up, a man of medium height with shadowed eyes. "But if we were to bond with the dolphin, it could pick something up from our minds. Maybe find a clue that we've forgotten ourselves?" He stopped as he heard murmurs of agreement all around.

Then Lux took off from above Andi's head. He flew out into the starry blackness beyond. He burst into flame. If he had been blazing before, this was an *inferno*! Andi licked her lips nervously.

Lux's words appeared in her mind. *Tell them watch.*

"He says to watch," Andi said to the hushed audience. "He's going to do something. I don't know what."

All the crewmen turned towards Lux, their eyes reflecting his fire. Lux flew, forming a shape out of the flame. The shape became a giant figure. A girl with overalls appeared outlined in the fire. *Why, it's me,* Andi realized, dazed. The enormous fiery figure of Andi stood bright and brilliant in the heavens. Then the figure began to move. The representation of Andi went from a smiling girl to one with a blank stare.

He's showing my death, Andi realized, now truly terrified.

The gigantic image of the now-dead Andi faded, replaced by a ship—a replica of the *Kronos*! She looked at her companions seated beside her. Artie's face went white while Jubal's mouth opened, slack in amazement. Donalys looked truly frightened.

A fiery dolphin appeared next to the replica of the ship. Then the image of the dolphin flew out far into space, leaving the fiery *Kronos* behind. The image of the dolphin disappeared. The faces of all the crewmen aboard the replicated *Kronos* dissolved into despair. Their mouths were open in silent screams of protest. Calz's face was the most prominent.

Andi understood. If something happened to her, Lux was telling everyone onboard the *Kronos* that all bets were off. They had come this far only because of him. They had no hope without him—*and me*, Andi amended silently.

The fiery vision dissolved into winking sparks. The crewmen turned back to Andi, their faces ashen. Looking at Captain Grubb for guidance, Andi saw that Lux had depicted his worst nightmare. Only Calypso smiled. Her face never left Andi's. The girl shot the selkie a grateful look before Calz broke in.

"You shouldn't have done that," he said through gritted teeth to Andi. "You shouldn't have done that."

Andi jumped up at this statement. She'd had enough. "Do you really think I put Lux up to this? He understood you all on his own. He figured it all out on his own. I had no idea he was going to do this."

She pointed up to space above them. "Look at what he did! Do you think he would've done that if he'd asked me to translate?" Andi was angry by now.

Calz refused to listen, keeping his head down. He stomped off, disappearing into the ship. Andi looked after his departing figure in amazement. Did he really think she had put Lux up to this? She knew that Lux was trying to protect her by not having her speak for him. This time he had spoken for himself quite clearly. Calz was unwilling to believe that.

Still looking up in the air at Lux, Andi jumped when he moved away, hurtling outward into space. He was leaving. Why? *Was this his way of showing the crewmen that this was what would happen if something did happen to her?* Andi tried to reach out to him through their shared mental bond. While she could still feel his incredible fury, she got no response. Sadly, she turned around to look at her friends.

Artie met her eyes first, his calm and questioning. Andi shrugged at her twin as if saying *What am I to do?* She smiled at him.

"You're here aren't you?" she asked.

The bemused expression that crossed his face showed that he did not understand. Andi laughed, then knelt before her twin, her hands on his knees as he sat in his chair.

"You're not distracted," she explained. "You're not lost inside one of those theories your head is always spinning out." Seeing Artie's ears turn pink, she added, "But hearing about those theories is always wonderful."

A relieved expression appeared on his face. Shaking her head to herself, Andi realized that Artie never wanted to disappoint her. Never wanted to let her down. *And he hasn't,* Andi realized with a broad grin.

Jubal walked towards her, dragging Donalys behind him. "That grin. You must be feeling better although I sure can't figure out why." He looked out towards space, where Lux's fiery display had taken place. "That was, well, *dramatic.*"

"No kidding," Andi answered dryly. Looking down at Donalys, Andi realized the boy was trembling. She put her hand on his shoulder. He was only a year and half younger than she was, Andi realized. Despite the fact they found themselves stuck for millions of years in some pocket universe... that didn't make Donalys any less a ten-year-old.

"I'm sorry, Andi," Donalys blurted out. "So sorry that—"

"You had no idea that was going to happen," she answered.

Jubal snorted. "You're lucky you played that joke on Andi," he told the younger boy. "I can think of some girls back home who would hold a grudge against you for, like, *forever.*"

Donalys' eyes widened as he heard this. "Andi's better than them," he declared. The adoring look he gave Andi made her uncomfortable. She felt responsible for him, but it was not a responsibility she wanted. Yet hadn't she taken that on when she found him inside the cave? The one at the bottom of the cliff she lived on. *Used to live on,* Andi reminded herself.

Jubal chuckled as he listened to Donalys. After seeing the expression on Andi's face, he quieted down immediately. "Andi..." he hesitated. "Where did Lux go?"

Andi raised her hands up in an *I don't know* gesture. Jubal nodded back at her. "They really ticked him off, didn't they." It was not a question.

That was the moment Captain Grubb chose to break into the conversation. "Do you think you could all come down from there?" His voice was plaintive.

Andi understood. What had happened had unnerved the captain. He was a man who always liked to show that he was in control of every situation. Calypso waved her down from the platform, so she ushered everyone off. She could tell the captain was very upset. *Whatever,* she shrugged.

Captain Grubb was deep in a quiet conversation with Calypso. Their heads shot up as Andi and her friends approached. Andi heard only one word and it was "mutiny." She looked at both Artie and Jubal to see if they had picked up on the word also, but their faces remained blank. Donalys had understood and his face shot up to hers.

"Okay, so," Andi began. "Will that keep them in line, or will it make them even angrier?"

Despite himself, Captain Grubb chuckled. "Direct and to the point, are you not, girl?"

Andi grinned at him. "What's the point of tiptoeing all around it? *They* sure didn't."

Calypso chose this moment to break in. "I am very angry, Andi. At them. This should not have happened. None of it should have taken place." Her bluish complexion darkened.

"They're scared," Jubal said. "What happened with Andi falling off and Lux dragging the ship down after her—it would upset anybody."

Captain Grubb hesitated. "But were they wrong?" he asked Jubal. Calypso's mouth parted in shock.

"Zare," she told him reprovingly, "she is a child."

"A child who can communicate with that dolphin while no one else can," Grubb said soberly. "They're actually talking about mutiny." Artie and Jubal shot startled glances at Andi.

"Space and sea," Captain Grubb rasped, losing his patience, his expression thunderous. "She isn't one of our crew! She rides with us, but she knows nothing about the ship. Nothing about us. The incident... I can't blame the crewmen for wondering after that happened."

"No," Calypso replied. "This incident may have made them come forward, but they've all been talking about it for a while now. Calz," she pronounced the name with a hint of distaste, "has been stirring them up. I've heard things. You know why he's doing this, Zare."

Artie finally spoke. "Frustrated," he said.

Andi looked at her twin. "Yes," she answered but Jubal's eyes had narrowed the way they always did when he had a flash of sudden insight. "Frustrated yes, Artie, but tell us why."

"We have not found it yet," her blond-haired brother explained.

"Our people," Captain Grubb said with a sigh. "The crew is only now starting to understand we may never find them. Our lost people. The universe is so vast..." he trailed off.

"Didn't you have a map of where you were going?" Jubal asked the captain.

"A path was created..." the captain began.

Jubal nodded impatiently. "Yes, yes. A wormhole. I *know*."

If Captain Grubb noticed Jubal's anger, he gave no sign. "We were all supposed to follow each other through it. We dropped out of it and... found ourselves trapped in that place where you and your Golden Creature found us." The captain addressed the final part of his statement to Andi.

"And now you have no idea where to go," Jubal concluded sadly.

"No," Captain Grubb answered soberly. "We don't."

"Isn't that your fault?" Jubal snapped. "Shouldn't you have taken that contingency into account? Anything could have happened."

Captain Grubb's eyes went flat. Iron. Andi knew there would be no response to Jubal's accusation.

Jubal looked at Andi and then said, "I don't care. I'm glad I said it." Andi tried to respond but then Lux reappeared far out in space. Turning her gaze upward, Lux was still wreathed in fiery anger.

"Lux," she whispered aloud, not caring if others heard her. Everyone's eyes turned up towards Lux, still floating at a distance above the ship. He did not want to consume them with his fire. *Could he control it?* Andi wondered. She wondered if it had to do with the bond they shared—any attack upon her was an attack on Lux himself. *And this is his line of defense*, she mused to herself.

A realization dawned on Andi. "He's not angry," she gasped aloud. "He's afraid."

Attack! Lux's voice echoed within her. Attack!

Author's Note

As far as the author knows, there is no island known as "Grey Cove" in the San Juan Archipelago of the Pacific Northwest.

Acknowledgments

It has been a very long journey from there to here and there are many people to thank.

I would like to thank Marianna Baer for her thoughts, incisive editing and daring me to rise to a greater level of writing.

Many thanks to Jack Cluth for looking over the manuscript in its early stages and encouraging me in my many subsequent drafts!

I would like to thank the editors and staff of lulu.com who worked closely with me in allowing this book to come to fruition. Thank you!

Deep gratitude to Talia Dugan for her wonderful drawings! She did all these while in high school and finished them up even while getting ready to graduate! We wish her much success in her future. Thank you to her family who supported her through all this as well.

A deep and profound thank you to the doctors who have saved my life:

Dr. Richards Lyon

Dr. Oscar Salvatierra

Dr. Robert Shimizu

Additional thanks need to be given to Dr. John M. Barry, Dr. Douglas Norman, and Dr. Jose Rueda. Also included are Dr. Pritham Raj, Dr. Wahba and Dr. Mary Meyer and of course Lynn Hoth.

To the Deaf Education staff of the Mt. Diablo Unified School District: thank you! This includes Gregory Gardens, Westwood Elementary, El Dorado Junior High and of course Concord High.

I would like to thank the teachers who always encouraged me, including but not limited to:

Ro Winfield, my preschool teacher who encouraged all of us to use our imaginations!

Cherisse Baatin, my 4th, and 5th grade teacher who later became a very dear friend.

Larry Bird and Katy Muus from 8th grade; both of you encouraged me in ways I can never repay.

Patricia Mortensen from Junior and Senior year who told me to "keep writing" — thank you!

And of course, our beloved professor Barbara Boyd who taught our first English classes in college — thank you! You are dearly missed.

I owe my childhood friends a special thanks —

The first goes to Jesse Phalen who always asked for a new story every year at his birthday party. He was always so kind and encouraging. It must run in his family! Jesse's mother Vikke was my sign-language interpreter for my first Creative Writing class and was supportive of my efforts.

To Jonathan and Gregory Bellusa who made childhood unforgettable for me. Their family was always so inclusive of me.

For Patrick and Michael Stuart and their family who made a great impact on my life. Patrick is still missed today. I am proud that my son has Patrick's name for his middle one.

With fond memories, I thank Liann Osborne, Jenny Nyguen, Lisa Harris, and Jill Roat. I also thank Eric Marks and Samuel Reynolds.

Many thanks to our Northwest friends—

- Irene Jazowick
- Billy and Dana Miles and their children.
- Aaron and Andrea Medlock and their children.
- Robert and Sharon Schniedewind and their children.
- John and Jil Yates and their children.

To the staff of Multnomah University/Multnomah Biblical Seminary, I will never be able to adequately thank you for all you did for me during my time there. Thank you for providing interpreting services and thank you for all the precious teaching you gave us students so that our walk with the Lord would become even stronger — and so that we could better and more effectively minister to others. My thanks will never be enough. I will always value my time there.

Many thanks to Paul and Anne Ogden for their support and prayers. What an encouragement you are!

A special thank you to Johnnie Burt, my supervisor and friend. Her thoughtfulness and gentle directness have been wonderful for me. I am very fortunate to have her friendship.

I want to thank a dear friend Jean Miller for her thoughtfulness and encouragement these many years. She was born to the craft of interpreting, and she has made it an art and a profound pleasure to witness.

Thanks to our family friend Christine Hearn for her amazing interpreting services and involvement with our family.

Thank you to Bob Ayres, my Deaf Teen Quest "boss" for many years. He and his wife Kathy Ayres have been dear friends who have mentored Shannon and I in so many ways.

Heartfelt gratitude goes to Marilyn Marcille for her love, dedication and support of our family. Most of all for sharing her love of God with us and our children.

Special thanks go to Kimberly Whetter, her husband Jevon and son Robbie for so many years of deep, fun, and loyal friendship. Thanks are given to Michele Jennings, now Michele Vincent. Special thanks also go to Irene Jazowick who has been so faithful at visiting me during my dialysis sessions.

For my goddaughter, Natalia - you have experienced much adversity in your life. I admire you. The day your parents decided to ask us to be your godparents was one of the best days of our lives. Thank you for blessing us as much as you have. We thank your parents Jil and John for including us in your lives.

My "Gentlemen's Club" has, at one time or another, told me to write a book! Here it is guys! For —

Monsieur Erick Howard Posner: you are an amazing father, husband, and best friend! You are tough on me, but it has made me a better person and writer! You have been there for me so often in and through my medical crises — I never thought I'd have a friend like that. I am grateful for all the memories we have together — yes, Erick — even I-5! I look forward to making more with your wonderful wife Sara and son Isaac.

Sir Andrew Sergio Leyva: Friend and brother, what can I say? Words seem inadequate. But I will try anyway. I thank you for chocolate cake. That has been a huge theme in our friendship and only you and I know the meaning of it. I thank you for missed plane rides, stays in the hospital with me, for understanding what I mean when what I say doesn't come out right. That's a true friend and you're it, ASL.

Errant Knight Randall "Randy" Rushing: Every time I see you or hear from you, I'm always reminded by how well you know me. The memories of us as pledge brothers together (EPSILON!) and then as fraternity brothers (LAMBDA SIGMA PI!) are amazing! And our bond continues today (two sons, both close in age). No matter where I am or what I'm doing, I am always thinking of you and thanking God for our friendship.

To Brady, Chhun, Chinkee, Chris, Christina, Monse, Savannah, and Sebastian — our youth group has become the stuff of legend. We all went through so much together. Jesus blessed us in you guys, and we are so grateful for all the time we spent together. Our little youth group deserves a book of its own but one of you must write it! We love you guys. Bella AKA "Izzie Belly" is a special gift from God.

A deep thank you to my in-laws, who are my "in-loves". To my mother-in-love, Glenna; to her husband Jim; to my father-in-love Phil; to his wife, Louise; to my siblings-in-love Sean and Janine; my nephew Mitchell, my niece Riley, and my niece Jalyn.

Deep thanks go to my dear godmother "Binky" Margot Scott who is now with the Lord. We miss your gentle, quiet yet fun nature.

Many thanks to my Aunt Connie and Uncle King who were very supportive of my education growing up. Aunt Connie filled a void left by my Grandfather Henry. Thank you for that.

I am blessed to have had so many meaningful and fun experiences with the Staples family growing up — Janet, Russell, Jeffrey, Katharine and now Elizabeth! We are thrilled with the addition of little Clara Jane and Malcolm to their ranks!

I must make special mention of Judy Jordan, my beloved mentor and friend during my high school years. I may be Deaf, but I know her laughter is the music of heaven. It has been more than 10 years since you went to be with the Lord. I've thought of you every single day.

How can I not mention Earl Palmer, my pastor, my mentor, my friend? Your letters and encouragement over the years have meant so much. Thank you for being there when Shannon and I got married. The time spent with you and your wife Shirley aboard the "Sea Cloud" will never be forgotten.

A special thank you to the uncles, aunts, cousins who supported me growing up. I have been overwhelmed by their generosity and support all my life. Growing up with Ben, Rebekah, Rachel, Anthea, and Laura was wonderful. Not many are as fortunate as I am. I know that.

For both sets of grandparents: Grandpa Henry and Grandma Lorraine Rudd; Grandpa Phil and Grandma Annette Reynolds - your legacy in Christ is very alive here on Earth in your children, grand-children, and great-grandchildren. Thank you for loving us as you did and thank you for your heritage of faith.

For my "Auntie Mar," who learned sign language for me and volunteered at my preschool and elementary school, thank you for being such a TURKEY! You have always been more than just the "fun" aunt; you are the aunt who was there for us more than any other. I have learned about Jesus by watching you all these years.

For my grandmother Laura: you were not only my grandmother, but you were also one of my dearest friends. You were so gracious in your love and so thoughtful and kind in your quiet way. Your willing-ness to learn sign-language for me showed me how much you loved me and thank you. I'm so glad you were able to stay with us so long. That doesn't make missing you any easier.

I am extremely grateful to my two kidney donors: the first one being my father Stephen; in the early '90s, transplantation was still so uncertain. Your donation allowed me to live in full while graduating high school, college, and my courtship of Shannon. The memories of us skiing, waterskiing, playing in the pool, watching movies have all contributed to the sense of FUN I try to bring to the lives of my children as their dad. Not to mention snorkeling and boogie boarding and all the trips over the country—no, the world! I love you very much.

Shannon and I would never have had a family if it were not for my second kidney donor, Fran. After marrying, I was given yet again a second chance at life through the donation of your kidney. Our children, whom we did not think would ever be born, are blessed to have you, Fran, as their godmother.

To my two boys, Evan, and Jared! We did not know if we could have you and when you entered the world only 20 months apart from one another, you changed our lives so completely. Thank you for your sense of imagination, fun, sensitivity, and thoughtfulness of others. We learn so much from you and you two are miracles.

For my mother, who has lent so much support to both me and my family. I am in awe of my mother and humbled that she is MY mother! So much of my writing is from how Mom is my meaning-maker. You are my biggest and best example next to God, and I thank Him for you. After my got my first transplant, it did not work right away. I was very depressed. I remember how you, my mother, taught me to appreciate the sixth floor of the hospital then: it was a beautiful garden that I was able to visit and appreciate while waiting for my kidney to 'kick in'. She taught me a very important lesson then: pull the yellow into the black. That's who my mother is. I owe her and love her so much.

Shannon, you made my dreams come true when you became my wife. You make them come true every day when I see you with our boys. We've been so blessed, Shannon. Thank you for your patience with me on this project, for knowing when to let me write, for knowing when to pull me away. We have grown so much together but you are still the same young woman who drove down with me to Ashland on our second date and got M&Ms all over your shorts! I love it when you laugh. I love it when you're a clown. I love it when I see you nurture our sons. I love it when you talk to me about your feelings and thoughts. I love it when you touch me when you're listening to me. I love how you say just the right thing that, when I'm figuring something out, helps bridge everything together. Yes, Shannon, the reality is better than the dream. And I know how much you've sacrificed to be with me! Not many wives would be as patient as you have! I've always felt your support and encouragement. I love you. *Ti Amo — all my love all of the time!*

Finally, thank you God, my Lord Jesus. I thank you for how you design every one of us to be so very different from one another, our different functions facets of Your own character. You've shown Yourself in my life so many times in so many ways. Thank you. Thank you, Lord.

About the Author

Matthew Rudd Reynolds lives in the Pacific Northwest with his wife Shannon and their college-age sons, Evan and Jared. Matt is profoundly Deaf and uses ASL to communicate. He has had three kidney transplants as well. In addition to swimming and skiing, Matt has become quite interested in kayaking and hiking. He is currently at work on his standalone novel, *All the Stilled Voices*, which takes place during the "Deaf President Now" protests in 1988. Matt is also focused on Andi and Lux's next adventure, tentatively entitled *Where Stars Cast their Shadows*. Matt is grateful to God and his donors for the second and third chances he has received in life. More can be found out about Matt at *matthewruddreynolds.com*.